Books by Chris Cavender

A SLICE OF MURDER

PEPPERONI PIZZA CAN BE MURDER

A PIZZA TO DIE FOR

REST IN PIZZA

Published by Kensington Publishing Corporation

CHRIS CAVENDER

REST IN PIZZA

KENSINGTON BOOKS

www.kensingtonbooks.com

For Patty,
We don't always have a lot of dough, but the
extra toppings are always there!
Enjoy!

Ideas are like pizza dough, made to be tossed around.
—Anna Quindlen

Chapter 1

At first glance through the large front window of A Slice of Delight, it looked as though the person inside the pizzeria was simply sitting at a table in the dining area, waiting patiently for food to be delivered.

But the pizzeria wasn't open yet and wouldn't be for hours.

A closer look revealed the chef's knife stuck all the way to its handle through the victim's chest, pinning the patron upright in place to the back of the chair, like a butterfly in a collector's case.

The murder weapon, taken straight from the kitchen but never before used in such a grim and dreadful fashion, was one all too familiar to the owner of A Slice of Delight.

There was no movement, no sound, no life surrounding the victim.

Murder had come back to the sleepy little town of Timber Ridge, North Carolina, and despite the warmth of the day, its cold breath was having its way with the citizens there.

One Week Earlier

"How's the lunch crowd doing out there now? Are we going to be able to take our break anytime soon?" I impatiently asked my sister, Maddy Spencer, who also happened to be one of my employees. I'm Eleanor Swift, and I normally work the kitchen while she handles the dining room of my pizzeria, A Slice of Delight, located on the square in the heart of Timber Ridge, North Carolina. My younger sister is tall, thin, and blond, three things that with all certainty could never be used to describe me. Maddy had come to help out when my late husband, Joe, had been killed, and she had kept everything going until I'd been ready to face the world again, and much to my delight, she'd decided to stay.

"We're all good. Greg is the only one out there besides me, Eleanor," Maddy answered. Greg Hatcher, along with Josh Hurley, were our only other two employees at the time, and though we were pressed on occasion with such a small staff, it allowed me to run the pizzeria on a tight budget, keeping my expenses pared to the bone. We didn't deliver pizzas or sandwiches anymore as a general rule, but if the occasion merited it, and the income it generated was large enough, I'd been known to make an exception from time to time. We'd had some bad experiences in the past with our deliveries, and it was something I wasn't willing to take a chance on these days without a proportionally sized payoff on the other end.

I glanced at the clock and saw that we still had seven minutes until we were officially due to close for our one-hour break, but that was just too bad. For some reason I needed a break, and after all, if I couldn't change our hours whenever I wanted to as the boss, what good were all the headaches I got that also came with the territory? "Go ahead and tell Greg to flip the sign and lock up," I said.

Maddy didn't wait around for me to second-guess myself as she bolted for the front with a grin on her face. She knew enough to take a golden opportunity like that when she saw it. Greg was a student at the local college, and Josh would be going even farther away himself soon. It meant that I'd be losing my connection to the nearby high school, and I always tried to keep at least one high schooler on the payroll all of the time, but for the two of them, I'd make an exception. I knew this "family" of employees wouldn't last forever, but I wasn't about to hurry the end of this particular era. That was the sad truth of it. Whether they were good, bad, or indifferent, no staff ever stayed the same. At least I had Maddy, a constant in my life since she'd first come to work for me.

Greg came into the back whistling and put his apron on the hook by the door. He was a big guy and could look fierce when he wanted to, but I knew that under that tough exterior was a gentle soul. "Thanks for the break, boss. You don't even have to pay me for the time I'm missing," he said with a smile.

The funny thing was, Greg had more money than I did. He'd come into an inheritance from his grandparents a while back, and I had worried that he'd leave me once he didn't need his job at the Slice anymore, but to my great delight, he'd decided to stay. The only thing that was really different about him was that he didn't have to scrounge food in my kitchen anymore, though that never stopped him from trying. Old habits died hard, I knew.

"Is there anything in this joint to eat?" Greg asked, reinforcing my last thought about him.

I looked around and said, "This is your lucky day. We've got a large cheese pizza nobody picked up, but I doubt it's any good now. It's been sitting there on the warming rack for awhile."

"How long has it been?" Greg asked, standing close to me. Sometimes I forgot just how tall and broad-shouldered he was, but it was pretty obvious when I had to look up to see into his eyes.

"I'd have to say at least forty minutes. Let me make you a new one before Maddy and I take off."

"No, it's fine," he said, grabbing up the box. "I like a pizza that's room temperature now and then. Good thing Josh is in class, or I'd be fighting him for it. I might grab a soda on the way out though, if you don't mind."

"Be my guest," I said.

Maddy came back just as I finished washing the last of the

lunch dishes. Most days we made something at the Slice and ate right there, but today we were treating ourselves to a lunch out on the town. Well, Brian's Diner wasn't exactly high-class dining; it was actually more like a greasy spoon café, but at least it wasn't a pizza or a sub. As much as I loved what we offered at the Slice, sometimes I just had to get away, and Maddy was all for it, especially since I'd offered to treat.

"Let's roll, Eleanor. Aren't you ready yet?" she asked. "We don't want to miss our reservation."

I looked at her and smiled. "Since when did Mark Deacon require lunchtime reservations at Brian's?"

Maddy grinned at me. "He doesn't, but I'm hungry, and I didn't want to sound like a pig. Are you coming, or what?"

I had to laugh. "I'm right behind you. Do you want to drive, or should I?"

"I will," she said as she shucked off her apron and grabbed her purse. "No offense, but sometimes you drive like an old woman."

"How could I possibly take offense to that? It doesn't even apply to me, since I'm not all that old," I said.

"You're older than me," she said with a laugh. "That's really all that counts when it comes down to it, isn't it?"

I fought to hide my own grin as I double-checked everything. The conveyor oven was turned off, and the toppings were wrapped and stored in the refrigerator. "Did you grab the till from the cash register?"

She snapped her fingers in the air. "I knew I forgot something. I'll be right back."

We'd been robbed once before, which had given me an incentive to install a safe from Slick's Hardware Store in our storeroom. Even with the generous discount my friend, Slick, had given me, it had still cost more money than I'd been comfortable spending, but in the end, I suppose that it was better than losing everything. "The money has to actually be in the safe for it to be protected, you know that, right?" I called out to her, not able to hide my laughter.

Maddy came back thirty seconds later, long enough for me to open the safe's door and make room for the cash till. As she slid it into place, I waited, then shut the door, spinning the dial twice for good luck.

"Now, who's ready to eat?" I asked. "I thought you were as ready as I was to get away for an hour." I glanced at my watch, and then amended, "Well, fifty-seven minutes, anyway."

Maddy arched an eyebrow. "Just for that, I'm going to order two specials. Especially since you're paying."

"Order whatever you'd like," I said with a grin, and then quickly added, "as long as our total bill isn't over twelve bucks."

"Is that with tip, or without?" she asked.

I grinned at her. "No, I'll cover the tip, too."

"Gee, Sis, you are all heart," she said.

"Come on, let's go before something comes up."

"Are you expecting anything to?" Maddy asked as we walked through the Slice, turning off lights as we went.

"I never expect it. That's why I'm always so surprised when something does," I admitted.

As I let us out the front door and locked it behind us, I nearly ran Cary Wilkes over. Cary owned a multi-state cleaning agency, but my ties to her were more personal than that. Her son, Rick, was away at college now, but he'd worked at the Slice before leaving home, and we'd become friends during his time at the pizzeria. Cary had been working on loosening her apron strings since he'd gone away, with admittedly marginal success so far, but clearly still not enough for Rick's taste.

"I'm sorry, Cary. I'd love to stay and chat, but we're closed for lunch, and Maddy and I have someplace we need to be," I said. There was no way I was going to work through our lunchtime, not even for a friend. My sister and I hadn't had a real break for the past several days, but I'd grown too used to the time off in the middle of the day since we'd implemented it to ever go back to our old hours. Most days it gave us all a nice hour away from the pizzeria, but sometimes we had to use it for sleuthing. Maddy and I were crackerjack amateur investigators, but only when the crimes involved us. The rest of the time, we did our best not to poke our noses into other people's problems. We managed to have enough on our own.

"Don't worry, I already ate," she said as she pulled a large envelope from her purse. "Rick wanted me to give this to you. I didn't even realize that it was your birthday, Eleanor."

"It's not for another two weeks," I said, taking the card from her. I slid it into my back pocket, something that clearly disappointed Cary. From the intent look on her face, it was clear that she was curious about what it said inside.

"Aren't you going to open it?" she asked eagerly.

"I will, but not until my birthday," I said with a smile.

"That's the way the Spencers do it," Maddy said. "No cards opened early, and no presents enjoyed until the thank-you notes have been written."

"The Swifts feel that way, too," I said, since I'd implemented the rule right after marrying Joe. He'd thought I'd been joking at first, but it didn't take him long to realize that I hadn't been kidding, and he quickly indulged me.

Cary grinned despite her disappointment. "You two are a real pair, aren't you?"

"Jokers, maybe," Maddy said as she glanced over at me. "I'd say that's a good fit, wouldn't you?"

I decided her question really didn't need an answer, so I turned to Cary and asked, "How's Rick doing these days?"

"I'm not sure he's eating enough, or getting enough sleep," she admitted, the worry showing in her face instantly.

"I'm sure that he's fine, Cary," I said, patting her hand. "I'm just curious, but why didn't Rick send my card directly here to the Slice instead of sending it through you? He knows my address."

Cary looked uncomfortable with the question, and I had a suspicion I knew why. I asked a little strongly, "You're still giving him space, aren't you?"

"Hey, I'm working on it," she said as her cell phone rang. As if arranged by providence, she started to answer it as she said to me, "Sorry, I've got to take this."

Cary was deep in conversation as she left us, and I had to wonder if some of it was so that she wouldn't have to address my question.

After she was out of sight, Maddy said, "I'm amazed Rick stayed close enough to Timber Ridge for his mom to drop in on him whenever she wants to. I figured he'd go to school in Hawaii or Alaska."

"We should cut her some slack, Maddy. She doesn't have anyone else, and Rick knows it. He wouldn't go very far away; that would be too cruel. He loves her, even if she does have a tendency to smother him."

"Well, she should give Rick his space and get someone of her own," Maddy said. "After all, even we've both managed to do that."

I wasn't sure I liked the assumption in Maddy's statement. "Slow down there, Sister. I never said I had anyone in my life."

Maddy arched one eyebrow toward me as we walked down the promenade toward the shortcut to our parking area in back. "Really? What would David Quinton think if he heard you say that?"

David had courted me for years, to no avail, and then he'd left Timber Ridge to try to make a fresh start. When he'd come back later, he was a changed man, and if I were being honest about it, maybe I'd changed some, too, in the time that he was gone. I'd been so in love with my late husband, Joe, that I couldn't imagine anyone else in my life, but David had somehow managed to find his way in. We were taking it slow, though—glacially, in

Maddy's opinion—but I was letting him into my heart a little bit at a time, and it was honestly the best that I could do. "He'd understand. He knows how I feel about him." I turned to look at her and asked, "Speaking of men in our lives, how are you and Bob getting along these days?" Bob Lemon was an excellent local attorney and the current object of my sister's affections. The question was fair game, since Maddy had been the one to bring our love lives into the conversation. After all, I figured that the more I could distract Maddy from asking questions about my private life, the better.

My sister didn't answer as quickly as I expected her to. "I'm not sure, to be honest with you."

That was an odd reply, even for her. "What do you mean?"

Maddy frowned, and then said, "I thought we were in a good place, but he's been acting kind of odd lately. Eleanor, we both know that I've been married more than a few times before, but I still can't figure that man out. You'd think I'd getter better with practice being around them."

"More than a few times? Did you just say that?" I asked with a grin.

"Okay, so it's four times, but who's counting?" Maddy asked.

"Not me," I said. "All I can think about right now is lunch."

"I'm right behind you."

As we walked down the promenade toward the shortcut together, I glanced back at A Slice of Delight. The previous occupant had painted the building mostly blue, and Joe and I had learned early on that it would have been prohibitively expensive to get rid of, so we'd kept it as is. I'd grown fond of it over the years, and doubted I would change it even if I could afford to now. We stood out among a cluster of shops and businesses, and really, what more could I ask for? The other buildings, normally sharing sidewalls and standing shoulder to shoulder, allowed a single break from the walls that otherwise touched on either side. Maddy and I used the bricked shortcut every time we came or left the pizzeria. In order to get there from the Slice, though, we had to pass several other shops along the way. One of buildings, a now-defunct exclusive wine and cheese shop that had lasted just six months, had lost its previous sign of The Winey Husband and was now going to reopen as a bookstore, something the square sorely needed, in my opinion. Adding even more to our excitement, the new owner was a friend of ours named Cindy Rankin. Her husband had died unexpectedly, and she'd come into some money from an insurance policy that she hadn't even known he had. After a year spent mostly in mourning, Cindy had decided it was time to get on with her life. It had been her dream to own a bookstore someday, and despite a generally gloomy financial outlook, Cindy had gone for it.

I was about to comment on how brave she was to Maddy when the door of the bookshop opened, and Cindy herself came out.

"I'm so glad I ran into you two," she said. "I was just coming down to the Slice. I'm in trouble, and I desperately need your help."

"What's going on?" I asked Cindy as Maddy and I walked inside. Visions of our lunch out dissipated like morning mist. "It looks like you could open today."

The new bookstore was in great shape as far as I could tell, with row upon row of shelves made of polished cherry wood and filled with books. There were clever signs above each section, with categories written in script on large bookmarks hanging from the ceiling. One corner of the place was devoted exclusively to reading, with big comfy chairs and a fireplace giving the entire space a warm glow, and another nook housed a coffee counter and pastry display area. Soft music played in the background, and the only thing out of place was a stack of boxes near the register.

Cindy frowned as she looked around. "I wish. We're seven days away from opening, whether we're ready or not."

I couldn't imagine what else she might be hoping to do in that brief amount of time, but I remembered when Joe and I had first opened A Slice of Delight how I found myself constantly wishing that we had one more week. Joe had assured me that no matter how prepared we thought we were, that extra week would never come. The only way we'd managed to get everything right was actually opening our pizzeria for business. "What can we do to help?"

"I just got a call from a publicist from one of the big publishers. They want to feature one of their A-list writers for my grand opening."

"Is that actually a problem? It sounds like a wonderful opportunity," Maddy said as she picked up a mystery and started flipping through it. My sister was a nut for mysteries, and despite her brash and bold outward appearance, she favored cozies, especially craft-based and culinary mysteries, above all else.

"You'd think so," Cindy said with a worried expression on her face, "but I don't know anything about cooking, especially Italian fare."

"Why should you have to?" I asked. "Leave that to the celebrity author. No one expects you to know how to cook or bake. After all, you're not making your own pastries, are you?"

"Of course not. Paul is supplying them."

"Good choice," I said. Paul was a good friend of ours, and he happened to run the best bakery, Paul's Pastries, in our part of North Carolina. "He makes our sandwich rolls for us. Trust me, you won't be disappointed."

"I'm not worried about that," she said. "The problem is, they're sending Antonio Benet, and I understand he can be difficult at times."

"The guy from the Food for Thought Network?" Maddy asked. Cindy nodded. "Have you seen his show?"

"I've watched it a few times," Maddy admitted. I knew she was addicted to all of the food-related channels on television.

"Then you'll be perfect," Cindy said with delight.

"For what?" Maddy asked, the suspicion clear in her voice.

"To help me," Cindy said after taking a lungful of air,. "Ladies, I hate to ask, but I need you both."

The poor girl looked as though she were about to collapse.

"What's your concern?" I asked.

"This," Cindy said as she thrust a sheaf of papers toward me. "The whole thing just came today."

I took the offered sheets of paper from her and scanned through them as Maddy read over my shoulder.

It appeared that Chef Benet was going to be promoting his new cookbook, *A Taste of Italian Heaven, Benet Style*, and he had a very specific list of expectations of any venue he'd be visiting.

"It looks pretty clear to me," I said as I scanned the list. He wanted cooking equipment, including a portable oven and other kitchen tools, to enable him to host a demonstration. I had a feeling Cindy could round up what she needed in town without much trouble at all.

"Flip the page," Cindy said ominously.

I did, and saw that the chef was more particular than any diva I'd ever imagined. The next page contained his list of personal demands, and they sounded as though they'd come from a madman holding hostages instead of a cook preparing a meal. I stopped after reading the first one. "He expects you to have a full kitchen mock-up for his demonstration? Where are you going to put it all?"

"I'm moving the middle of the store into storage for now, but that's not all. Keep reading."

I did, and soon saw the reason she'd probably wanted to talk to us. "You want us to be his assistants, don't you?" The contract stipulated that two trained cooks had to be at his disposal to do his prep and clean up, and to basically keep him happy the entire time he was in Timber Ridge. He also required a greenroom before his "performance," and another kitchen, one with an electric pizza oven, at his disposal off-site to test some new recipes.

"I know it's a lot to ask," Cindy said. "You can say no if you want to. I'll manage somehow."

"You can do it. We have faith in you," Maddy said, and I shushed my sister.

"Don't worry. We'll help," I said. I'd had Joe to fall back on when we'd opened our place, but Cindy had no one but her mother, Janet. If I could, I was going to be that rock for her. Cindy had lost her husband, but that didn't mean she had to lose her dream. If I couldn't help out another widow when she needed me, I wasn't sure I could justify occupying space in this world.

Maddy touched my arm and whispered, "Eleanor, can we talk about this first?"

"I'm sorry," I said to Cindy. "I should correct that. I'll help, but I really can't speak for Maddy."

"I'm in, too," my sister said, though in my mind she still sounded a little reluctant.

Cindy didn't hear it in her voice, though, or chose to ignore it. "You two are lifesavers," she said with a broad grin.

"When do you need us?" I asked.

"The day before the signing would be great. Not all day, but just to make sure I've got everything I need. Chef Benet is coming in later in the day, but his front person will be here early. I feel bad about having you shut down your restaurant for two days."

"We can't afford to do that," I said. "But we shouldn't have to. Maddy and Greg can run the Slice while I'm over here, and we can shut down during the few hours he needs for his demonstration the next day. At most we'll lose three or four hours, and we can afford that to help a friend."

Cindy hugged me and then Maddy in turn. "I can't thank you both enough."

"We're happy to help," I said.

Maddy and I left, and once we were out of sight of the bookstore, I turned to her and said, "You really don't want to do this, do you?"

"What are you talking about? I'm happy to lend a hand."

"Madeline Spencer, I know you better than that. What's wrong?"

My sister shook her head. "I just hate to see you lose sales you can't afford to give up. I don't have to remind you how close we balance between red and black ink every month, do I?"

"There are more important things in this world than money," I said.

Maddy grinned. "In that case, how about a raise?"

I wasn't entirely sure she was serious, so I chose to treat it as a joke. "You know what I mean. Is that really it?"

Maddy frowned, and then stared at the brick pavers under her feet as she finally admitted, "Sis, I know how you feel about widows. Why shouldn't you help her? I admit that I'm a little worried about Benet, though."

"Why is that?" I asked. I'd have to catch one of his television shows before he came to town, but weren't all of those TV chefs perky and happy all of the time?

"From what I've read on the Internet, he's a bigger prima donna than seven divas in the same room."

"He can't be that bad, can he?" I asked.

"Trust me, if what I've read on-line is even close to the truth, he's worse. Much worse. That's what I was trying to warn you about. I'm thrilled to give Cindy a hand. I just wish she'd asked us to help stock shelves or something."

"It'll be fine," I said, wishing that I could believe it. After all, how bad could it really be?

Chapter 2

"Eleanor, do you have a minute?" Art Young asked me as Maddy and I finished our abbreviated lunch at Brian's Diner. Art had a reputation for being on the shady side of Timber Ridge society, but I'd never seen any evidence of unlawful behavior myself, though I honestly hadn't looked that hard for it. Art and I had formed an odd friendship over the past few years that even Maddy didn't understand, but that was okay with me. I certainly didn't agree with every choice my sister had ever made, so there was no reason to believe that she had to approve of mine. Art was a thin and dapper man, always dressed impeccably, and no one would ever suspect he could be labeled a criminal based on his outward appearance alone, nor by the way he communicated.

"Go ahead. I've got to call Bob anyway," Maddy said as she got up and made a quick exit.

"Your sister still isn't all that fond of me, is she?" Art asked.

"I'm not concerned one way or the other what she thinks, so you certainly shouldn't be. How are you?"

He looked weary as he answered, "I'm honestly not quite sure."

"What is it?" I'd never seen the man worried for a moment since I'd known him, so I was more than a little alarmed by his statement.

"May I join you for a moment?" Art asked, and then looked around the dining room at the folks who were trying their best not to be seen watching us. "Or would you be more comfortable meeting me somewhere more discreet?"

I shoved Maddy's dishes out of the way and said, "They can all bark at the moon, as far as I'm concerned," I said. "Go on. Sit."

Art smiled at that. "There aren't many folks who would dream of ordering me around with impunity the way you do."

"What can I say? I've always known I'm special." I looked closer at him, and saw new worry lines in his face. "Now tell me. What's wrong, and how can I help?"

"I'm going away," he said, his voice lowered to a softer tone.

"For good?" I asked. For some reason I couldn't fathom, Art's friendship was important to me, and I'd truly miss him if he were gone.

"No, nothing that dramatic," he said with a small smile. "I'm touched that you would miss me, though."

"Surely I'm not the only one," I said.

He shrugged slightly. "Let's just say the list is small."

I didn't want to add to the morose tone the conversation had taken. "So, how long will you be gone?"

"I'm afraid that's still undetermined as of yet," Art said.

"Longer than a day, but shorter than a month? How about a year?" I asked, trying to make him smile. My friend had a problem, and it pained me to see it in his eyes.

"Let's just hope for the best, shall we?" he asked.

"I was serious about the offer I just made, so don't take it so lightly. Is there anything I can do to help?"

He patted my hand briefly, and then quickly withdrew it. "I'm afraid not. At this point, I'm not all that certain that there's anything I can do myself."

"Well, I do appreciate you warning me that you won't be around for awhile," I said.

Art looked at me oddly for a moment, and then said, "Funny, but it was important to me that you knew I'd return someday." He reached into the vest pocket of his suit and withdrew a business card. As he slid it across the table to me, Art said, "If you need me, call that number. Ask whoever answers if it is the button factory, and then hang up. I'll get back to you as soon as I can."

"The button factory?" I asked as I picked up the card and studied the number embossed on it in gold. "What kind of code is that?"

He shrugged. "Let's just say that you might not want your name overheard on that particular call. The button factory. Remember it, Eleanor. It's the only way you can reach me if it's urgent."

"I won't forget," I said. It was certainly cryptic, but I knew better than to ask him any more questions about it. "Art, no matter what your troubles are, I hope everything works out for you," I said as I tucked the card into the front pocket of my jeans.

He stood and picked up our check before I could stop him.

"Hey, you don't have to buy my lunch every time you see me out, you know. Our friendship isn't conditional on you treating me to free meals."

"I understand that I don't have to do it, but it pleases me," he said with a smile. "Why not indulge me and just enjoy it?"

"Thanks so much," I said.

After Art was gone, Maddy came back. I had to wonder if she'd even called Bob at all, or if she'd been spying on us from afar.

"That was quick," she said.

"I was about to say the same thing to you. How's Bob?"

"In court," Maddy said. "I couldn't get through to him. What did Art want?"

I thought about retelling the conversation to Maddy, but I really didn't want to get into my friendship with Art with her, especially with everyone around still staring at me. It wasn't easy being Art's friend, and I may have lost some business at the pizzeria over the past several months because of it, but I wasn't about to let Timber Ridge dictate my friendships any more than I'd let Maddy do it. They could live with it, or stop coming by the Slice; either way, I was fine with it. "It's not that important."

She shrugged, and then looked around the tabletop. "Did you already grab the check? I wanted some pie. Hand it over."

I had to laugh. "You'll just have to live without it. Art picked up the tab this time before I could stop him."

"He bought us both lunch?" Maddy asked, and I wasn't exactly sure how she felt about the prospect.

I nodded. "Sis, if you have a problem with that, tip your waitress the cost of your meal. It doesn't matter to me."

She just shrugged. "I don't want to start any dangerous precedents," Maddy said. "They might start expecting me to be a big tipper, and you know how much I hate disappointing people." She glanced at her watch, and then added, "I hate to break up our little party, but it's time to get back to the Slice."

"That hour flew by, didn't it?" I asked as we approached the register.

Maddy just shrugged. "We didn't have an hour to start with, so yeah, it was quick. And don't forget, we get the pleasure of helping keep an egomaniac in line for the trouble. Maybe next time we'll stay at the Slice and eat."

"And miss all of this atmosphere?" I said, doing my best to smile. I'd backed my sister into a corner, and I knew it. She was helping Cindy out because of me, and I'd try to find a way to make it up to her.

Mark Deacon, the owner of Brian's and a longtime friend of ours, said as we approached the front register, "If you two left a tip on the table, you should go get it. Art covered it, too."

There was no judgment in his voice as he said it.

Maybe I'd found someone else who took the man at face

value, and did not base their feelings on rumor and innuendo. "Is Art a friend of yours, too?"

Mark smiled at me. "Hey, everyone who comes through that door and pays for his food is a friend of mine," he said. "How was lunch, by the way?"

"Excellent, as always," I said.

"And it's not pizza, right?" he asked with a grin.

"You could come get a slice yourself sometime," I said with a smile.

"You know what? I just might take you up on that sometime," he said. "As much as I love the food we serve here, there are times where I'd kill for something else to eat. Save a slice for me someday. I'm going to visit you both soon."

We all knew better than that. Mark was devoted to his restaurant, and if his doors were open to the public, he was there, too.

"You, sir, are a big fat liar," I said as I grinned at him.

"Hey, I just might surprise you both one of these days."

"I'll believe it when I see you walk into my pizzeria and order a slice," I said. I lowered my voice as I added, "Tell you what. If you ever do make it over to our corner of town, the pizza's on me."

When Maddy and I got back to the Slice, Greg had already gotten there and was patiently waiting for us. He was sitting at a table out front watching people and enjoying the day, but I still apologized as I unlocked the door. "Sorry we kept you waiting outside," I said.

"That's okay. I'm just glad it wasn't raining. You know, you could trust me with a key," Greg said. "I'm a dependable kind of guy."

"You're absolutely right." I turned to Maddy and said, "Do me a favor. Give him your key."

"Hey, when I did I get demoted?" she asked in protest.

"You didn't. I'll have another one made for you later."

Maddy handed me her key, and I saw that she was really reluctant to do it. Did she honestly think that I'd ever cut her out of my pizzeria? "Take it easy." I handed the key to Greg and then said, "Do me a favor and run this over to Slick's. He's got a key machine. Have him make a copy for you, and then give the original back to Maddy."

"Are you sure? I don't want you to do anything you're not comfortable with," he said.

"Greg, I trust you." I thought about it a second, and then said, "Don't let anyone know you have it though, okay? I don't want to have to start handing them out."

"Are you worried about Josh wanting one?" Greg asked. "You don't have to. Trust me, he doesn't want the responsibility."

"How could you possibly know that?" Maddy asked him as we all stepped inside the pizzeria.

"On quiet nights here, we talk about the strangest things," Greg said. "Don't worry about me. I'll be right back."

Greg took off, and I locked the door behind him. When I turned back to Maddy, I saw that she was watching me. "What's that look for? Don't you think I'm doing the right thing?"

"I'm just wondering what took you so long. Eleanor, I'm glad you're trusting Greg. It's about time, isn't it?"

"I guess so," I said with a sigh. "You know how hard it is for me to give up control of anything."

"You don't have to tell me," she said. "Remember when you got your first car? It took you years before you'd let me drive it."

"Maddy, you didn't have your license," I said.

"Details, details," she said as there was a knock at the front door.

It was Greg.

"That was fast, even for Slick," I said.

He handed the key back to Maddy and then said, "Thanks anyway, but I changed my mind."

I couldn't believe what I was hearing. "You honestly don't want a key of your own?"

Greg shook his head. "Josh is right. The responsibility of having it isn't worth the inconvenience of waiting out here for you two now and then." He added a big grin as he said, "I do appreciate the offer, though."

"You're welcome," I said as I walked back into my kitchen to prepare for our afternoon and evening crowd. I had five minutes to get ready for our second opening, and I planned to take advantage of every second of it. I wasn't quite sure I understood what had just happened, but Greg was happy, Maddy was pleased, and I was satisfied. I couldn't remember the last time I could say that about the three of us, so I decided to take it as a victory and leave it at that.

We'd been open about an hour when I heard noises coming from the dining room. Ordinarily I couldn't hear much through the closed kitchen door, but there was a group out there that was making it too easy for me to hear them.

I opened the door to see what all of the ruckus was about, and saw that twelve people had taken the liberty to shove three tables together in the middle of the pizzeria. I looked at Maddy, who just shrugged. She walked over to me, and asked, "Why didn't you tell me we booked a party today?"

"Mainly because I didn't," I said. "What's it all about?"

"I figured you'd want to ask yourself."

"Okay, I will." I approached the group, and they began applauding.

"Hey, look, it's the owner herself," one of the young men said.

An older woman with hair the most startling shade of blue said, "I need to speak with you, young lady." She said it in a voice that exactly matched my high school principal, in tone if not in timbre.

"That sounds good to me," I said, "but would you mind keeping it down to a dull roar? We have other diners."

One of the other boys took that moment to yell, "Ashley Fox is a rock star."

One of the women at the table, a young lady in her early twenties, looked embarrassed by the attention, and I had to believe she was the Ashley in question. "Would you guys keep it down?" she asked, to no avail.

But then the older lady spoke up. "Family, I know we have a great deal to celebrate, but there's no excuse for rudeness. Jason, Phil, do you both understand what I'm saying?"

The two young men nodded, and each had the decency to look chastened.

Once they were quiet, the matriarch said, "As you've already deduced, we are the Foxes, here to celebrate my granddaughter's college graduation."

"Congratulations," I said, and I saw Jason and Phil begin another celebratory whoop when the older woman iced them with one glance.

"Thank you. I apologize for the disturbance, and we'll do our best to keep it down. Now, are our pizzas ready?"

"I'm sorry, but I didn't realize that you've been here long enough to order," I said, confused by her question.

"We called yesterday to let you know we were coming."

I shook my head. "You didn't speak with me." Since Josh hadn't worked yesterday, they must have either talked to Maddy or Greg.

"Either one of you take an order for Fox yesterday?" I asked them.

They both denied it, and I turned back to the lady. "I'm sorry, ma'am, but there seems to be some confusion."

"Please, my name is Louise." She looked down the table and spotted a middle-aged woman dressed a little too nicely for my pizza place. "Michelle, are you certain you called yesterday?"

"Of course I did, Mother," she said, sounding for an instant like the teenager she must have been at one point in her life.

"You called A Slice of Delight?" Louise asked.

"I've got the number stored right here on my phone," Michelle said, and then recited seven numbers. They did indeed make up a telephone number. Just not mine.

"I'm sorry, but that's not our number."

Louise's gaze narrowed. "Michelle? To whom did you speak?"

"I got a recording, so I left a message."

I shook my head. "We didn't get it, since it wasn't our phone number. If you have half an hour, we'd be glad to make something special for you."

"We'll wait," Louise said.

"Give Maddy your order, and I'll be glad to get busy making it," I said. "Thanks for coming to A Slice of Delight."

"You're most welcome."

I went back into the kitchen, and less than a minute later, Maddy came in with their order. As I got busy making pizzas, Maddy lingered and asked, "Is it just me, or did that woman remind you of Principal Jeffries?"

I laughed as I worked. "It gave me the willies," I admitted. "She had to be a principal at one point in her life."

"Or a teacher, at the very least. She surely knows how to keep that crowd in line, doesn't she?"

"I could take a lesson from her," I said as I slid the first pizza onto the conveyor.

"I don't know, you've got a pretty commanding voice yourself," Maddy said.

"Shouldn't you be getting their drink orders?" I asked.

Maddy headed back for the door with a grin. "See? Goosebumps," she said as she headed back out front.

After the pizzas were in line on the conveyor, I took some of my cookie dough out and made them a specialty dessert pizza, on the house. After all, it was a big deal for them having a member of their clan graduate.

When it was finished, I brought it out, with a single candle on top. "Happy Graduation," I said as I slid the treat pizza in front of Ashley.

Louise looked touched by the gesture, and I didn't even mind the brief cheer that went up from the group.

As I walked back into the kitchen, Harry Tompkins, an irascible old goat with a thick skin, said, "Hey, don't I get something, too?"

Bob Hygart, who was sitting with him, said, "Charm school doesn't count, and besides, you flunked out, remember?"

"At least they let me enroll," Harry said with a grin.

I knew the two of them could go on that way for hours, so I ducked back into the kitchen, just partly because I needed to get back to work.

Maddy came back twenty minutes later with a new order, and a request. "Her ladyship requests an audience," she said.

It took me a second to figure out that she must be referring to Louise. "Send her back."

Louise came in, and said, "I hate to bother you, but I just wanted to thank you for taking such good care of my family. The celebratory pizza dessert was an especially nice touch, but I won't let you donate it. We Foxes pay as we go. We always have, and we always will."

"I really didn't make it to drum up business," I said. "It was a gift."

Louise seemed to take that in, and then said, "Then my tip will be generous to the point of covering its cost as well."

She started to leave when I asked, "Louise, where were you principal?"

"Jenkins Elementary," she said automatically, and then caught herself. "How on earth did you know? Were you one of my students?"

"No, ma'am, but you have that voice that's filled with authority."

She smiled at that. "Good to know that I haven't lost that. Have a pleasant evening, Eleanor."

"And you as well," I said, fighting the urge to curtsey, of all things.

Despite the initial volume of their party, I was glad they'd chosen A Slice of Delight to celebrate. It made the place feel like a part of someone's family, something I always cherished.

We were closing for the night when the kitchen door opened. Without looking up from the pizza I was making, I said, "I hope this is our last order tonight. We're locking the doors after I make that one."

"As long as I'm on the right side of the door, you can shut it all down now if you'd like," said a voice I was learning to enjoy.

"David, when did you get back into town?" I rushed over to him and gave him a big hug, despite my less than pristine apron. He'd been at his main office in Raleigh, and though he'd only been gone three days, I'd already found myself missing him. It was taking some getting used to, having a man back in my life, but for the most part, I was enjoying it. It was tough, but I was finally beginning to see that letting someone else into my heart didn't mean that I was shutting Joe, my late husband, out of it.

"Don't get too excited. I've got to go back tomorrow," he said, "But I missed you too much to stay away. Any chance we could get a pizza to go and eat it on your front porch? I've always enjoyed doing that."

"I think that's an absolutely wonderful idea," I said. "What kind of pizza did you have in mind?"

"A kitchen sink pizza sounds good to me," he said. "I've been eating too much junk lately, so a few veggies might just be good for me. I always loved your garbage pizzas."

I didn't take offense, because I knew that he wasn't using the term in a derogatory way. Maddy and I often referred to our super deluxe pizzas that way ourselves. As I prepped a crust for us, I said, "Some folks around town are serious when they classify what I serve here that way."

David looked at me with mock surprise on his face. "Your garbage pizza has more vegetables on it than a well-stocked salad bar. Point me to the rascals who say otherwise and I'll thrash them soundly for you."

"You're in a good mood," I said with a smile as I topped the pizza with anything and everything that sounded tasty to me.

"Why shouldn't I be?" he asked as he hugged me from behind and nuzzled my neck for a few seconds. "My professional life is going well, and my personal life isn't half-bad, either."

"Is there anything in particular that you're thankful for?" I asked.

He pulled away and looked at me intently as I turned around. "Eleanor, are you fishing for compliments? If you are, I don't have a problem with that. Just say the word, and I'll bury you in words of high praise."

I laughed at David as I threw a nearby towel at him. Since he'd come back to town, he was a different man in so many ways. Most of all, the things I liked best were that he'd found his sense of humor, and he'd developed a willingness to give me as much space as I needed, whenever I required it. David had told me that he was just happy to be in my life, and so far he'd proved it, with no demands on my time or attention. Whenever we could get together was just fine with him, an attitude that made me want to spend even more and more time with him.

"Save your flattery for a day when I really need it," I said with a smile. "Right now, I'm good. It's going to be about twelve minutes, and if we all pitch in and hurry, we'll be able to get out of here by then."

David grinned. "Maddy and Greg have already taken care of the front. The tables are clean and the floor is swept. Is there anything I can do to help expedite things around here so we can go to your place and eat that pizza?"

I knew that it wasn't an idle offering. David had proved time and time again in the past that he wasn't afraid of sweeping up or even doing dishes if the occasion called for it. I decided to take him up on his generous offer. "You can finish those dishes, and I'll try to balance out the cash register, if you really want to get out of here early."

He grabbed a spare apron on the rack and said, "Just watch me."

I found Maddy and Greg finishing up the front when I went to run the report on our cash register and take out the till. Everything out front looked good to go for tomorrow, and I was pleased yet again about how well my team worked together. "Everything looks perfect. You two can take off."

Greg didn't wait around, but Maddy lingered for a moment after he was gone. "Planning a little late-night rendezvous, are we?" she asked.

I gave her a big smile. "Yes, but not here. As soon as I balance the register, we're heading out."

"I can stay and do the dishes if you want me to," Maddy offered.

"Thanks, but David's already doing them."

Maddy just smiled as she handed me her apron. "Wow, I can't believe you convinced him to do the dishes."

"I didn't have to," I said smugly. "He volunteered."

"Then I'd say he's a keeper."

"Bob's done dishes here before, too," I said, remembering a time he'd helped out in order to make up with me after we'd had a squabble.

"That might just be one of the reasons that he's still around," she said with a smile. "It sounds like you have things covered here. I'll see you tomorrow, Sis. I'd say don't do anything that I wouldn't do, but why limit the amount of fun you might have tonight?"

I let her out. "Good night, Maddy."

After she was gone, I ran the report, and found to my delight that it balanced out the first time. After making out the deposit slip, I came back into the kitchen to find David drying the last pan.

"The pizza's ready," he said. "It just slid out of the oven, and the only thing I have left to do is wash the pan it's on."

I moved the pizza to an open box, cut it, and then closed it. As I did, David picked the pan up with a dish towel and slid it into the water, along with the wheeled cutter. A short burst of steam rushed up from the sudsy water, and as I put the money in my safe, David finished drying the pan.

"Should we grab a few drinks on the way out?" I offered as I turned off the kitchen lights and we moved into the dining room.

"That sounds good. You might want to get something for you, too."

I laughed as I got drinks out of the cooler, and then walked him to the front door.

"Where's your car?" I asked as I looked around the promenade. There was parking there, a wide expanse of it, but you had to walk over several yards of pavers to get to the lot.

"I'm parked back beside you," he said. "Tell you what. Why don't I drive you home, and then I'll bring you back here later," David offered.

"That's just crazy. We'll take both cars." I had a sudden idea. "Why don't we make it interesting? I'll race you to my place."

"That sounds intriguing. What do I get when I win?"

I shoved his chest lightly. "You mean if, right?"

"Okay, if," he conceded in a mockingly condescending voice.

"I'm not sure, but I'm certain I can come up with something suitable for the victor. Do you trust me?"

"You bet. You're on," he said with a grin.

I ended up winning the race, but just because I'd driven over the speed limit. The last thing I wanted was for Kevin Hurley to catch me and ticket me, but if he was out on the road that late, he wasn't anywhere near my place.

I tried to race up onto the porch before David could get there, but I didn't make it before I saw his headlights approach.

"No fair," he said good-naturedly. "You broke the law getting here so quickly."

"We didn't set any ground rules."

David shrugged. "So, what did you win?"

I put the pizza down, and then kissed him with my full attention. After we broke apart, he asked, "Remind me again. Who won?"

"I thought we both deserved a prize," I said.

"I agree wholeheartedly. What should we race to next?"

We both laughed at that, and then we shared the pizza on the porch, using the glasses and utensils David always stored in a basket in his trunk for just such occasions.

After we finished eating, David leaned back in his chair and said, "Eleanor, that's the best thing I've had in days."

"Because of the company?" I asked, teasing him.

"That, too, but you really can make a great pizza. Have you ever thought about going into business?"

I laughed. "No, it sounds too much like work." As I said it, David yawned. "I'm not keeping you up, am I?"

He shook his head. "No, I'm just a little tired. I had to start work at six this morning so I could justify the drive back here tonight so I could see you."

"Do you really have to go back right away?" I hated the thought of him driving three hours on the interstate when he was clearly exhausted.

He nodded. "I'm afraid so. I was lucky to carve out enough time to come back tonight, and I'm going to be paying for it tomorrow," he said as he stood and stretched.

I walked him to his car, and then gave him my best good night kiss. "I'm glad you did."

"Me, too," he said. "Trust me, you're worth every bit of the effort."

For some reason, I just couldn't seem to let him go. "You're not driving back tonight, are you?"

"No, I'd never make it," he admitted. "I'll go back to my apartment and see if I can steal a little sleep before I tackle the drive. I'm glad I never gave up my lease on it."

I hated the thought of what he'd given up just to see me. "How soon do you have to leave in the morning?"

He groaned softly. "It'll have to be around five, if I'm going to make it to the morning meeting in time."

"I hope it was worth it," I asked.

"I'd leave right now, if I had to. That's how much this all meant to me."

"But you won't, right? You need at least some sleep first," I said as I gave him another kiss, and then pushed him away. "Don't worry about the basket. I'll do the dishes and have it ready for the next time you come over."

"That sounds promising," he said.

"Quit fishing," I said. "You know there's going to be a next time."

"I always hope so," he said. "But I don't want to take anything for granted."

"You're not," I said.

I stood on the porch and waved to David as he drove away, and then gathered the dishes and basket and walked inside.

I'd fought his presence in my life for a long time, but it was good having him in it now, and I knew in my heart that Joe would have approved.

Chapter 3

"Eleanor, I don't know why we can't shut down for a few hours today, too, so I can come with you. We won't lose that much business."

I couldn't believe that Maddy was actually arguing with me about closing the Slice while I helped Cindy to get ready for her grand opening and book signing. My sister had been the one urging me all last week to keep the place open while Chef Benet was in town, but now that we were on the eve of his visit, she was clearly beginning to have second thoughts.

"That's not what you said before."

Maddy shrugged. "I know, but a girl has a right to change her mind sometimes, doesn't she?"

I laughed at her. "Come on, tell the truth. You're just not all that crazy about running the kitchen while I'm gone, are you? Have some faith in yourself, Sis. You're good at it. You've proven that before."

She acted as though this wasn't news to her, but she was clearly still unhappy about the arrangements. "I know I can handle it, but I still think that you could use my help dealing with Benet. You don't know what he's like."

"Don't worry, I've done some research," I said. I had, too, checking out his name on the Internet. If half the stories I'd read were true, there was a part of me that was starting to think that

Maddy was right. The man might really be too much for me to handle on my own.

"Tell you what," I said. "We'll keep things like we planned them for now, but if I feel like I'm in over my head, I'll send you a 911 text and you can rush right over."

"I'll be waiting for it," she said.

"Come on. You'll be fine," I said, trying to buoy her spirits.

"I'm not the one I'm worried about," she said as I left her alone in the kitchen.

Greg was prepared to wait on tables by himself, since Josh was still in school for another hour, but so far, we hadn't had a customer all afternoon.

"What's up, boss? Heading over to the slaughterhouse?"

"Keep an eye on her, would you?" I asked. "If things get too crazy, give me a call and I'll see if I can come over and lend a hand."

"Don't worry. She'll be fine."

"Josh is still coming as soon as school's out, right?"

"He'll be here. He texted me about ten minutes ago, and I can handle this madhouse by myself until he shows up. Not that it's anything to worry about at the moment. Why the lull? Have any ideas?"

"Who knows? Our customer base is capricious at best. I'm sure someone will show up soon."

"I hope so," he said. "I've already done the crossword puzzle in today's paper, and I'm going to start on the brainteasers next, and I hate doing those things."

I nodded. "Maybe our lack of customers isn't necessarily a bad thing."

He looked at me oddly, and then asked, "Are you feeling okay, boss? Do you have a fever or something?"

"I'm fine," I said a little self-consciously. "Why, do I look bad?"

"No, but that's the problem," Greg answered. "I just figured if you stopped worrying about the bottom line around here, something must be horribly wrong with you."

I had to laugh. "I may pinch pennies, but we both know that there's more to life than money."

Greg kept looking at me strangely. "If you're trying to persuade me that you're okay, you're using the wrong words."

I had to smile, mainly because he was right. "Okay, I get it. Seriously, though, we might end up shutting down a few hours today, along with tomorrow's signing. Are you okay with that?"

"I'm fine with it. It's not exactly like I need the money to get by, remember?" he asked with a grin.

"I know. I'm just grateful you keep coming in at all," I said, sounding a little more sincere than I'd planned. "I've been afraid to ask, but why *do* you keep coming back?"

It was his turn to look serious as he asked, "Eleanor, you're not trying to get rid of me, are you?"

"No way. I'm just not sure I'd act the same way if I were in your shoes."

Greg just shrugged. "You might be surprised. I'd go crazy with nothing to do but go to college, and besides, where else would I find the kind of entertainment that's around here every day?"

"I'll grant you that," I said with a smile. "Maddy and I both love having you here. You know that, don't you?"

"I do, but it's always good to hear," he said.

Josh came in as we were talking, and he looked excited as he asked, "Did you two see the fire?"

I was about to ask him if he was cutting classes again to work at the pizzeria when his initial question cut through my mind and moved to the head of the line.

"What are you talking about? Where did you see a fire?" I asked, having a feeling of dread sink into my stomach as I imagined the books at the new bookstore going up in flames. "Is it in the Bookmark?"

"Believe it or not, it's closer than that," Josh said as he pointed outside. "Somebody must have just torched the trashcan out front."

We all raced to the front window, and Maddy must have heard the commotion, because she soon joined us. "What's going on?" she asked as she dried her hands on her apron.

I pointed outside as the flames in the trashcan leaped higher into the air. "It appears that there is an arsonist loose in Timber Ridge."

"Well, hot dog, grab some marshmallows and let's have ourselves a roast," my sister said as she headed out the door.

We all followed her, and I found myself wondering what kind of craziness we'd see next in Timber Ridge. The ground around the can was covered in brick pavers, and there wasn't another structure within two dozen feet, so I knew if we just left the fire alone, it would burn itself out soon enough. Not that there was any chance of that happening with the two young men I had working for me.

"Should we try to put it out?" Greg asked, just as I heard sirens coming from nearby. "I've been dying for the chance to use that fire extinguisher of yours."

"No need," I said. "This will give our volunteer firefighters something to practice on that they didn't set themselves."

"I'm taking bets about how many people they use to put it out," Greg said. "Anybody want to make a friendly wager?"

"What's your over and under number?" Maddy asked.

I swatted at my sister. "Don't encourage him," I said.

"Seven," Greg added.

Maddy looked at him and said, "Knowing this town, I'll take the over."

"No way they'll use more than four," Josh said.

Greg looked at me and asked, "Eleanor, do you want to get in on this? The betting window is about to close."

"You know I don't approve of gambling," I said, "but this is a sure thing. Maddy's right. They'll send at least nine."

Maddy grinned at me, and I smiled back. We stood far enough away not to get in the way, and as the fire truck rolled up, I was amazed to see that there were only three firefighters on it.

Josh smiled. "It looks like I win."

"Hang on a second. The fire's not out yet," Maddy said.

"No way. Only the ones on the truck count," Josh said.

"Judges?" Maddy asked Greg.

He grinned. "The number has to be the total firefighters that show up until the blaze is out. Sorry, Josh."

His best friend just laughed. "That's okay. I can live with that."

The hose was hooked up to a hydrant at the edge of the promenade, and by the time they got it unrolled and in front of the trashcan, which was now slowly burning out all by itself, there were exactly seven volunteers. They absolutely buried the can with water, snuffing out the last remaining ember and sending debris all over my section of the promenade. The force of the blast was so hard, I was afraid they'd knock the can off its chain, but it held fast. I looked around and saw that the activity had drawn quite a crowd, including Cindy from the Bookmark.

I called over to her, "Today's the big day."

"Are you coming?" she asked, the nervousness clear in her voice.

"No worries; I'll be there soon."

Cindy managed a halfhearted wave, and then disappeared back into her bookstore. I had to wonder just how bad her day had been so far, and how much worse it was probably going to get.

I just hoped that I was wrong. Now that the excitement was over, I decided that there was no point in putting it off. As the crew of volunteers rolled their hose up and put it back in the truck, I said, "Well, it looks like all of the entertainment is over, so I'd better take off. I'll see you all later."

"Have fun," Maddy said with a hint of the devil in her eyes.

"You, too," I answered.

"Remember the secret number if you get in a jam," Maddy said, mouthing *nine one one* to me.

I just laughed as I left them there.

As I walked down the promenade toward the Bookmark, I took a deep breath.

It was time to follow up on my promise to help.

I just hoped Chef Benet wasn't as bad as I'd heard.

But I wasn't counting on it.

I had to knock on the Bookmark's door three times before anyone came to let me in. Cindy finally heard me, and she looked frazzled already when she unlocked the door, something that was definitely not a good sign.

"Are things really that bad?" I asked.

"I don't know how they could get any worse. Chef Benet's assistant just got here, but the star of the show isn't even in town yet. What am I going to do if Benet doesn't show up tomorrow?"

Cindy looked as though she wanted to cry. It was time to do my best to calm her down. "Take it easy, and tell me what's going on. Were you honestly expecting him to get here the day before his event? He's probably busy with his television show responsibilities."

"But they told me he'd be here today," she said, as though repeating it enough would somehow make it happen.

I tapped my watch. "Don't borrow trouble. Today's not over yet, not by a long shot, Cindy. Has anything good happened so far?" I had to do my best to cheer her spirits.

"Well," she admitted, "at least his personal assistant is here."

"That's good, right?" I asked, trying to reach for anything I could.

Cindy's frown just deepened. "I'm not all that sure. From what he's been saying so far, we're going to be in for a rough ride. Eleanor, I'm so sorry I got you into this."

"Nonsense, I'm happy to help. Now, let's go see what we can do to make this go more smoothly and take some of the worries off your mind."

"I'm not sure that's even possible," she admitted.

"Tomorrow is a big day for you, and you need to do your best to enjoy it."

As we spoke, a tall, thin young man with ginger hair came out biting his lower lip and mumbling softly to himself.

When he spotted me, he asked Cindy, "Who is this? One of your clerks?"

"I'm Eleanor Swift," I said, extending my hand.

He either didn't notice it, or chose to ignore it, as he said, "I'm sorry, I should have guessed. Listen, I don't mean to be rude, but we've got a ton of work to do before the event tomorrow. Why exactly are you here?"

"I asked her to come over to lend a hand. She's going to be helping us out as one of Chef Benet's assistants," Cindy said. "She runs A Slice of Delight just down the promenade."

"Right, the pizza place," he said with a worried expression on his face. "I have to tell you, the chef is not at all happy about that."

Okay, somehow this conversation had started off badly, but I wasn't going to keep it that way. "I'm sorry. I introduced myself before, but I still don't know who you are."

"I'm the assistant to Chef Benet," he answered a little too stiffly for my taste.

"I didn't ask you what your job description was. Let's try this again. I'm Eleanor Swift. And you are?" I asked with my brightest smile.

The young man sighed as he returned it and shrugged. "Forgive me. When I'm setting up for one of the chef's events, I kind of get in a zone. I do apologize, and I'll try to be a little less intense. My name is Oliver Wills, by the way."

"So, how long have you worked for Benet?" I asked.

He flinched as I said the chef's name. "It's Chef, always Chef, and nothing but Chef. He won't even answer to his name, if you can believe that."

"From what I've heard about him, I have no trouble believing that all," I said, still smiling.

Oliver laughed. "You think you know what he's like, but you're wrong. He's a thousand times worse than his reputation."

What an odd thing to say about an employer. "If you don't mind my asking, why do you continue to work for him, then?"

Oliver looked as though he'd contemplated that very question a million times before. "He's a celebrity, and I'm just a nobody. Not that I'm not a good cook in my own right," he added hastily, "But Chef has the fame, and the reputation, and at our little network, that seems to be what matters most. Talent and ability both take a backseat to star power."

"How sad," I said. "It shouldn't be that way."

Oliver smiled as he turned to face Cindy. "You know what? I like her."

"I do, too," Cindy said with a relieved expression. I wasn't sure how Benet was going to be, but Oliver seemed nice enough once we broke through his frosty shell.

It was time we all got busy. "Now, what can we do to make Benet, er, Chef, happy?"

"If I knew that, I'd have my own show by now," Oliver said with a smile. "The test kitchen isn't going to arrive for another hour. Would it be possible for us to visit your pizzeria while we're waiting? I need to do some recon work there, too."

"You're not going to tear the place down, are you?" I asked.

"Not me, but I can't speak for Chef."

Oliver and I started to walk out, when Cindy asked, "Do you need me? If I may, I'd rather stay here while they're setting the kitchen up for tomorrow's demonstration."

"Stay," Oliver said, and then paused a moment to add, "I'm

sorry if I was too hard on you before. Working for Chef has a tendency to do that to people."

"You're forgiven," Cindy said with a broad smile.

After we left the bookstore, I said, "I'm curious about something. I was under the impression that celebrity events were planned well in advance. This kind of happened at the last minute, didn't it?"

Oliver nodded. "Tell me about it. We were all set to debut the book in New York for the morning talk-show programs, but Chef decided at the last second that he had to come to North Carolina."

"And you don't know why?"

Oliver frowned. "No offense, but he turned down a massive amount of exposure, something that's completely out of character for him. Plus, if he had to go someplace in North Carolina, why here? Bookstores in Raleigh, Charlotte, and Asheville all put in requests for him, but he insisted on coming to this little burg."

I couldn't let that comment slide, not with the way he'd said it. "I know we have a small town. That's why so many of us like it."

Oliver looked around at the shops, the brick promenade, the trees, the statues, the obelisk, and the captured cannon. "I didn't mean anything derogatory, trust me. I can see why you all love it. It's charming, and there's no denying it."

"But it's not exactly a place for a proper book launch, right?" I asked.

"No, not in my mind. Is that your place?" he asked, pointing to my blue building.

"It is," I said as we neared. "We're open right now, so I'd appreciate it if you didn't disrupt our business any more than you have to."

"Of course," he said, and then said, "Why blue, if I might ask?"

"You can ask, but I honestly don't know myself," I answered honestly.

He studied the painted brick, mortar, and stone, and then said, "It looks as though it would be expensive to remove. I'm guessing you were stuck with it when you got the place."

"Right in one," I said. "How could you possibly know that?"

Oliver laughed. "You might have your own hidden sense of whimsy, but you look far too sensible to paint the structure blue yourself."

"I might just surprise you," I said, grinning at him. I held the door open, and after he walked in, I followed him.

During the time I'd been at the Bookmark, my pizzeria was now over halfway full. Greg and Josh were both waiting on customers, but both young men looked at me with matching inquiring glances as I walked in with Oliver. I smiled and nodded with as much reassurance as I could muster that all was right with the world, and they both went back to work. It was nice having them both look out for me, even if I didn't need it as much as they thought I did.

"They're worried about you," Oliver said softly.

"I didn't realize you caught that," I said with a smile.

"Believe me, I don't miss much." He looked around, and then said, "I may have spoken too hastily. This place is really quaint."

"We like it," I said.

"May I see the kitchen?"

"This way," I said, leading him to the back.

Maddy was surprised to see me, and before she noticed that we had company, she asked, "How bad was it? Is the man as dreadful as we thought? I can't believe you're already back here. I didn't get any texts."

I didn't know what she was talking about at first, and then I realized that she was talking about the 911 call I was supposed to make at the first sign of trouble.

As the chef's assistant joined us, I said, "Maddy, this is Oliver Wills. Oliver, this is my sister, Maddy, the best front person we have, and a rather excellent backup in the kitchen as well."

They shook hands, and then Maddy said, "You must be special, Oliver. Eleanor doesn't let just anyone come back here during working hours."

He shrugged. "I don't know about being special. I'm the chef's personal assistant and food-prep man. It's not really all that much of a claim to fame."

"I assume you're talking about Chef Benet," Maddy said. "I've got to tell you, I just loved his Chicken Parm Twist from the show last night."

"Can you keep a secret?" he asked.

I was about to answer for her when Maddy said, "Try me."

Lowering his voice, Oliver said proudly, "That was actually one of mine."

"Really?" Maddy asked, clearly happy with the backstage information.

"Well, at least it was my basic idea. The chef expounded on it and made it his own, of course, but I thought of the twist."

"You're good," Maddy said.

Oliver seemed pleased with the praise, and then noticed the conveyor oven. "Is this how you make your pizzas?" he asked.

"Yes, it works fine for our needs," I chimed in.

"You don't have a wood-fired oven?" he asked.

Why did everyone believe that pizza had to be baked on a stone by the fire to be authentic? "There's actually one on the square, but it's in another restaurant."

Oliver nodded. "May I see that one instead?"

"I'm sorry, but the owner is out of town until further notice."

It was true. Nathan Pane had left town after losing his nephew, a man who had opened a rival to our pizzeria, and as far as I knew, the pizzeria's true owner had no immediate plans to come back.

"That's too bad," Oliver said. As he looked around, he said, "I suppose this will just have to do."

"It works for us," Maddy said coldly, clearly not enjoying

Oliver's take on our kitchen. Whatever goodwill he'd amassed so far was now gone, and what's more, he could tell it from our expressions.

"Please, don't misunderstand," Oliver said. "I learned to cook in a kitchen a great deal like this that my parents owned when I was a young boy. I personally think that it's just about perfect. Chef is the one that is so hard to please."

"He'll just have to learn to live with a little disappointment, then," Maddy said, some of the coolness easing out of her voice. But it was still clear that she wasn't happy about having me, or Oliver, in the kitchen when she worked.

"Thanks, Maddy," I said as I led Oliver out. "I'll talk to you later."

"It was truly nice meeting you," the chef's assistant said.

"You, too," Maddy said, and she even managed a slight smile.

"I'm sorry about that," I said as we walked out into the dining room.

"About what?"

"We tend to take things personally around here, and my sister doesn't mind expressing her feelings when she's not pleased about something," I explained.

"There's no need to apologize. Actually, I thought she was quite charming," Oliver said.

"Boy, you really are used to abuse if you think my sister is pleasant," I said with a smile.

"What can I say? We all have to put up with things we don't like in order to do the things we do."

"Wow. So, you're a chef *and* a philosopher," I said.

"No, I'm a cook. Just a cook," he repeated as though it were a mantra. "We should get back the bookstore and see how Cindy is doing."

"Do you think Chef will approve of our kitchen?" I asked. Blast it all, now he had me doing it.

"Don't worry about it too much. He'd complain if you had a

culinary institute at your disposal instead of a pizzeria. It seems to just be his nature."

"I won't sweat it then," I said. "Listen, no matter what, this event is really important to Cindy, so if there's anything I can do, just let me know."

"I will," he said.

His smile turned into a frown when we got back to the Bookmark and saw the new demonstration kitchen's layout. "What happened? This doesn't follow the plan at all. It's all wrong. We have to redo everything."

Cindy was about to break down, but I stepped in and said, "Then let's do it. Why don't you go tell them exactly what you need, Oliver?"

I gave her a quick hug as he talked to the moving men, who were thankfully still on site packing up their equipment.

"Do you really think that it's going to be all right?" Cindy asked me, the hope bright in her eyes.

"I can't guarantee that, but at least it will be quick," I said with a grin. "In three days, it will be just like he'd never been here."

Only I was wrong saying that then.

I just didn't know it at the time.

Chapter 4

"I'm truly sorry about all of this," Oliver said to us as Cindy and I worked with the installation people to get everything in order for the demonstration the next day. "I just know that if we don't get it right the first time, Chef is going to be insufferable, and you don't want to see what that man can do when he's not happy. It's bad enough when he's in a good mood."

"Any examples you might like to share about the man at his worst?" I asked as Cindy and I worked at unboxing the bowls, pans, and utensils for the big event.

Oliver shook his head in disbelief. "Where do I start? Once, in Virginia, he intentionally locked the bookstore owner in a storage closet without telling anyone what he was doing, and the place was in a complete panic over the missing woman as he continued serenely on with his demonstration," Oliver said.

It was clear that story wasn't going to help Cindy's peace of mind. I asked, "Why would he do something like that?"

Oliver frowned as he explained, "Chef said that she kept asking too many questions, and he was beginning to lose his focus. He didn't even try to lie and say that it was an accident." Oliver ran a hand through his hair as he added, "I can't tell you what we had to do to make that problem go away."

"Come on, we won't share the story with anyone else," I said.

"No, you don't understand. I signed a nondisclosure agreement harsher than any writer ever had to agree to in their lives. If I say a word about it, I'll not only lose my job, but I'll most likely go to jail, too."

"That's pretty bad," I said. "I'm amazed no one ever took a swing at him."

That brought a smile to Oliver's lips. "Trust me; you wouldn't believe the number of people who have done just that. Chef claims that his arrogance is one of the things that make him a great creator of dishes, but I don't believe it for a second. I think he just enjoys being a bully."

I shook my head. "And yet you stay on with him. If you don't mind my saying, I have to believe that you can do better than this."

Oliver looked around, and then lowered his voice. "This has just been a means to an end all these years. I haven't just worked as his researcher and main assistant on the show and for his cookbooks. I've constantly been pitching my own ideas to the execs at the network, too." I noticed that his fists were clinched as he added, "If they'd only given me one shot at my own show, it would have given me the career I should really be having, instead of working for Chef."

It appeared that having an oversized ego wasn't just his employer's problem. "But in the meantime, you've been paying a pretty big price for an opportunity that might never present itself," I said.

"I like to think of it as paying my dues," he answered, "But trust me, I won't be paying them that much longer. I've just about had enough."

"Well, then, I hope you get exactly what you deserve in the end." Oliver could interpret that statement however he wanted to, but if he took a moment to really think about what I'd just said, he'd realize that I hadn't exactly wished him the best of luck. In my mind, it was the perfect curse. Who among us would truly be happy if we actually got what we deserved in life, both the good parts and the bad?

"It must be frustrating watching him take the stage every day, when that's where you want to be," Cindy added.

"Deserve to be," Oliver corrected. He took a deep breath, and then his voice faltered a little as he said, "I know it must sound crazy to you two. But it's not going to keep going on like this for-ever. Honestly, there are some days when I don't know if it's ever going to happen, but if it does, it's going to have to occur quickly." He looked all around us, though we were alone at that moment, and explained, "I've decided that I'm going to try one last pitch to Chef's executive producer tomorrow after the dem-onstration, and if she turns me down again, I'm moving on to an-other dream, and she can find someone else to hold Chef's hand."

"What will you do if you leave this job?" I asked.

"Who knows? I might just work in a real restaurant where I can actually get credit for what I cook," he said. "I'm better than most people could imagine, but I'll never be able to prove it if I can't get out from under Chef's thumb." Oliver must have real-ized just how much of his thoughts he'd been revealing to us. As though he needed to break a spell we had him under, he shook his head and looked over the setup we currently had. After nod-ding, he said, "I think this will do great. Ladies, you were a huge help today. Thanks so much. I couldn't have done it without you."

"You're most welcome." I'd been touched by Oliver's confes-sions, and how hard he worked for a man that he clearly didn't like. He deserved at least something for all he'd done today. "Would you like to come by A Slice of Delight for a bite to eat? It's on the house, and you can order whatever you'd like."

He took a moment to consider it, and then reluctantly said, "Thanks, but I'm worn out, and I've still got to work on tomor-row's presentation for Chef. I think I'll just go back to my hotel room and work there, if you don't mind. I'll see you bright and early tomorrow, ladies. Have a nice evening."

"You, too," we said as Oliver left the bookstore and we were alone.

After the chef's assistant was gone, Cindy hugged me.

"What was that for?" I asked after I pulled away.

"Are you kidding? Eleanor, you saved me today."

I could hardly call the little bit I'd done anything that dramatic. "Oliver wasn't all that bad."

My friend shrugged, and then said, "Not after you got here. How did you manage to handle him so well?"

"All I did was talk to him," I said. "I asked a few questions, and then listened to what he had to say. That's all most of us want these days, someone who will listen to us. It's amazing how intoxicating the feeling can be." I touched her shoulder lightly, and then added, "Cindy, you really shouldn't worry about tomorrow."

"Not even a little bit?" she asked me with a grin.

I smiled back at her. "Okay, a little is okay. Heck, I'd even say that it was normal. You should know that when Joe and I started the Slice, I don't think I slept more than ten minutes at a time the week before we officially opened."

Cindy got quiet for a moment, and then asked me in a somber tone, "Eleanor, do you ever stop missing him?"

I realized that the question was less about my late husband than it was about her feelings toward hers, so I was very careful when I answered her. "I miss him, and I always will, but it's not the same gaping wound that it once was. I know it doesn't feel like it at the moment, but it does get better over time. It's kind of the great equalizer."

She looked troubled by my statement. "That sounds as though I'm going to forget him, and I never want to do that."

I touched her hand. "I'm not saying that at all. What time does is it gives you perspective. Instead of feeling mostly pain when you think of your late husband and turning him into some kind of saint in your mind, you begin to remember him as a man, flaws and all, the good right along with the bad. When those thoughts start to occur, you're on your way to healing. At least that's how it's worked for me." I was a little embarrassed by the way I was lecturing her, but Cindy had asked me for my take on things, and I owed her the most honesty I could muster.

"Do you think you'll ever fall in love again?" she asked, her voice sounding almost frightened as she posed it.

"That's a complicated question," I said. "As a matter of fact, I just started dating someone, and we're still just finding our way, but I have a feeling that it's going to be worth it in the long run."

"I know I shouldn't be grilling you like this, but there's no one else I can talk to about what I'm going through."

"I don't mind," I answered. "If I'm not comfortable with your questions, I may just not answer them." I tried to add a slight smile, but I knew that it wouldn't do much to ease Cindy's troubled mind.

"What motivated you to ever date again? I can't imagine doing it," she said, and I could see tears forming in the corners of her eyes.

It was an answer I'd sought myself, and one that I was comfortable giving her now. "Joe would never have wanted me to spend the rest of my life alone. He was too full of a strong spirit to want me to waste away longing for the past. I finally realized that I was actually doing him a disservice by the way I was living my life."

Cindy hugged me again, and as she did, I could feel a shiver go through her. "It's so hard, Eleanor. How do you get through it?"

"It's like everything else. You take things one day at a time, and you rely on your friends," I said. "I'm here for you, Cindy; I know that Maddy is, too, and at least a dozen other people in Timber Ridge. If you need help, all you have to do is reach out and ask for it."

"I'll try," she said as she pulled away and wiped her cheeks.

"It's not easy, is it?" I asked, smiling at her. "The best way to do it is just practice."

"Hey, I asked you, didn't I?" she asked, a slight grin warming her face. I was glad to see it.

"Baby steps are all right," I said. "Just as long as they're all heading in the right direction."

"I'll do my best," she said.

When I got back to the Slice, business had definitely picked up. Greg and Josh were busy up front waiting on customers, and it was pretty easy to see that they could use Maddy's help out front, too. For a split second, I considered giving them a hand myself and letting my sister continue to work in the kitchen, but I knew how stressed-out Maddy got when the orders started piling in, so I couldn't do that to her. It was easy enough to understand why she felt that way. I'd had a lot more practice coping with it than she had, and it still managed to get to me sometimes.

"I'm back," I said as I grabbed my apron off the hook once I walked into the kitchen.

"I'm not even going to pretend that I didn't miss you," Maddy said as she gladly gave up her spot at the prep table. "How did things go at the bookstore?"

"I was about to give up ever making things right, but we finally got everything in place over there," I answered. "Now all we have to do is wait for Chef Benet to grace us with his presence." I glanced beside the oven and saw that something was obscured by a dish towel. When I pulled the cloth off, I saw that it was Chef Benet's last book.

"What's this?" I asked with a grin as I picked it up. "I didn't realize that you were that big a fan of the man."

Maddy smiled back at me. "Sue me, I like autographed books. Do you think there's any chance that he'll sign this for me tomorrow?"

"All bets are off, but it couldn't hurt to ask," I said as I handed it back to her.

"I know that there are all kinds of terrible stories about how the man acts in public, but honestly, I can't wait to meet him," Maddy said. "I've got a dozen signed books from quite a few authors, but they are all mysteries. This will be my first cookbook."

"Then it's going to be a big day for all of us," I said.

Greg came through the door with another order. "Man, the natives are getting restless out there. How's the food coming along back here?"

I glanced in the oven and saw that two pizzas were close to coming out. "Give us two minutes and we'll have something for you."

"What do I do in the meantime?" he asked with a smile. "I know one thing. I'm not going back out there without food in my hands."

"You could always tap dance, sing, and just generally try to entertain us with your amazing talent," Maddy suggested.

"Hang on, I thought our goal was to keep our customers," Greg answered. "Not the cooks."

"You may call us chefs, if you please," I said in my haughtiest tone. We all cracked up at that as I reached in and pulled the first pizza out, since it looked good. Checking the order, I saw that it was for the dining room, so I slid it out onto a serving trail, cut it deftly, and then handed it to Greg.

"How's that for timing? You are saved from embarrassing yourself," I said.

"At least for now," he answered, and then took off with the pizza.

"I'd better get out there and give them a hand," Maddy said. "Can you deal with this by yourself?"

I looked at the stacked orders. "Don't worry about me. I can handle it. Thanks for holding down the fort. I mean it. I really appreciate it."

"I was happy to do it." As Maddy started to go out front to join Greg and Josh, she hesitated long enough to add, "Just do me a favor and don't make a habit of it."

"Look on the bright side. At least we'll be closed tomorrow until four," I said. "The demonstration will be over by then, and we'll get our pizza parlor back."

"If you want to know the truth, it can't happen soon enough for me," she said.

"You and me and Cindy, too," I said as I started knuckling a new ball of cold dough into one of our large pans to fill the bottom order on the stack.

"Is she freaking out over there?" Maddy asked.

"On more levels than I can explain," I said. I didn't want to get into all of the things Cindy and I had discussed, particularly my love life.

"She'll be fine," Maddy said with the gentle smile I loved so much. "As long as we're beside her, how can she go wrong?"

"I'm glad you're on board all the way," I said.

"Hey, I'm a big fan of the woman myself, but honestly, if something, or someone, is important to you, they matter to me, too."

I finally caught up with the pizza rush, but the kitchen was a mess the rest of the night, and by the time we served our last customer, I was ready to throw in the towel myself. Maddy and I had different philosophies when it came to running the Slice's kitchen, but I couldn't exactly fuss at her after she'd done me such a huge favor by covering for me. It was going to take some real cleaning efforts to get things right again, but at the moment all I wanted to do was go home and go to sleep. It suddenly occurred to me that I'd at least get to sleep in the next day, so that was something.

Taking a deep breath, I started tackling the mess. It helped that Maddy pitched in, too, and we got it taken care of sooner than I would have believed, without skipping a single step or cutting a corner.

I had to admit, though, that by the time I got home, I was too tired to even take a shower. A part of me was suddenly glad that David was out of town, because I was in no position to entertain.

I collapsed on top of my bed, not even bothering to undress, and did my best not to dream about pizza and difficult chefs.

As promised, I met Maddy the next day in front of the Slice a little after eleven. "It feels odd not being open today," she said. "Did you enjoy sleeping in, Sis?"

"I tried to, but I couldn't help myself; I got up at my regular time. It was all I could do not to get dressed and come to work this morning." As I let us in and then locked the door behind us afterward, I added, "Maybe I should have listened to my instincts. We still need dough for later this afternoon and tonight."

"You're just making half a batch, though, right?" Maddy asked.

I'd already considered, and rejected, the idea. "No, I'll make a full recipe, and then I can freeze whatever we don't use. I'm getting low on backup dough, so it will be nice having a cushion again. How about you? Did you enjoy sleeping in?" I asked as we walked into the kitchen and I started pulling the ingredients we'd need from our pantry.

"Not a chance," Maddy said with a frown. "Who would have believed it? I used to be able to sleep through a fire alarm, but not this morning. I knew I had time off, but my body refused to accept it. I woke up at my normal time, and then stared at the alarm clock, trying to will myself to go back to sleep the rest of the time."

"Did you have any luck at all?" I asked as I started measuring flour into the mixer. "Sometimes those last stolen minutes are the best."

She stifled a yawn, and then asked, "What do you think?"

"I believe we're both going to be a little groggy today, but take heart. Where there's hope, there's caffeine."

"Why don't I make us a pot?" she volunteered, and I wasn't about to disagree.

By the time I had the first batch of dough ready to rest, Maddy handed me a cup. I wasn't ordinarily a big coffee drinker, but today I needed it to get myself started.

Maddy clinked my coffee cup with hers and said, "Here's to a good day, despite what we've been told to expect."

I took a deep sip and then shrugged. "You never know. Honestly, I've got a good feeling about today."

"Then we're in trouble," Maddy said as she began prepping vegetables for later.

"Why do you say that?" I asked, honestly curious about my sister's reaction.

"Eleanor, every premonition you've ever had in your life has ended badly, and you know it."

"That's not true," I said in protest. "I dreamed that I was going to meet the man I was supposed to marry the very night before Joe came into my life."

She nodded. "Okay, so you got one in ten thousand right. Good for you, but I'm still not convinced."

"There have been more times than that," I said. "I just can't list them all off the top of my head."

"Well, let's both just hope that you're due to have another one," Maddy said.

After we had everything ready and the dough was stored away in the fridge, I asked, "That should take care of things until we get back. What do you say? Are you ready to go meet your idol?"

"It's not like he's my hero or anything," Maddy said, but I noticed that she did grab her book on the way out of the kitchen. "I just think it could be nice to meet him."

As I hung my apron back on its hook, I said, "Let's just hope that he exceeds our expectations, and in a good way, too."

"I'm sure he's just a little temperamental," Maddy said. "They say that all the great ones are."

I laughed a little, but not enough to offend my sister. "I'd argue with you about that, but I really don't care one way or the other. I just want today to be as uneventful as it can possibly be."

We turned off the lights and locked the exterior door to the Slice as Mark Deacon walked up. "You're not closed, are you?" he asked incredulously. "What about that free pizza you offered me yesterday?"

"I am so sorry, but we're working the book signing at the Bookmark," I said, "But if you're here to eat lunch, I'll make one just for you. No one can say that my word isn't good. When I make a promise, I follow through."

"No, don't bother," Mark said. "It's okay. I'll catch you another time."

I knew that Cindy would be expecting us at any minute, but this took precedence, as far as I was concerned. Who knew how long it would take Mark to come back if I turned him away this time? "You're not getting away that easily. Maddy, you grab one arm, and I'll get the other."

I unlocked the door and glanced at the clock. We'd left the Slice a little early, and now we'd get to the bookshop a little late, but we still had two and a half hours before the big event. What harm could it do to stop to make one of my friends a pizza?

"Would you like a booth or a table?" Maddy asked as we all walked in together.

"If it's all the same to you, I'd rather eat in the kitchen with you two."

I had to laugh at that. "Mark, you left the diner to have lunch with us. You can eat wherever you'd like. If the kitchen is where you want to eat, you've got it."

"That would be great," he said.

I flipped the oven on, glad that it had a quick-start feature. If

I'd had to build and stoke a fire in a brick pizza oven, Mark wouldn't be eating for quite a while.

He looked at the conveyor oven, and as I kneaded dough into a pan, he asked, "Aren't you going to throw it up in the air like they do on TV?"

I had to laugh as I said, "Sorry, we knuckle our dough here. There's really nobody to show off for usually, and besides, I like this way better."

"That's okay," he answered with a laugh. "I wasn't expecting a floor show."

"What would you like on your pizza, sir?" I asked as I added a layer of sauce to the exposed dough.

He shrugged. "Just throw some veggies and some meat on it. To be honest with you, I'm not all that picky."

I did as he asked as Mark took a seat on a barstool by the prep counter, and Maddy pulled out my office chair so she could join us.

"I'm not used to working with an audience," I said.

"Me, either," Mark replied.

"I don't know what you two are so afraid of. I do my best work with a crowd of onlookers," Maddy said with a broad grin.

Just as I finished making the pizza, the oven's preheating cycle was finished, and I slid it onto the moving conveyor belt.

I wiped my hands on my apron, and then asked, "I'm dying to know. How did you manage to get away from the grill?"

He shrugged. "I finally decided that I've been turning you down long enough. Besides, my customers just rave about your pizza, and I just had to try some of it for myself."

"Your food is great, too," Maddy said.

"Let's face it. We're both good at what we do," Mark said. "But I just had a yen for pizza, and I can't get Laney to make it." Laney had worked at the grill forever. In fact, she'd been there longer than Mark had, and had become kind of an institution there over the years. I knew that it took a lot for Mark to break away from work to visit us, and I greatly appreciated it.

"I'm glad you came. Are you going to the big book signing later?" I asked.

Mark looked at me with the distaste clear on his face. "No, to be honest with you, I tend to stay away from crowds when I'm not at work. I get tired of being around people all of the time."

"You don't have to tell me. That's why I hang out in the kitchen," I admitted. "I like people, but there's nothing like being back here and making things happen."

We were still chatting when the pizza slid out the other side. I cut off the oven, and then asked Mark, "It's not too late to change your mind. Would you still like to eat this here, or should I slide it into a box so you can take it with you?"

"Are you pressed for time?" he asked.

"Not at all," I said, hoping he hadn't seen me just glance at the clock on the wall near his head.

"Then I'll eat it here, on one condition."

"What's that?" Maddy asked.

"You two have to join me. There's no way that I can eat all of this by myself, and if I bring it back to Laney, she'll smack me with her spatula."

Neither one of us had eaten yet, and it would probably be a long time before we got the opportunity again. "That sounds good to me," I said. "How about you?"

Maddy nodded her approval as well, and the three of us had a slice apiece.

Mark took his first bite, and then grinned broadly. "Hey, this is really good."

I had to laugh at his reaction. "Don't act so surprised. It's not the first one I ever made, you know."

"I didn't mean that," he said. "I heard it was good, but I didn't think it was this tasty."

"Thank you, kind sir," I said. "Maddy makes a mean pizza, too."

My sister shook her head as she finished another bite. "You can give me all of the credit you want to, Eleanor, but you are the pizza guru around here."

"Well, it's pretty clear that I don't know what I've been missing all these years." He looked at the half pizza that was left after we finished eating, and then asked, "I changed my mind. For pizza this good, I'm willing to risk the wrath of Laney. Could I possibly get this to go?"

"You surely can," I said as I boxed it up for him.

"What do I owe you?" Mark asked as he reached for his wallet.

"Put away your money. There's no charge for the first one," I said.

Maddy grinned and added, "That's the way we snag you as a customer. First we get you hooked, and then you have to come back for more."

"It's a pretty sure bet that I will. Thanks again. You both made my day."

As we walked him out, I felt good that Mark had finally made the trek to our pizzeria.

That glow died pretty suddenly, though, when I saw a man dressed in a chef's outfit storm out of the Bookmark, throwing things as he left.

It appeared that Chef Benet had finally arrived, and we were late for his big entrance, though it appeared that we were catching his grand exit.

Chapter 5

"Chef, it's an honor to meet you," Maddy said before I could even get a word in myself to try to stop his hasty retreat. Chef Benet was dressed in his white smock and high hat, standing on the sidewalk in front of the Bookmark looking up and down the promenade as though he wasn't exactly sure where he was. All that was clear was that he wanted to be just about anywhere else. Maddy grabbed his arm and continued, "May I say that you are a true genius in the kitchen."

It certainly got his attention, but more importantly, Maddy's assault froze him in his tracks. He shrugged off her compliment, and then said, "I don't dispute it, but if it is true, then how can they expect me to create anything of worth in there? The demonstration kitchen that they've set up is subpar on so many levels I can't even begin to correct it in the minuscule amount of time I've got left."

"Surely someone with your talent can take the worst setup imaginable and still make magic," I said, doing my best to emulate my little sister and mollify him. If he walked away now, Cindy's bookstore might never recover from it.

He studied me closely, and then turned his attention back to Maddy. "Who exactly are the two of you?"

"We're thrilled to say that we're here just for you," I said. "I'm Eleanor, and this is my sister, Maddy." I held out my hand, hoping to get a grip on the man myself before he could bolt away on us.

Instead of taking my offered hand, Benet looked at it as though it were an undercooked cabbage and pointedly ignored it. "You both are responsible for this mess, then."

"Then let us make it right for you," I said.

"How could you possibly manage to do that? You aren't chefs. You make pizza for a living," he added, making it sound as though there was something fundamentally wrong with our line of work. I could see how the man could alienate people so quickly. He seemed to have a real knack for it, and I was having a more and more difficult time swallowing my own sharp retorts. Maddy must have been medicated to keep her mouth shut so completely.

"It's not gourmet Italian food like you prepare," I admitted, "but we do serve good food for a fair price, something that shouldn't be treated lightly."

He looked at me with open disdain. "And is that all that you aspire to in this life, to create food that is just good, not great?"

"I'm not a genius," I said, "But I've got my fans, too."

Benet looked as though he was having a difficult time believing that. "No doubt they are all philistines and ruffians who don't know what real food is supposed to taste like."

As he continued to verbally lash out at us, Oliver finally came out of the bookstore, followed closely behind by Cindy and another woman I didn't recognize. She was a little older than the rest of us, dressed in a fancy outfit and sporting some nice earrings and a bracelet that cost more than my car.

When she spoke, there was an air of long suffering in her voice. "Antonio, please come back inside."

"We can fix this, Chef," Oliver said, adding his own voice to the mix.

"Patrice, you need to stay out of this," he said to the woman, dismissing her with a flick of his eyes, and then Benet turned and focused his withering gaze on Oliver. "How exactly could you possibly correct this now, when you had all day yesterday to do it right the first time?"

I had to give Oliver some credit. Most folks would have collapsed under the assault, but he stood his ground and took it. In a soothing voice, as though he were coddling a delicate child, he said, "Come in and tell me, and I'll make it work."

The chef shook his head in refusal, and the older woman tried again. "You are under an obligation here, Antonio. You simply must not walk out now. It is unprofessional."

"Need I remind you yet again that you are my wife, and not my business manager?" he asked. "There is an option in my appearance contract that allows me to decline to sign or demonstrate at any venue if the set is not done to my satisfaction. Well, it's not, so I decline," he said.

"You can't do this to me," Cindy said, the despondence thick in her voice. She was close to tears, and I believed that everyone there knew it. "I'll be ruined."

"I can't concern myself with your problems. If this was so important to you, then perhaps you should have done a better job preparing for me," Chef Benet said. He studied her with an air of smug superiority that made me want to throw a pie in his face.

"We did everything you asked," Cindy said, sniffing a few times to keep her emotions in check for as long as she could manage it.

I knew it wouldn't take much more pressure to make her crack like an eggshell. I stepped up and said, "Chef, if you leave, your fans won't have a chance to tell you how much they love you. Wouldn't it be criminal to deprive them of that?"

He bit his lip, and then said, "Perhaps."

It was the most ground he'd given yet, and I decided to push my luck a little further. "It would be tragic if they didn't have the opportunity to see you in person." Wow, I almost choked on those last words, but I wasn't doing this for me; I was trying to protect Cindy from failing before she even had a chance to succeed. We had drawn quite a bit of attention where we stood from folks innocently strolling down the promenade, and I didn't think this debate would do anyone any good being held out on the sidewalk. "Could we at least discuss it inside?"

"Where do you suggest, in your pizza joint?" he asked with as much scorn as I thought he could gather.

Heaven forbid we taint our delicate feet by stepping inside there. This guy was every bit the prima donna we'd been told he was. "I thought we might go back inside the bookstore so we can work out a solution to all of this," I said.

"Fine," he said in annoyance, and managed to lead the rest of us back in.

Cindy grabbed my arm as we hurried in after him and whispered, "Thank you, Eleanor."

"We won a battle, but there's still the war," I said.

As soon as we were inside, a woman in her twenties dressed entirely in black came in after us, carrying an overnight bag over one shoulder. A telephone was in her free hand, and it looked so natural there that I doubt she ever had it very far away.

"Sorry, but the signing isn't due for another two hours," Cindy said as she stepped between the newcomer and Chef Benet.

The woman looked at her watch and then said, "Actually, it's supposed to occur in one hundred and eleven minutes, to be exact." She turned to Chef Benet, and then said, "I just got into town, Chef, but this is too important to let slide. We need to talk, and I mean right now."

"Everyone, I'd like you to meet my executive producer, Jessie Taylor," Benet explained graciously, and then he turned to her. "Jessie, I'm afraid you wasted a trip. I told you last night that we have nothing to talk about."

She clearly wasn't happy with his reaction. "Oh, no? The network and I believe otherwise, and if you know what's good for you, you will, too."

Benet sneered a little, clearly an instinctive reaction to most of his exchanges with lesser beings. "Believe what you will," he said. "Right is on my side."

Jessie turned to me and asked plaintively, "Is there someplace we can talk in private?"

"I don't quite understand why you'd want to talk to me. I don't have anything to say to you," I said, knowing full well that wasn't what she'd meant. I was trying to diffuse the situation, but from the way she reacted to my humor, I may as well have saved my breath.

"I'm talking about us," she said, pointing to Benet and then to herself.

"Why would you ask me? I don't own this place," I said, "You'll have to ask the owner," as I pointed to Cindy.

"That would be fine. You're more than welcome to use my office," Cindy volunteered. "It's just through there."

Jessie started for the office door, but Benet didn't follow her.

She stopped and turned, looking hard at him. "Chef, I won't ask again."

"If only I could believe that," Benet said, and then he followed his producer into Cindy's office. He must have tried to shut the door, but it was new, and the hinges were clearly out of alignment. It began to close, and then slowly swung until it was open a few inches, enough for us to hear whatever they were saying, no matter how much privacy they were under the impression they were enjoying.

I had my doubts that they even realized what had happened, especially after listening to a few moments of their conversation.

"Enough browbeating," Benet said to her fiercely, not keeping his voice down a bit as far as I could tell. "You may as well stop trying to bully me into doing what you want me to do. You don't own me, and neither does your network."

"That's funny, we've got a contract that says exactly that," Jessie said. "Do I even need to remind you that you have an obligation to film two more seasons of your show, and we still have the option to extend that to two more after that?"

"You can't make me be creative for you!" There was a hard edge to his words now. "You are trying to tie my talents up in a yellow-dog contract that I can't and won't fulfill. I won't do it."

"Then you'll be in breach of that yellow-dog contract," she said, her voice and tone matching his now, "and we'll hold your feet to the flames until it is satisfied. If we let you go, you shouldn't even think for one second that anyone will touch you after we're finished with you."

"We'll just see about that," Benet said. "My attorney informs me that we have several legal precedents on our side. I am walking away, and the sooner you people accept that, the better off we'll all be."

Jessie sounded confused by that. "I don't understand why you're so adamant about leaving a successful and proven show, anyway. What are you planning to do if you leave us?"

He looked almost proud as he answered, "Whatever my heart tells me to. The lawyers can settle it amongst themselves, but you can't keep me against my will. I'm going to the Food Bites Network, and I'm leaving you and your pitiful minions behind me."

When the door burst open, we were all trying to pretend that we hadn't heard what had just been said, but it was impossible to do.

Benet's wife took a step toward him, but one glare from the chef sent her scurrying backward as though she'd been slapped.

Benet stopped in front of me and held out his hand. "Give me the key to your restaurant."

I wanted to refuse, but no matter how I felt about the man at the moment, I'd promised Cindy that he could have the place as his greenroom. Who knew what kind of mess he was about to make of it, but I'd just have to hope that my kitchen would fare better than his confrontations had today.

As I handed the key to him, I said, "I don't want to find a thing in my kitchen or dining room touched while you're there, do you understand me?"

He laughed in my face. "Are you actually threatening me? You're nothing but a pizza maker."

I had had just about enough of this windbag's attitude, and I started to say something when my sister, Maddy, of all people, put a restraining hand on my arm. I took a deep breath, smiled gently at her, and then allowed myself to speak with the chef in a voice that wouldn't reflect how I really felt. "I treat my restaurant like it's my baby, and trust me, you don't want to get this mother mad at you."

He took the key, stared at me another second, and then stormed out without another word.

"I'd better go after him," Patrice said, and hurried out the door.

Maddy punched my shoulder lightly. "Wow, I thought you were going to smack him right there. That took guts."

"You know how protective I am about the Slice," I said.

"Just don't get angry with me," she said with a grin.

Cindy turned to Oliver and asked, "What are we going to do? Is he even going to bother coming back?"

The assistant just shrugged. "To tell you the truth, I'm really not sure. In the meantime, we'll have to plan for both contingencies." An idea seemed to blossom in him as Jessie came out. "If worse comes to worse and he doesn't make it back in time, I'll do the demonstration myself."

Jessie heard it, as I was certain she was meant to, since he'd said it with enough volume for folks out on the street to hear him. "Forget it, Oliver. If Benet bails out on this, the show is cancelled, and I'm not just talking about this book launch."

"I could take over his show, Jessie," Oliver said, the pleading thick in his voice. "All of Chef's best creations were inspired by me, and I can prepare them better than he could ever dream of doing."

"I've told you before, Oliver, it's Ms. Taylor to you," Jessie said. "And to be honest with you, I don't care if you're the best chef that's ever been born; you're not getting your own show, at least not as long as I'm running things there."

"Why not?" Oliver demanded. "I've got talent. You've tasted my dishes and said so yourself."

She nodded impatiently, the irritation of this distraction clearly starting to bug her. "In the kitchen, you might just be as good as you keep telling me that you are, but all that really matters is that the camera doesn't like you. If you want to keep the petty little job you have now, I suggest you go find Benet and try to persuade him that it's in his best interest to give his talk and demonstration today."

Oliver looked crushed by her ruthless assessment of his chances to have a show of his own in the future, and as he walked out of the bookshop with shoulders slumped, I couldn't help but feel a little sorry for the guy again.

"Wow, you are a real toad, aren't you? You didn't have to be so hard on him, you know," I said.

Jessie appeared not to have heard me at first. She examined me as though I was something on the bottom of one of her shoes, and then asked, "Excuse me, but were you talking to me?"

"You're the only one trying to be a bigger jerk than Benet is, and if I hadn't just seen it for myself, I never would have believed it," I said, not caring what the producer thought of me at this point. I doubted we were even going to have a signing and a cooking demonstration anymore, and if we did, it was clear that Benet would do it, or not, because of the way he felt, not based on someone else's input.

She frowned as she said, "Perhaps you should just worry about your own little corner of the world, no matter how small and insignificant it might be, and leave me to mine."

"Was anything served by being so mean to Oliver just now?" I asked. "That was just plain cruel."

Jessie shook her head, and with more sadness than anger, she explained, "Listen, I've tried to let him down easy a dozen times over the past two years, but he keeps asking. It sounds to me like he's been crying on your shoulder. Did he tell you that I gave him a screen test when he came up with a really good idea?"

"No," I admitted. "He didn't say a word about that."

Jessie just shook her head. "And why should he? The man couldn't have been any stiffer if he'd been carved out of wood. He has so little stage presence that I almost lost him in the shot a time or two." Jessie waved a hand in the air then, as though she were shooing away a cluster of gnats. "Listen, I'm really upset about what's going on with Chef Benet, but you're right, I shouldn't have taken it out on Oliver. When he comes back, I'll apologize and do my best to smooth things over, but in the meantime, we need to find Benet."

"Was Oliver really that bad?" Maddy asked. "He seems fine to me when he's talking about cooking."

Jessie grimaced. "He nearly set the kitchen on fire during his audition, which would have been bad, but not as bad as his personality on tape. It's never going to work, and the sooner he gives up that particular dream, the better off he'll be. You may not believe me, but at first, I was just trying to help him."

"And now?" I asked.

"Honestly? I've done everything I can to discourage him. It may sound cruel to you people, but stringing him along is a lot harsher, at least in my opinion."

She started for the door, and then turned back and looked at the rest of us. "Why are you all standing around just looking at each other? We need to find Benet."

I'm not sure why we all obeyed, but we did. There was something in the executive producer's voice that eliminated all consideration of defiance.

"Where should we look first?" Maddy asked as we hit the sidewalk together.

"I think the first place we should check is the Slice. After all, he just took a key from me."

"You want to make sure he doesn't trash the place, don't you?"

That was exactly what I was trying to prevent. Who knew how Benet might react if he felt as though he were being thwarted. "Maddy, if he so much as breaks a toothpick, the man's going to have a world of problems that he hasn't even dreamed about yet."

As I'd said the last bit, Jessie walked past us, glancing at my fiery promise with one eyebrow raised. I didn't care if she thought I was capable of violence or not. I'd meant every word I'd said. The Slice was so much a part of me that I swore if someone wrecked it, I believed I'd feel the pain myself, like some kind of psychic connection between my mind and the business I ran.

We hurried to the pizzeria, and I peeked in the window as Maddy handed me her key. I should have had Slick make an extra one for me after all. Not having my own key to the pizzeria was disturbing on a level I hadn't even contemplated before.

Was someone there?

I used the key and unlocked the door. When I looked around the dining room, I didn't see any evidence that anyone had been there since Maddy, Mark, and I had left earlier, and I had to wonder if the sun coming through the window had cast a shadow of something that had looked like a man.

"Hello?" I called out as we went back to the kitchen.

Nothing in the kitchen had been touched since we'd left it.

"At the risk of being Captain Obvious, he's not here," Maddy said.

"That doesn't mean he won't show up here eventually. We can check back later," I said. "In the meantime, we can start hitting other places on the promenade."

"Why just around here?" Maddy asked as we started back toward the front door.

"Come on, Sis. You saw him searching for a way off the square. He was clearly confused. How far do you think he'd get on his own? Let's go."

Maddy smiled at me. "Are you sure you wouldn't rather just stay here and stand guard over the place?"

"It's tempting," I said, "But I can't let Cindy down. We need to do everything in our power to salvage her grand opening. Come on."

We left the pizzeria together, locked up, and then stared up and down the promenade.

I tried to hand Maddy her key back, but she refused. "You keep it. I know it's more than just a key to you."

"Just take it, okay?" I wasn't in the mood to argue with her.

My sister did as I asked and took the key back, albeit reluctantly, and then said, "Thanks."

I just nodded. As I looked around, I said, "You take one way, and I'll take the other."

Maddy glanced up and down the broad expanse, and then said, "That's fine by me. I'll head this way, and you go the other."

"Call if you find him," I said.

"You do the same."

I headed in the other direction, and decided that while I was out anyway, I might as well stop in at Paul's Pastries and see if the owner had seen the wayward chef since he'd stormed out of the bookstore. Paul was a good friend of ours, and besides supplying us with buns for our sandwiches, he also catered to our sweet tooths.

What I didn't expect was to find Chef Benet himself inside, arguing about beignets, of all things.

"These are dull and lifeless," Benet snapped as I walked in. He tore one of the donut treats between two hands and looked disgusted by what he saw. "Look at this. They should be light, fluffy, and full of air, not little brick missiles to hurl through windows."

"If you want to see a brick, I'll show you one," Paul said as he started to step out from behind the counter. Paul was an accomplished baker, something he was rightfully proud of and passionate about, and I knew that he'd defend his pastries to any extent he felt necessary.

"Take it easy, guys," I said as I stepped between them. "It's okay to have a difference of opinion."

"Do you actually know this joker, Eleanor?" Paul asked as he stared Benet down.

"Of course she knows me, you fool. Ask anyone. I am Chef Benet, king of the kitchen."

"What you are is delusional," Paul said.

I interjected. "He's doing a signing and a demonstration for Cindy at the Bookmark for her grand opening today," I said. In a lower voice, I added, "She really needs this, Paul. Can you back down just a little?"

I was counting on my friend's support of a fellow shop owner on the promenade to trump his indignation.

At least I was hoping it would.

"Just get him out of here," Paul said in a softer voice as he retreated to the other side of the counter.

Benet must have overheard him, though. He said, "I would be delighted to leave. In fact, it will be the most pleasant part of my experience meeting you as far as I'm concerned."

Paul grinned wickedly at the man as he said, "Right back at you, chief."

"It's Chef," Benet corrected.

"Sure. Whatever you say, Chef."

I could see Benet bristle at Paul's comment, so I decided to get the chef out of there before more than a beignet was destroyed.

Once I got Benet on the sidewalk, I asked, "Do you *have* to alienate everyone you meet?"

I doubted the chef even knew that I was displeased with him, and even if he did, I knew in my heart that he didn't care. "If that man can't deal with the truth about his inferior products, he shouldn't try to push them on unsuspecting customers."

"I *like* Paul's confections," I said, defending my friend.

"Then again, you run a pizza stand," he said, his feelings about my livelihood coming out strong and clear. "Your opinion hardly matters."

I felt my blood pressure spiking, but I couldn't let this pompous blowhard bother me, at least not until after the signing. "Here's a thought. Why don't you go to the Slice and wait until it's time for your presentation. No one will bother you there, and you can compose yourself before you're due to go on."

"I don't need to isolate myself for that," he said. "I am always willing to share my knowledge with those less fortunate. But I'm still not at all certain that I'm even giving my presentation today."

Where did this guy get such a grand opinion of himself? And then I looked down the promenade toward the bookstore. To my shock and amazement, at a little more than an hour away from his talk, I saw that a line was already forming. As much as I hated to do it, it was time to make a plea to the man's vanity. "Think of your fans," I said, trying to stroke this man's sizable ego a little harder. "They deserve the best you've got, don't you agree?"

Wow, to my surprise, his head actually could get bigger. He waved a hand in the air as he said, "My least effort is more than most people are capable of at full capacity."

I honestly didn't know how to respond to that, so I kept quiet, though I continued to herd him back to the Slice.

"Then we don't want to cause a riot if folks see you walking out on the promenade without a bodyguard," I said, the sarcasm oozing from my voice.

"You have a point there," Benet said. "Perhaps I could use a little time for myself before I begin."

We got to the pizzeria, and the chef stood there waiting for me to open the door for him.

"I'd love to help you out, but you have my key, remember?" I said

"Yes, of course," he said.

I waited until he had the door unlocked and was stepping inside, but I didn't go in with him. As a matter of fact, as soon as he locked the place up from the inside, I started toward the bookstore to tell Cindy that I'd found her wayward chef, and that from how it seemed at the moment, her store's grand opening was back on schedule.

If she wanted to walk down and babysit Benet herself, she was welcome to the job.

As for me, I'd had my fill of the iron-mouthed chef.

Chapter 6

"**D**id you find him?" Cindy asked me as I walked into the bookstore. The expression she gave me for just a moment was really strange. For a second, I wasn't sure if she was hoping that I'd tracked the chef down or wishing that he was gone for good.

"He's at the Slice even as we speak. That reminds me," I said as I grabbed my cell phone. "I've got to call Maddy and tell her that she can come back."

"You don't need to. She's already here," Cindy said, pointing to the mystery section, where my sister had her nose in what I saw was the latest brand-new Death on Demand book from Carolyn Hart. I knew that Mrs. Hart was one of her favorites, and every time she published a new book, Maddy was there.

I walked up behind my sister and said, "Okay, there is no way that you knew I found Benet, and yet here you are ahead of me."

Nothing. No reaction at all from her.

I touched her shoulder lightly. "Maddy, did you hear me?"

What?" she asked, looking up from the book and putting her finger on a line to hold her place. At least she was making eye contact now. While I had her attention, I asked, "What happened to you?"

It was clear that my sister barely registered my presence, and I had a feeling that nothing I said could break through Mrs. Hart's spell. Maddy waved me away as though I were a gnat. "Hey, I tried, but I couldn't find him, so I came back here to see if he'd turned up on his own," she said, barely acknowledging my presence. "Why are you here?" She glanced around the room, and then added, "I don't see Benet around. You should keep looking." And then she went back to her book, forgetting that I was even in the room, let alone that we'd just been talking.

I knew she wasn't listening to me. "He was on the cannon, trying to do a jig. The poor man fell off three times before he managed to stay up on it for more than ten seconds."

"That's nice," she said as she continued to read.

"He wants to buy me out and run the pizzeria himself, so we have to be out of the Slice by five."

"Sure, yes, I get it." Three seconds later, she nearly dropped the book in her hands. "What did you just say?"

"I was just trying to get your attention," I said with a smile.

Maddy frowned at me. "That's not very nice, Eleanor." She took the book up to Cindy, and I decided to follow her.

"I'd like to buy this, please," Maddy said.

"We're not ready for sales yet," Cindy said, and then turned to her mother. "Mom? Can we go ahead and make a sale?"

Janet, Cindy's mom, was working on the register with a tech of some sort. "Not yet. We need a few minutes before we'll be able to do that."

"I don't mind waiting," Maddy said, clutching the novel as though it contained the secrets of the universe.

"Probably all week," I added. "I have a feeling that my sister isn't leaving this bookstore until she owns that book."

"It's not just that. I want the privilege of being the first customer," Maddy said.

"How sweet of you," Cindy said.

"We've got it," her mother said as the technician stood. "We're ready now."

Maddy smiled, pushed the book across the wooden counter, and said, "I'd like this, please."

My sister put two twenties down alongside the novel, and as Cindy's mom made change, she took a single from the register and handed it her daughter.

"What's this for?"

"This is a big moment in any small business person's life. It's the first dollar you earned here," her mother said. "You should frame it and put it in your office."

"I just hope this isn't all I make," Cindy said, though she pocketed the bill nonetheless.

Her mother smiled softly at her. "You'll be fine, Cynthia. This town has needed a good bookstore for years. You're filling a real need around here."

Cindy just shrugged. "Let's hope you're right." After Maddy got her book, her change, a receipt, and a bag with the Bookmark's logo on it, she was happy as could be.

"Hey, Sis, don't forget. We're here to work, too, remember?"

"Of course I do," Maddy said. "Let me just tuck this under my jacket and put it somewhere, and I'll be ready to help." She did as she promised, and then looked around the store. "Where is Prince Charming, anyway? You did find him, didn't you?"

"The last time I saw him, he was at the Slice grumbling about the world," I said. I glanced at my watch and saw that we were fifteen minutes away from the presentation. As I did, Cindy said loudly to the folks there working, "If I could have your attention, please. First, I want to thank you all for your help this past week. I couldn't have done it without you, so give yourselves a round of applause."

Everyone did as they were asked, though I thought Maddy's applause were a little too boisterous. Once everyone settled down, Cindy said, "In one minute, I'm going to let them in. We need to finish putting the chairs out, and get rid of the last box. Thanks again."

She looked as though she might be starting to cry, and I could sympathize with her. It was an emotional time, and if she couldn't let a tear out now, her heart would have had to be made of stone.

Cindy walked to the door, opened it, and then said to the crowd gathered outside, "Welcome to the Bookmark. The demonstration with world renowned Chef Benet will begin in ten minutes, so come in, find a seat, and get ready to have some fun."

A crowd of over three dozen was waiting, three-quarters women and a quarter men. They came in one rush, taking the seats they thought would offer the best view of the chef's demonstration. Say what you will about the man, but it was clear that he had a legion of his very own fans. Maddy and I stood in back, not to get a particularly good view, but to get as far away from Benet as we could and still be in the building.

To my great surprise, Chief Hurley walked into the bookshop and headed straight to me.

Oh, no. What had I done, or neglected to do, this time?

I decided a preemptive strike might be in order. "Hey, Chief, I didn't know you were a fan of cooking shows."

"Are you kidding me? They're the best thing on television these days," he said.

"Really? I never would have figured you for a foodie. Why's that?"

"They put me to sleep every night," he said with a slight smile.

What an odd thing to say if he truly were a fan. "If you really feel that way, then why are you here?" I asked.

"Truth be told, I'm looking for my son," he said. As one of my employees, Josh Hurley had been a bone of contention between the two of us ever since he'd come to work for me at the Slice. Kevin had never been particularly happy about it, and when I found myself in trouble time and time again, the chief of police did everything he could to distance his boy from me.

I looked around the room, knowing that I'd seen Josh slip in with the crowd just a few minutes earlier. "He's over there," I said as I pointed to him where he was hanging out with Greg and talking to a pretty young woman who was working behind the coffee counter.

"Good," he said, but before he could join Josh, I touched his sleeve lightly and asked, "You're not going to embarrass him, are you?"

"What are you talking about?"

"Come on, Kevin. He's clearly enjoying talking to that girl. I thought you might want to give him a little space."

The police chief shook his head. "Eleanor, you don't need to protect my son from me. I won't give him a hard time. I just need to ask him something."

I just shook my head, but it was all I needed.

The chief's good mood was quickly dissipating. "What is it? If you've got something to say, just spit it out."

"Remember when your dad came to school to give you your lunch money when we were in high school?" Kevin and I had been dating then, and the whole school had spent two weeks waving five dollar bills at him and laughing.

Kevin frowned. "Okay, you've got a point. Listen, why don't you do it for me, then? Ask him if he ever found his car keys. The last time I saw him, he was tearing up the house searching for them."

"He must have found them, because I saw him driving today," I said. "When did he lose them?"

"Last night," the chief said.

"There you go. Case solved." I looked over and saw that Josh spotted us talking. His face reddened slightly, and he quickly turned away from us. Kevin must have caught it, too.

"When did I become my old man?" he asked wistfully.

"You haven't, and you won't," I said sympathetically. "We both know that you're nothing like him."

"Thanks for that," Kevin said, clearly meaning it. His father hadn't been the best dad in the world, but he hadn't been the worst, either. I guess we all see things from our own perspective, and in Kevin's mind, his dad had not been someone he wanted to emulate. George was still around town, and still giving his son a hard time every time he saw him, despite the fact that Kevin had a serious job with grave responsibilities. I would have loved to have my own father alive. We'd had a bond that had been unbreakable, and I missed him most days, but not as much as I missed Joe, though both men had been cut from the same cloth. While David Quinton wasn't like either one of them physically, he had shared the two most important traits they'd had, the two that mattered the most to me: they had both possessed truly kind hearts, and they'd both had a funny, if skewed, sense of humor.

Kevin looked around the shop at the crowd of people waiting for the demonstration, and then said, "Cindy's getting close to an occupancy violation here."

Leave it to the cop to look for trouble where there wasn't any. "You're not going to shut her down, are you?"

"What?" he asked, clearly startled by my question. "No, of course not. I know what this means to her. I'll say something to her if too many more people try to jam in here, but it's going to take a whole lot more than this to make me do anything to stand between her and her dream."

"Thanks," I said, touching his arm lightly. "It's nice to know that there's still a heart beating under that uniform."

He shook his head a little sadly. "Eleanor, it's my job to uphold the law, but there's a difference between arresting an armed robber and breaking up someone's grand opening party. I'm not a complete ogre, you know."

"I know," I said. "Sometimes I forget, though."

Kevin just shrugged. "It's a tough job, I'm the first one to admit that. Sometimes I let it get to me, no matter how much I try not to let it."

Wow, that was the most emotionally revealing thing I'd ever

heard Kevin say since he'd told me that he loved me. Of course, that was after I caught him cheating on me, but still. It was nice to know that there was still a part of that boy in this man today. Maddy drifted over to us, and Kevin took the opportunity to leave us, no doubt in search of Cindy to let her know that the crowd was getting a little too large.

"Was it something I said?" Maddy asked with a grin as she watched him retreat into the store.

"No, why do you ask?"

"If it was, I want to remember what it was the next time I need it," she replied with a grin. "He took off like a shot, didn't he?"

"It wasn't you. He had to talk to Cindy."

Maddy nodded, and then looked around the room. "This is some grand opening party, isn't it?"

"Cindy could have done a lot worse." I glanced at my watch, and saw that Benet was now four minutes late. "Where is the chef, anyway?"

"He's probably waiting to make a grand entrance, no doubt," Maddy said. "The man is a born diva if ever there was one."

Cindy came over to us a few seconds later, a worried expression on her face. I had a pretty good idea what that was about.

"Don't worry. He's not going to shut you down," I said, trying to offer her a little comfort. It was hard to imagine how Kevin had couched his warning to her, and clearly it had upset her.

It only served to confuse her, though. "What? Why would he do that? I don't get it."

"Neither one of you is making the slightest bit of sense," Maddy said. She looked at Cindy and asked, "Who exactly are you talking about?"

"Who else? Chef Benet, of course," Cindy said. "He should have been here by now. Why, what were you talking about, Eleanor?" she asked as she looked at me.

"The police chief was worried about your occupancy rate," I admitted. "Didn't he say something to you about that?"

Cindy nodded, still clearly distracted by the chef's absence. "Yes, and we're going to open the doors so folks can still hear him from in front of the shop. It's not going to be a problem, though. There's not going to be anything to hear unless we get him over here."

"Send his assistant over to the pizzeria to fetch him," I said, as I pointed to Oliver, who was in a deep conversation with Jessie Taylor.

"He's tied up," Cindy said as she looked toward them.

"Then send his wife," I said as I looked around for Patrice. "I don't see her, but she can't be far off."

"Would you do it?" Cindy asked me.

"I suppose I could," I said reluctantly. I couldn't wait until this was over, so in a way, finding Benet was in my favor. The quicker he gave his talk, the faster I could reopen my pizzeria and get life back to some semblance of being normal.

"Thank you," Cindy gushed, and disappeared back into the crowd. I had to wonder if one of the reasons she'd left so abruptly was to steal my opportunity to change my mind.

I grabbed Maddy's arm and started pulling her toward the door.

"Hey, I don't have to go, too, do I?" she protested.

"Sorry, it's your sisterly duty," I answered.

"How did you come up with that? It's not exactly playing fair, is it?"

"Hey, blame the sister's handbook," I said with a smile as we left the bookshop. "If I have to tackle that arrogant jerk by myself, I might not trust myself to behave."

"In that case, I'm definitely coming," Maddy said. "Could I hang back and watch the fireworks?"

"Come on," I said. We got away from the crowd and started walking down the promenade to the Slice. The crowd thinned to nothing by the time we were in front of the pizzeria, and I wondered if I shouldn't try some kind of promotional gimmick myself to drum up a little business sometime. We could certainly use the income, and the exposure, too.

I reached into my purse for my key, only to realize that I'd loaned mine to Chef Benet.

"I need your key, Maddy," I said.

She was staring into the big window up front, and I had to repeat myself to get her attention. "Maddy? Did you hear me?"

"That's kind of odd, isn't it?" she asked as she kept looking inside.

"What?" I asked, trying to see around her.

"Is that Benet? He's just sitting at a table with his back to us."

"Maybe it's part of his process," I said.

"Do you think?"

"Who knows?" I asked. "Give me your key so we can get him and get this thing going."

Maddy handed me her key ring, and I found the right key and opened the door. As I handed her keys back to her, I said loudly, "Come on, Chef, you're late."

He didn't respond to my voice. In fact, he didn't even move a muscle.

"Chef, it's time," I said, this time more forcefully than before.

I suddenly had had enough of his prima donna attitude. I put a hand on his shoulder and shook him a little. "Enough with the attitude. Let's go, buster. You're keeping everyone waiting."

And then I looked over his shoulder and saw one of my kitchen knives sticking in his chest all the way to its hilt.

I felt his neck, but not only was there no pulse, his skin was eerily cold to the touch.

"Get the police chief, Maddy," I said. "Someone murdered Chef Benet."

Chapter 7

Maddy didn't move, though. She just stood there staring at Benet. "Eleanor, are you sure he's dead?"

"There's no doubt about it in my mind, but if you want to check for a pulse yourself, be my guest." We were wasting time, and I was done debating what our next course of action should be. "Maddy, if you don't want to go get Chief Hurley at the bookstore, you can always stay here with the body and I'll go get him myself."

That snapped Maddy out of her funk. "No, that's okay. Thanks for offering, but I like your plan better."

Before my sister could get out the door, I thought about the best way to handle it, and then suggested, "Ask him to come over here, but don't tell him why. We don't want to cause a panic if we don't have to."

"I'll try," she said, and then Maddy was gone, leaving me alone with the dead body of a man I had never liked much in life.

I tried not to look at Benet, but it was hard not to. It was no secret to anyone that I hadn't been a fan of the man, but even he had to have deserved better than he'd gotten in the end. It couldn't have been a pleasant way to go, facing your killer as they stabbed you face-to-face.

A thought suddenly struck me. What if the killer was still in the pizzeria? We'd never even made it into the kitchen, and there was a lot of room to hide back there. By sending Maddy off to get Kevin Hurley, I'd left myself vulnerable and open to attack. The dining room was clearly empty, except for the dead body, but that still left too many places for a murderer to hide.

I was walking softly toward the door that separated the two areas when I heard a voice behind me ask, "What exactly is it that you think you're doing?"

"Chef Benet is dead, and the killer might still be here," I said softly to Chief Hurley as he walked into the Slice.

He drew his revolver, and then motioned me back behind him. I wasn't sure if he wanted me by the door, or on the other side of it, but I wasn't going to leave him alone, not that I had a chance if an armed murderer managed to overpower him.

I listened carefully as he disappeared into the kitchen, taking in every imagined whisper of sound. I must have been holding my breath, because when the chief came back out, his weapon was holstered. I nearly passed out from the strain.

"Nobody's back there. You're all clear," the chief said as he duplicated my earlier effort and checked for the chef's pulse.

"He's cold to the touch," I said.

"I still have to check."

Once the chief of police was satisfied that the chef had put on his last demonstration and cooked his own last supper, he looked at me. "Eleanor, did you touch anything?"

I thought about it, and then asked, "Are you kidding me? I'm here every day, remember?"

"I'm talking about since you walked in the door and found the body," he explained.

"Let's see." I thought about what I'd done since Maddy and I had found the chef, and ticked off the items that I could remember touching since I'd been there. "All I can think of are both sides of the doorknob, the lock, and his neck." I shuddered a little as I recalled the icy touch of his skin, but I buried it just as quickly as it had surfaced. That was one memory I was going to do my best to suppress.

"You didn't touch the knife handle, though, did you?" Kevin asked as he took his radio out and made a call in code. The only thing I got was "the Slice," because the numbers he used didn't mean a thing to me.

"No," I said simply. "At least not today."

"Does that mean that you recognize the murder weapon?" he asked as he bent forward to study the handle of the knife.

"It's one of mine," I admitted.

That got his interest. "From here, or from home?"

"It's part of a set I've got back there," I said as I pointed to the kitchen.

Kevin Hurley nodded as he looked around the dining room. "As far as you can tell, is there anything out of place?"

I looked around, but everything looked normal to me. "Not out here. At least not that I can see at first glance."

The police chief nodded. "Good. You've been helpful, but why don't you go outside and wait with Maddy while I finish up here? She trailed behind me, and I know she wants to see you. I'll be back out as soon as I can."

I nodded, happy enough to get as far away as I could manage from the body in my pizzeria.

Maddy hugged me the second that I walked outside. "I shouldn't have left you by yourself in there," she said in a rush. "I regretted it the second I walked out. Eleanor, I'm so sorry."

"Hey, there's no reason to beat yourself up about it. I asked you to do it, remember? Someone had to get the chief, and the other one needed to stay with the body," I said.

Maddy shook her head, a frown still plastered on her face. "We should have called 911 from the dining room," she said. "Eleanor, I don't mean to be an alarmist, but as I went to get Kevin, I realized that we didn't even check the kitchen. Whoever killed Benet could have been waiting there for you."

"But they weren't," I said, calming my sister as much as I could. Maddy was a rock most of the time. It was only when she felt she'd put me in jeopardy did she ever react the way she was at the moment. I pulled away from her and stared into her eyes. "You didn't do anything I didn't ask you to do, and it all worked out fine in the end."

"Not for Benet," she said as she glanced back inside the dining room. "Who would want to kill the Chef?"

Who wouldn't? I thought, one of the most uncharitable things I'd thought recently. I felt ashamed of my reaction, but it was still a valid point. "If you ask me, it might be easier to count the people who knew Chef who might not want to see him dead. The man didn't exactly exude kindness or inspire love, did he?"

She shrugged. "I feel horrible even thinking it, but I'm honestly surprised someone didn't do something to him sooner." Maddy must have realized how that sounded, because she quickly added, "You know what I mean, Eleanor."

"Trust me, you're not saying anything that I haven't been thinking," I said. "But I don't know how much of that I should say to the chief. I wasn't a fan of the man myself, and more than one person heard us arguing. I'm not in any mood to volunteer going on his list of murder suspects."

"Got it," she said. "I agree."

I looked up the promenade and saw Patrice Benet fighting her way toward us through a pair of police officers who were holding the crowd back.

Had someone told her already that her husband was dead?

Jessie and Oliver showed up a second later and were trying to restrain her, but it didn't appear that they were having much luck.

If anyone was going to stop her from rushing in to see her husband's dead body, it was going to have to be Maddy and me.

"You can't go in there," I said as I blocked Patrice from coming anywhere near the front window of the Slice. "How did you even hear about it so quickly?"

"Someone shouted it out from the sidewalk, and we all heard it inside the bookstore," she said. Her eyes were pleading as she asked me, "It's not true, is it? Please tell me they were lying."

How was I supposed to handle that? I had to wonder who had announced the chef's murder to the world, when we'd just discovered the body ourselves. Had someone overheard Maddy talking to Kevin Hurley and put two and two together, or had they seen me inside with the body? Worse yet, could the killer have brazenly announced the crime to confuse things as quickly as he could? I'd have to think about that later, but it didn't help me deal with the problem I had standing in front of me at the moment. Right now, I had a brand-new widow to deal with, and I had to deliver the worst news I'd ever had to in my life.

She must have read my expression, because Patrice broke down right there on the promenade in front of my pizza parlor. I guess my expression of sorrow and sadness must have been enough of an answer for her.

Jessie and Oliver sandwiched her in a hug, more police officers began to arrive on the scene, and most of the folks from the book signing had followed Patrice and everyone else to us. It was a bad day for my pizzeria, an even uglier one for Cindy, but it was honestly a tragic day for Patrice.

And for Chef Benet, it was his last.

"I need to get away from here," Patrice said as she watched the chief put police tape around the door to the Slice. We'd all moved out of the way and we were now standing farther down the promenade where we wouldn't bother the stream of officers coming in and out.

"I'm sorry, I just can't deal with being here right now," Patrice said, her words coming out between her sobs. She managed to pull herself together, at least a little, and then said in a steadier voice, "Everywhere I look reminds me of Antonio. Can someone give me a ride back to my hotel room?" She frowned again, and before anyone could answer, Patrice added, "No, I can't go there, either," she said, giving it a moment's consideration. "What am I going to do?"

I don't know what made me suggest it, but before I knew what I was saying, I said, "You can come home with me. It's not far, and you can have some time to wrap your head around what happened today."

"I can't impose on you like that," she said, almost automatically.

I should have kept my mouth shut then, but I pushed forward. "It's no imposition. I live alone, so you won't be disturbed."

Maddy said, "I hate to interrupt, but Eleanor, can I talk to you a second?"

"It's fine," Patrice said. "Go on."

I stepped away with my sister and asked, "What is it, Maddy? The woman's in some serious pain. If we can help her, we should."

Keeping her voice low, my sister said, "Think about this before you do it. For all we know, Patrice could have murdered her husband half an hour ago, and you just invited her into your home."

"Do you honestly think she's a killer?" I asked softly as I looked over at her. The woman didn't look capable of killing anyone, especially by driving a chef's knife into his chest. Then again, it could have been a crime of passion, facing the victim and skewering him as she watched him die. I had to remember that the killer hadn't stopped halfway in when, there was no doubt in my mind, the job was done; they'd continued until the knife had been buried all the way to the hilt, pinning Benet to the chair he'd been sitting in like a butterfly on a display board.

"Tell me something. We've dealt with murderers before. What exactly does a killer look like?" Maddy asked. "If we've learned anything, it's that you can't tell what someone might do just by looking at them."

She was making some good, solid points, but I didn't see any way out of rescinding my offer. "Okay, for the sake of argument, let's say you're right. What am I going to do now? I've already invited her to stay with me."

Patrice came over to us before we could come up with a solution to my dilemma and said, "Excuse me, but I'm going to have to decline your kind offer. Oliver and Jessie have offered to take me to another hotel. I don't feel right imposing on you, and I need to be among people I know at a time like this."

"It's no problem at all," I said. I felt as though I'd just dodged a bullet, though from what Maddy had said, I wasn't sure how sincere I sounded.

"I appreciate that. You understand then, don't you?"

"Perfectly," I said. It might have been nice having Patrice close enough to question now that I realized what a good suspect she was, but I didn't want to have to watch my back in my own home every second I was there, either.

"Don't worry. We're all staying, at least until the police are done with us," Oliver volunteered. "We'll be at the Ridgecrest Inn in Mountain Lake. It was one of the places I scouted out when I came here a few days ago."

"That's a great idea," I said. A thought occurred to me that I needed to be around these people more, since they were all the most likely suspects in Benet's murder. "Let me bring you some pizza tonight," I said. "It's the least I can do, and none of you are going to feel like going out." And it would offer me a chance to talk to them again. It didn't take a genius to realize that with Benet being murdered in my restaurant, some folks were going to think I had something to do with it, and I couldn't afford that. I wished I could say that it was the first time I'd found a dead body in the Slice, but I would have been lying.

"That would be comforting, somehow," Patrice said.

"Excellent. I'll see you at seven," I said.

After they were gone, Maddy said, "That's a great idea and all, but what makes you think Chief Hurley is going to release our kitchen in time for us to follow up on your offer and make pizza tonight?"

I did my best to smile at her. "Maddy, we don't have to use the oven at the Slice. I can make a good pizza at home, even if we don't have access to our regular things. Joe and I bought a portable brick-lined pizza oven before we ever opened the Slice, and I've still got it sitting in the basement. It makes fine pizzas, trust me." I touched my sister's shoulder. "Thanks for stepping in before Patrice agreed to come home with me. I don't know what I was thinking making that offer."

"You were thinking about a woman who'd just lost her husband," Maddy said. "Your reaction makes sense on that level, but I couldn't let you take that kind of chance."

"That's just one of the reasons why we need each other," I said.

We lingered out front awhile, and Jenny Wilkes, the woman who owned our local flower shop, Forever in Bloom, stopped by and saw the police tape in front of the Slice.

"I can't believe what happened," Jenny said. "You found another dead body here? You must feel cursed, Eleanor."

"I try not to think about it, but how did you hear about what happened?" I asked.

"You're kidding, right? It's all over town," Jenny said. "I'm sorry. Was it supposed to be a secret?"

"No, of course not," Maddy answered.

"Well, I don't care what folks are saying, I know the two of you had nothing to do with that man's murder."

"People are already saying that one of us killed him?" I asked, incredulous that anyone could believe that.

"Hey, don't shoot the messenger. I said I'm on your side," Jenny said.

"I'm sorry," I replied, trying to calm my voice down. "I didn't mean to attack you. As a matter of fact, I appreciate you telling me."

Jenny was satisfied with my apology. "Like I said, there's no way everyone believes it. You've got a core group of people in town who believe in you, including me."

After Jenny was gone, I told my sister, "You know what this means, don't you?"

"That Jenny Wilkes is on our side?" Maddy asked. "It's good to know that at least somebody's got our backs."

"It is, but that's not what I'm talking about. There's no doubt in my mind that what she said is true, and it just confirms what I've been thinking. If so many people around Timber Ridge believe that we could have had something to do with Benet's murder, we're going to have to dig into this ourselves."

"What's the chief going to think about that?" Maddy asked.

"It's a little too late to start worrying about that now," I said. "We'll do what we have to do, and if we step on a few toes in the process, then so be it."

The chief of police finally came out of the restaurant again. Kevin Hurley barely noticed us at first, but when he did, he walked over and joined us. "What are you two still doing here?"

"We were wondering when we could get our restaurant back," I asked.

"Not today, and maybe not tomorrow," he said flatly.

That was not the news I wanted to hear. "What? You can't do that to me. I need my business to be open."

He sighed as he ran his hands through his hair. "Eleanor, we'll do what we can, but I can't make any promises. All I can say is that you'll get it when you get it. The coroner's on the way, and my crime scene guy is already in there taking videos and pictures of everything. As it is, they're going to be working awhile. I really am sorry," he added, and I believed him. "I'm not trying to hurt you, but murder is murder, and we aren't cutting a single corner."

"Just do what you can," I said.

"I'm glad you're still here. We're going to need a key to the place so we can lock up for you."

I turned to Maddy and said, "Go on. Give him yours."

"Where's your key, Eleanor?" Chief Hurley asked.

"I gave it to him," I said, pointing toward the dead chef, but not even looking in his direction.

Hurley nodded. "We'll be sure you get it back when this is all over."

"You can keep it, for all I care," I said, thinking about it being in the dead man's pocket. "I'll have Slick make another one for me from Maddy's."

"Exactly how many keys are floating around town right now?" the chief asked. It was clear there had been another reason he'd approached us.

"As long as I've owned the place, there have just been two," I admitted. "I tried to give Greg one, but he decided not to take it. He said it was too much responsibility."

"That's smart of him. How about Josh?" he asked, softly.

"No, it never came up," I admitted.

"Good," he said, and I could understand why. Who wanted their child tied in closer to a murder than they already were? Because he worked at the Slice, I knew Josh had to be on the list of suspects, though I doubted he was very high up, since he'd never even met the chef. Maddy and I, on the other hand, had to be closer to the top of any list that the chief made, and my name in particular might be one of the headliners. While I didn't have a real motive to kill the man, we had argued, and in public at that. When I thought of it that way, I knew the police chief had to at least consider the possibility that I'd done it, no matter how unpleasant that prospect was for me.

"I'll call you as soon as I can about when I can turn the restaurant back over to you," he said.

He walked away, and I turned to Maddy. As I did, I looked at my watch, and then said, "I have some time before I have to go shopping for supplies. Do you mind giving me a hand?"

"With the pizza, or the investigation?" she asked.

"I was hoping we might be able to do a little bit of both," I admitted.

"You can count on me," Maddy said. "You know that."

"Then why don't we go back and talk to Cindy about what happened to Benet?" I suggested.

Maddy looked at me askance. "Eleanor, do you honestly think that she might have done it?"

It was not as easy a question to answer as I might have liked. "I wish I could say no, but I just can't, not yet. Cindy's the real reason he was here, after all. I'm still not sure why Benet canceled a national television appearance to come to Timber Ridge instead, but I have to wonder if she's not a part of that decision somehow."

"Why do you say that?" Maddy asked.

"I don't know," I replied. "It just doesn't make sense unless there was some kind of personal connection between them."

When we got to the bookstore, it was empty. Everyone had cleared out, including the staff. At least there was no police tape across the door, like there was at my place. I glanced back in again, and saw something that I'd missed at first glance. Cindy was sitting among a mess of things, surrounded by empty chairs and a demonstration kitchen that would never be used. There was clearly a general pall of doom around her, not that I could blame her. Her grand opening had turned out to be one huge nightmare, and I wondered if her shop could ever recover from such an inauspicious start.

I tapped on the door, and had to do it twice before she even looked up.

As she stood, I saw the weariness in her, and wondered if Maddy and I should wait until later to talk to her. No, the sooner we got started investigating the chef's murder, the faster folks would forget that we'd ever been involved.

As she unlocked the door and let us in, I asked, "Where did everybody go?"

"I sent them all home. We obviously can't open the store now," she said. As she looked around at the mess, she added, "What am I going to do? This is bad on so many levels, I can't imagine ever making it all go away."

"Take a week before you hold your grand opening," I said. "That way, you can get the place in order and try again."

"I'm not sure I have the heart to do that," she said. "Let's not kid ourselves. The chef's murder is going to hang over the bookstore like a black cloud. I might as well just shut the place down and get it over with."

"We've dealt with it ourselves in the past," I said as diplomatically as I could. "You can come back from it. I'm not saying that's going to be easy, but it can be done." She had problems today, there was no denying that, but at the end of the day, the body hadn't been found in her store. It had been discovered at the Slice, and that put Maddy and me right in the middle of it.

"I'm sorry, I didn't even think about what this is going to mean to you," she said quickly. "Is there anything I can do to help you?"

"Funny, that's why we're here," Maddy said. "What say we get started on making things right again now?"

"I guess we should," Cindy said halfheartedly.

"That's the spirit," Maddy said, trying to drive a little enthusiasm into her words. "When are they coming to take the kitchen apart?"

I looked over and saw that it was indeed a stark reminder of what had happened, or had failed to happen, earlier.

"Not until tomorrow," she said sadly.

I knew that Maddy loved a challenge, and this gave her something to sink her teeth into. "We'll see about that. Where's your paperwork?"

Cindy pointed to the counter. "It's all over there in that mess."

Maddy dove into the pile of papers, and I quietly thanked her. As she sorted through the stack and got the right number, I told Cindy, "Don't worry. My sister is a whirlwind when it comes to handling something that needs to be done."

"That's nice," she said calmly, as though it didn't matter to her one way or the other. As I looked closer, though, I saw that she'd been crying earlier, if the redness in her eyes was any indication. "How are you taking the murder itself?"

"It's devastating, of course," Cindy said.

"Had you met Benet before he came to town?" I asked, trying to keep my voice and tone even as I asked.

"No, not really," she said after pausing a moment.

What an odd response. "What exactly does that mean?"

"It's complicated," Cindy said.

Maddy's voice suddenly rose as she spoke on the telephone, and I heard her say, "I don't care what the contract says, get someone over here this afternoon to remove your things, or you'll find them out in front of the bookstore in one hour. Oh, and it's supposed to rain tonight, not to mention the possibility that it won't be here when you finally show up tomorrow." She paused, and then nodded as she said, "Okay, but after two hours, it's all going. Trust me, you don't want to call my bluff."

She hung up, and then noticed we were watching her. "It's all taken care of. They're coming this afternoon," she reported.

I grinned at my sister and asked, "And, how are we going to get all of this out front if they don't?"

Maddy grinned at me. "Hey, we all know that I was bluffing. They probably suspect as much themselves. But do they have the courage to prove it? How much do you want to bet they beat the deadline?"

"No way I'm betting against you," I said.

"I'll get started on making things ready to go, then," she said.

"That sounds great to me. We'll help you," Cindy said.

"Hang on. We're not done talking yet." I needed to find out just what Cindy had meant by saying that she hadn't really met Benet before. How could you not really meet someone? You either had or you hadn't, as far as I was concerned.

Cindy looked as though she might start crying again at the slightest provocation. "Eleanor, I don't want to talk about it. Is that okay?"

"We can postpone it, but we're going to have to talk about it sooner or later," I said. I'd give her a little time, but the two of us were not done talking about her relationship with Benet.

I had a feeling that Cindy had lied to me before about it.

It might not have mattered before the chef had been murdered, but it had become significant now, and I wasn't about to just drop it.

Chapter 8

"I can't believe we pulled it off," Cindy said in amazement as she surveyed her shop two hours later. The movers had come and gone, the folding chairs were taken away, and we had the Bookmark in good enough shape to open the next day if Cindy wanted to. I wished I could say the same thing about the Slice, but I still hadn't heard from Chief Hurley. It looked like Maddy and I would be winging it in my kitchen tonight, making pizzas the old-fashioned way in my portable pizza oven. I didn't mind, though. Somehow it was a fitting way to remember my late husband. Joe and I had tried out a dozen different recipes for dough and sauce in that kitchen before we'd opened the Slice, so in a way, it might be a nice way of revisiting my roots and how the pizza parlor had come to be.

"I can't thank the two of you enough for everything that you've done for me," Cindy said. "You continually keep saving me."

"We've been glad to help. After all, what are friends for?" I asked. Maddy and I had earned some real credit with her, and I planned on using every bit of it soon to speak to her again about Benet.

As Maddy and I started to leave the bookstore, I looked at the clock near the door. Once we were outside, I said, "We need to get home so we can start on the dough," I said.

Maddy must have seen the clock, too. "We're kind of pushing it, aren't we?"

I nodded. "We've been known to do that in the past, though, haven't we? We'll make accelerated dough and modify our sauce. It might not be perfect, or even up to the Slice's standards, but it will be good. I can guarantee that."

"I'll say this for you, Sis. I like your confidence," Maddy said.

"Don't forget, this won't be my first time making pizza at home," I said. "Joe and I tried our recipes there first."

"This won't be too sad for you then, will it?" Maddy asked softly as we walked down to the grocery store. My sister struck most people as brash and more than a bit flippant, but I knew deep down that she had a heart as big as the great outdoors.

"I thought about that for a second, but in a way, it's going to be perfect."

"Something's changed about you, Eleanor," Maddy said as she took me in.

"These are new jeans," I admitted, "and I got a haircut last week."

"I'm talking about the inside, not outside." She hesitated, and then said, "You're finally healing, aren't you?"

I nodded, having come to that very same conclusion myself earlier. "I admit that David's helped some, but I've finally come to realize that Joe wouldn't want me to stay broken for the rest of my life. I'll never forget him, but it's time that I started making a real life for myself. Maybe I'm finally getting some perspective."

"Well, whatever it is, I approve," she said.

"I'm glad. Now let's shop."

"Well, it's not clothes, but it still might be fun," Maddy said.

Maddy and I had fun buying what we needed, and then we got into my Subaru and headed to my place. It was a Craftsman-style Arts and Crafts home that Joe and I had remodeled ourselves, with lots of nice homey touches. My place was the perfect house to call home, and I was glad about it again every time I walked in the front door.

As I pulled the last pizza out of the portable oven, Maddy glanced at the clock and said, "If we're lucky and don't hit any red lights, we just might make it after all."

"I never had any doubts," I said.

"Boy, I must have had enough for both of us, then," she answered as I slid the last small pizza onto the cooling rack with the pizza peel.

"Too bad we didn't have time to make one for ourselves," she said as she stared at the pizzas we'd already made. The pizzas were smaller than I usually made, but the oven would only hold a medium-size crust, so I'd had to plan accordingly.

"Hey, you said you liked the way I made your peanut butter and jelly sandwich," I protested with a smile. We'd eaten them while the pizzas had been taking their turns in the oven.

"It was good," Maddy acknowledged, "but it was no pizza."

"As soon as we get back into the Slice, I'll make you something special," I said, looking around for something to carry the food in.

Maddy must have read my mind. "Eleanor, how are we going to get these pizzas to the hotel? We can't exactly carry them in like this."

I suddenly remembered the boxes Joe and I had tested out before we'd placed our first order for the to-go boxes we used now. I looked in the back of the pantry, and sure enough, three unused boxes were still there, along with a worn-out insulation bag that had seen better days. It was all buried under a pile of dishcloths that had gotten too worn for the restaurant. I'd been meaning to clean out the pantry for ages, but now I was glad that I hadn't.

"How about this?" I asked as I opened the box and showed it to Maddy.

That's when I saw the letter inside.

"What's that?" Maddy asked as she reached for it.

"I have no idea," I said as I pulled it out myself, "but it's addressed to me, and it's in Joe's handwriting."

The pizzas now forgotten, I pulled out the envelope and started to read a handwritten note I never thought I'd ever see again.

> *Ellie,*
>
> *I just wanted to tell you how very much I love you. I know I'm not the most romantic guy in the world, but having you in my life has made it complete. If I die tomorrow, it will be as a happy man. I've built a business, rebuilt a house, and even changed my life, and I couldn't have done any of it without you beside me.*
>
> *If I don't tell you enough, please know in my heart that I'm thinking it all of the time nonetheless.*
>
> *Joe*

I started crying from the first word, and as I looked up at Maddy, I saw that she was worried about me. I handed it to her, and when she looked to see if I was certain about letting her read it, I nodded my acceptance.

By the time she finished it, she was crying, too.

"He really was something, wasn't he?" Maddy said.

"The find of a lifetime," I answered. "I must have put this in the box when he gave it to me, and then promptly forgot all about it." I took the note back from her, caressing the paper, touching each written word as if it still had a connection with my late husband.

"Do you want me to take the pizzas myself? If you want me to, I completely understand," Maddy said.

I gently folded the note back up, treating it like the precious thing that it was, and then gently slid it back into the envelope. "Thanks, but we need to do this." I wiped the last of my tears away, and then put the letter on the counter where I'd never forget it again.

It was clear from the look in her eyes that Maddy still wasn't sure, but I was certain.

I would have that letter from my husband forever to cherish, reread, and memorize from that moment on.

But at least for right now, I had to put that on hold.

Maddy and I had a killer to catch.

After we drove the fifteen minutes to Mountain Lake, we got Patrice's room number at the front desk and knocked on the door.

No one answered. Was she sleeping? Sedated? Or even gone?

Maddy knocked again, louder this time, and Jessie answered the door.

"Hey, look at you. We'd just about given up on you, but here you are," she said, slurring her words a little as she did.

Maddy and I had been watching the dashboard clock the whole time over, so I knew that we'd made it with at least a minute to spare. "We're right on time, and don't forget, free delivery is included, too," I said, smiling.

"Do you mean that people usually have to pay extra for delivery?" she asked, clearly confused.

"No, like I said, it's included," I said, and then got tired of standing out in the hallway. I'd tried to be a little funny, but it was clear that I'd failed. "May we come in?"

"Sure thing," she said as she stepped aside. It was a spacious suite, and I could see why Oliver had chosen it. I could imagine that it must have fit Benet's personality better than where he'd ended up staying, but the commute to Timber Ridge had probably been too far for him.

In the living room, I saw the reason for Jessie's intoxicated behavior. On the table between the sofa and two chairs was a collection of liquor bottles, not a single one unopened. Patrice had a bit of a glazed look on her face, and Oliver sat there nodding and smiling, but making no real sounds at all.

"Pizza's here," I announced as Maddy moved some bottles around to make room for the boxes.

"Join us," Patrice said, shaking her head as though she was trying to get the cobwebs out of her brain.

I knew there wouldn't be enough for all of us, but I couldn't pass up the opportunity to talk to these people when their tongues were a little loose.

"Thanks so much for your kind offer. I don't mind if we do," I said.

Maddy looked at me curiously, since we both knew that we hadn't brought enough pizza for all five of us, but my sister played along. As she plated up a piece for each of them on the tough paper plates we'd brought with us, she took one slice and cut it in half, dividing it between us. It would give us something to nibble on to look sociable, but not detract much from their pizza or our conversation.

"Have a drink," Jessie insisted after we were all settled down. "Goodness knows that we have."

"Thanks," I said, trying to decline as politely as I could, "but we've got to do some driving after this."

"Just a little one, then," Patrice said. "I insist."

"You've convinced us," Maddy said. "I'll take care of them myself."

I wasn't sure what she had in mind, and then I saw a large bottle of Coke on the table behind one couch. She filled two cups with soda, and then grabbed a bottle of bourbon. I tried to warn her off before she poured some into our cups, and then she showed me that she'd planted her thumb over the opening. To the rest of them, it must have appeared as though we were getting a healthy dose of booze, when in fact our sodas were still pristine.

I was glad that Maddy knew as well as I did that we both had to be at the top of our game right now.

I took a sip after she handed me my cup. "Um, that's good."

"Only the best," Jessie said. She tried to stand, but must have realized that she'd never make it. Instead, she lifted one of the hotel glasses and said, "I'd like to propose a toast, to Antonio."

We all lifted our cups and said in unison, "To Antonio," and then we drank.

I moved over to Patrice, and asked carefully, "How are you holding up?"

"I still can't believe he's gone," she said. "He wasn't the best husband in the world, and I knew he had at least one woman on the side most of the time that we were married, but in his own way, he loved me. I know it with all my heart."

Jessie came over and put a hand on Patrice's shoulder. "I keep telling you, he was faithful to you."

"As far as you know," Patrice said, puckering her lips slightly.

Oliver was still silent as he sat there eating pizza, and it was pretty clear he had no interest in joining the conversation. We'd see about that later, but at the moment, Patrice and Jessie were willing to talk, and I was going to take advantage of it.

"I knew when I married him that he wasn't the kind of man who'd ever be satisfied with just one woman," Patrice said. "What a shame."

She started nodding off then, and Jessie said, "You are clearly exhausted. Let's get you into bed. You'll feel better in the morning."

"I don't think that I'll feel better ever again," Patrice said, though she let herself be led away.

Jessie hesitated, turned to us at the door and said, "I'll be back in a second."

That left Oliver in the room, and Maddy decided to finally take a shot at him. "Did you ever figure out why Benet wanted to come here in the first place?" my sister asked him.

"I didn't have to figure it out," Oliver said, and then smiled broadly. "I knew," he added, tapping his temple with an index finger. I imagined he was just as drunk as the other three, but I never would have been able to tell it from his voice.

"Would you mind telling us?" Maddy asked, acting as though it were the most important thing in the world he could say.

"It was for some important business," Oliver said. "Very important business."

"About his television show?" Maddy prompted when it was clear that he wasn't going to explain any further.

"Not television. Family business," Oliver elaborated.

This was a potential blockbuster. "Did Chef Benet have family in Timber Ridge?" I asked, forgetting for a second that I'd decided to let Maddy question him.

"He sure did," Oliver said, just as Patrice's door opened and Jessie came out. "He didn't want to tell me, but I found out." Oliver nodded his head slightly, and then turned toward the television producer as she spoke, effectively killing our conversation.

"I'm sorry," she said, "But I'm going to have to ask you to leave now. I'm afraid Patrice had a little too much to drink, and now she's feeling a bit under the weather."

Like that was some kind of news flash. "Can we help?" I asked.

"No, Oliver and I can take care of it ourselves." I wasn't sure either one of them was capable of doing much, but I couldn't very well insist that they allow me to lend a hand.

"We'll talk to you tomorrow, I'm sure," I said as I stood.

"I'm afraid that won't do. We'll be busy making arrangements," Jessie said, "But we'll see. Thanks for the pizza."

The funny thing was, she didn't sound drunk at all as she ushered us out of the suite. Had she pretended to be hammered to see what we were up to, or had something happened in Patrice's room that had sobered her up?

I honestly couldn't say.

On the drive back to Timber Ridge, Maddy asked, "What did you make of that little scene back there?"

"They were a mess, weren't they?" I swerved to avoid a squirrel, and then asked, "Was Jessie really drunk when we got there?"

"I'd say without a doubt," Maddy replied. "She seemed to sway just the right amount, and I could smell liquor on her breath when I gave her a slice of pizza."

Maybe I'd been wrong about her. "Then what sobered her up so fast? Could Patrice have said something to her out of our hearing that shocked her sober?"

Maddy took a moment before she answered. "I don't know. I can't quit thinking about what Oliver said. What did he mean about family business? Benet's not from around here. I saw his bio on the back of his cookbook. He grew up in Atlanta, and from the sound of it, it's as close as he ever got to our part of North Carolina."

"There's something there, though," I said as I tapped my steering wheel. "We need to do a little more digging into that."

"You know me," Maddy said. "I'm all for it, but I'm not exactly sure how we should go about it. What did you have in mind?"

"I'm not sure yet," I admitted. "But give me some time. I'm sure that I'll be able to come up with something."

"There's no doubt in my mind that you will. You're kind of gifted that way, aren't you?"

"Is it a gift, or really a curse?" I asked with a slight smile.

"I guess that all depends," Maddy said.

My cell phone rang, and I reached for it, but Maddy was quicker.

"Eleanor Swift's phone," she said with a smile before I could protest.

Whoever it was, the call ended rather quickly. "Yes. Yes. I understand. Okay. Fine."

That was all she said during the course of the telephone call, and after she was finished, she put my cell phone back where it had been without saying a word.

I gave her a full ten seconds until I asked, "Care to share what that was about with me?"

"It was Kevin Hurley," she said.

"What did he want?" I had visions of having the Slice quarantined so long that I lost my business, and realized that it was a very real possibility, given the razor-edge of a profit margin I worked under.

"Don't worry. You'll like hearing this. He said they finished up with their investigation sooner than he expected, so we can have the Slice back now if you want to reopen. He's leaving the key at your place."

Maddy frowned as she delivered the last bit of news, her smile dying quickly.

I glanced over at her and asked, "What's wrong with that? You should be happy we got the Slice back. It's good news, isn't it?"

"I don't know. I'm kind of beat, and you're going to want to open tonight, aren't you?" she asked as she glanced at my clock dash. I looked myself, and saw that it was almost nine.

"You know what? Forget it. It's not worth our time to go to all of that trouble for an hour or two," I said, "Even if we stay open late. We just found the body this morning. I think folks might need a little time to get over that, don't you? As a matter of fact, I was thinking about staying closed tomorrow, too."

Maddy looked at me sideways with clear confusion on her face. "Who are you, and what did you do with my sister?"

"What do you mean?"

"Eleanor, I've never known you to pass up the opportunity to make a buck."

I shrugged. "It appears that finding a dead body in my dining room has that effect on me. Who knew? So, what do you think? Should we open tomorrow, or not? If we keep the doors closed another day, we should be able to get a lot more snooping in."

Maddy thought about it, was obviously tempted by the prospect, and then said, "I'm just worried about the message it sends if we don't reopen. We don't want folks in town to think we're doing it because we're guilty of something, do we?"

"I suppose you're right," I said with a sigh. "But I meant what I said before: we aren't going to do it tonight. I'm every bit as worn out as you are. Why don't we just call it a night? That way we can make a fresh start in the morning."

"That sounds like a great plan to me," Maddy said. "I might call Bob and see if he wants to come over. Are you calling David?"

I considered it for a moment, and then said, "No, I'm going to take a long, hot bath, and then I'm going to bed."

"Suit yourself," she said. She grabbed her cell phone, and after a brief conversation, she hung up, still frowning.

"What did Bob do, turn you down?" I asked, never believing that it was even in the realm of possibility.

Maddy nodded. "That's exactly what he did. Bob just told me that he hadn't realized that I'd be free tonight, so he agreed to play poker with some friends."

"That doesn't bother you, does it?" I asked my strong-willed, independent sister, surprised that she was acting as though it did.

"Of course not," she said as she put her phone back in her bag. "He should spend some time with his friends."

It didn't ring true to me, but I wasn't about to say anything else about it. I had enough to deal with on my own without taking Maddy's problems on, too. She acted so aloof most of the time that it was hard to read her, even for me. I didn't envy Bob the task he must have had figuring out what was on my sister's mind.

As for me, the note I'd found from Joe had hit me harder than I realized, and the last thing I wanted to do was spend time with another man. I'd call David tomorrow, but for tonight, I just wanted to be alone with my memories.

When we got back to my place, Maddy got in her car and left, and I went inside to clean up the mess we'd made making pizzas. It delayed my bath a little, but I knew that there was no way I was going to feel like doing it in the morning.

I had enough to do tomorrow as things stood now without adding more chores to my schedule. I had a pizzeria to open, and if things went well, I might still have enough time to investigate a murder.

Chapter 9

"There, that should do it," Maddy said as we finished mopping the floor in the dining room of the Slice the next morning. We'd come in early to set things right again, but I had my doubts that anyone would even show up after there'd been a murder there so recently. We'd done everything we could to cleanse the memory of it away, and if scrubbing the place down counted for anything, we should be set. I knew that wasn't the case, though, so for good measure, we mixed the tables up so much that even I couldn't pick the one out where Maddy and I had found the murdered chef. The police, for whatever reason, had taken only the chair he'd been pinned to, but that was just as well as far as I was concerned.

I didn't need any reminders, myself. My sister and I had decided to change the layout of the dining room dramatically so nothing occupied the space where the murder table had been, and I wasn't sure that I was all that fond of the new arrangement. In general, I wasn't all that big a fan of changing anything that Joe and I had so carefully created, but then I realized that it was silly trying to keep things the same as they'd always been. This place was an ongoing business venture, not a shrine to the past.

Maddy stood back and looked at the results. "I like it. It's quirky," she said.

I took in the new arrangement and asked, "What exactly makes it quirky in your mind?"

"It's something you have to be able to recognize on your own without explanation," Maddy said a little condescendingly.

"You don't know either, do you?" I asked with a smile.

"I don't have a clue," she said with a laugh. "It just seemed like the thing to say," she added, matching my grin.

As I studied the dining room one last time, I realized that I was as satisfied with the arrangement as I was going to be. It was time to get back to work—not cleaning, but getting ready to serve pizza and sandwiches to whoever was brave enough to come in after what had happened the day before. "Are we ready to go ahead and start our prep work in the kitchen? I doubt that we're going to be overrun with customers. As a matter of fact, I'm not entirely sure that anyone's going to show up at all."

Maddy shook her head. "Eleanor, never underestimate the taste of the general population. Unless I miss my guess, we're going to be jammed; trust me. Is Greg coming in early?"

I thought about the work schedule I'd posted a few days ago, and then nodded. "He'll be here when we open, so we've got that covered, just in case."

Maddy nodded. "That's good, because we're going to need him. We should make extra dough, too."

My sister was convinced that there would be a mad rush of diners, but I had some serious doubts about that myself. But honestly, what would it hurt to indulge her? "I still think you're probably wrong, but if I make a double batch of dough, I can freeze it along with the dough I made yesterday morning before . . . you know. It wouldn't hurt to have some extra put back, just in case, so I'll make enough fresh dough this morning to give us a good supply. How are the veggies?"

That was Maddy's area of responsibility, telling me when we

needed to order more, and how much. "We should be set. We've got a delivery coming tomorrow, but if we run out, I can always go to the store and get whatever we need to hold us over."

"Then let's get busy."

As my sister and I worked in back, Maddy prepping the veggie toppings and me creating the dough that would soon become crust, we chatted about a great many things, but the topic we discussed most of all was, unsurprisingly, who we thought might have killed Chef Benet.

"The first question is," I said as I started setting out my ingredients, "why would anyone want to kill him?"

"You actually met the guy, right?" Maddy asked as she cut up fresh green peppers. "Hang on, I know you did, because I saw you arguing with him myself."

I had to give her that. Benet hadn't been the nicest man I'd ever met. "Granted, he wasn't very pleasant, but I have to believe someone had a better reason to kill him than just because his personality was a little grating."

"Well, why do people commit murder, anyway?" Maddy asked. "There are only two reasons that I can think of off the top of my head—love and greed, right?"

"That's a little too simplistic for my taste," I said as I started measuring out the ingredients for the dough.

She finished cutting the green peppers and started on the mushrooms. "Hey, I'm willing to listen if you've got anything better to add to the conversation. Go ahead, be more specific."

I thought about it for a few seconds, and then said, "His murder could have been related to his business, his family, or his love life."

"Who exactly does that broad list leave out?" she asked. "You're adding more people to the list, not subtracting from it."

"Hey, I never said this was going to be easy," I said as I flipped the mixer on and raised my voice so that Maddy could hear me over the motor. "No matter how we look at it, his wife has to be our first suspect. After all, you'd have to believe that she had the most to gain from his death, especially if there's insurance, which I'm betting there is. I wonder how much Benet made with his TV show and his books."

"I don't know about that," Maddy said, "but I have to wonder if the woman is even physically capable of killing him that way. Do you honestly believe that Patrice is strong enough to drive a knife clear through the man? I wouldn't think that it would be easy. It would have to take someone really strong."

"Or really motivated," I added. "I keep my knives sharp, but not that sharp. Still, if Patrice thought that her husband was cheating on her, she'd have incentive, at least in her own mind."

Maddy nodded as she moved the cut mushrooms into the covered bowl where they'd stay in the refrigerator until we were ready for them. "So, she tops our list, but we're not going to stop there, are we? We can't forget Oliver and Jessie. They each had their own reasons to want to see the man dead."

I nodded as I turned the mixer off. The silence that followed was a nice change of pace from the mixer's powerful motor. Had it actually been getting louder lately, or was it just my imagination? I dreaded the thought, and the expense, of replacing the floor unit, but I'd have to find a way to do it somehow if the motor ever died. Mixing as much dough as I needed every day by hand would be a nightmare. I'd find the money, one way or another, but I wasn't looking forward to it. "It's true that Benet treated his assistant like dirt, but Oliver wasn't going to be around much longer. He hinted that if he didn't get his big break soon, he was going to quit anyway, so why kill his boss?"

Maddy said, "Maybe he thought that the only way he'd ever get on the air was by taking Benet off himself."

I just shrugged. "Oliver knew that he wasn't going to get his own show, no matter what happened, remember? On the other hand, if Jessie had died instead of Benet, Oliver would be at the top of my list. Jessie spanked him pretty thoroughly, didn't she?"

"She did. Then what would her motive be to kill Benet? He was her bread and butter at the network," Maddy said.

"We can't forget the fact that he was leaving," I noted. "She could have easily been mad enough to kill him."

"Agreed," Maddy answered. "That leaves us with the odd 'family business' clue we got from Oliver, and Patrice's conviction that Benet was having an affair. A scorned mistress can be just as dangerous as a neglected wife."

I pulled the beater out and covered the mixer so the dough could raise, and then said, "So, we've got two more suspects. The only problem is that we don't know who they are."

"Or have any way to find out," Maddy added. "But besides those few minor difficulties, it's going to be a piece of cake."

"Hey, give us a little credit, Sis. We've done it before," I said, reminding her of some of our past exploits.

"Not without a little help from our friends and loved ones," Maddy said. "You can't exactly call up your buddy Art Young at the moment, can you?"

"Not unless it's an emergency," I said reluctantly. "It sounds as though he's got problems of his own."

"I don't even want to think about what they might be," she said as she shivered a little, though the kitchen was plenty warm enough.

I knew that my sister was not Art's biggest fan by any stretch of the imagination, so I decided not to add anything to that particular conversation. "At least we still have David and Bob."

Maddy frowned for a second, and then she took a particularly vicious slice at a poor defenseless onion she'd been chopping. "I'd rather not ask Bob at the moment, if that's okay with you."

"It's fine by me," I said. "Honestly, the more I think about it, I'm not exactly sure what we could ask them to do to help out, anyway. Why don't we keep digging on our own before we start bringing other folks into it. For now, we should both just focus on what we do best."

"Get married?" Maddy asked with a smile. "Between the two of us, we've done it five times."

I shook my head, though I smiled a little. "That may be true, but I'm responsible for just one of those trips down the aisle."

"I know, I'm the romantic of the family," Maddy said. "Don't worry. I'll wait until you catch up."

I rolled my eyes, but just a little. "You're in for a long wait, then."

"That's something I could live with, no problem at all. Okay, if you weren't talking about getting married again, what did you have in mind that the two of us are supposedly so good at?"

"I was thinking more along the lines of selling some pizza and subs," I said.

"You know what? I like your idea better," Maddy said.

"Have you honestly had your fill of holy matrimony?" I asked, trying to keep my tone light. Maddy usually joked about her four trips down the aisle, but lately she hadn't made any self-deprecating cracks about it, and this was the first time she'd opened up in ages.

"There are too many factors that are out of my control, and too few I can change myself. The short answer? I'd have to say, who knows?"

It was an odd response that I wasn't at all certain I wanted to dig any deeper into. Maddy and I had our differences from time to time, as nearly all sisters did, but in the end we were there for each other when it counted. It was okay if I didn't know every opinion she held, and I was fairly certain she felt the same way about me. If she did decide to talk about what was troubling her, I'd be there, ready to listen. And honestly, it was just about the only thing I knew that I could do these days.

We left it at that, and before I knew it, it was time to open our doors and see if the public awaited, or if Maddy, Greg, and I were going to have the chance to catch up on our cleaning.

In the end, I just hoped that someone besides Greg Hatcher showed up.

* * *

Half an hour later, Maddy came back to my busy kitchen with another three orders. We'd had a crowd from the very start, to my amazement. I had to give my sister credit. She hadn't said one "I told you so"; at least not yet. "And you were afraid folks would stay away because of the murder," she said.

"I've got to say, I have to wonder about their motives," I replied as I started on another thin-crust pizza.

She looked at me oddly. "Who cares? They're spending money, and we missed an entire day of sales yesterday, don't forget that," Maddy said as she plated a pizza for me and cut it into slices to prepare it for a customer.

"Don't tell me you're worried about the bottom line now," I said. That was just too much to take in.

"Hey, I draw a paycheck here, too, remember? I care about the Slice doing well enough to keep a roof over my head and keep me fed."

"Don't worry. I can't imagine that either one of us is going to miss any meals," I said as I finished the pizza I'd been working on and slid it onto the conveyor. It was at times like these that I loved the convenience of the conveyor oven Joe and I had purchased when we'd decided to open A Slice of Delight. The pizzas went in as a combination of raw dough, sauce, uncooked toppings, and shredded cheese, and they came out transformed into pies full of bubbling goodness, the crust baked, the sauce heated, the toppings cooked, and the cheese melted into a delicious covering for it all. The best part about it, at least in my mind, was that once something got on the conveyor, it didn't need any more attention from me until it was time to plate and serve.

As I started on the next pizza, Maddy grabbed the finished one she'd just cut and left again.

Greg came into the kitchen a second later waving more orders at me. "Wow, I didn't know that many folks in Timber Ridge even liked our pizza."

As I took two more orders from him, I asked, "What's not to like?"

"I agree, trust me, but if someone else asks to sit at the table of death, I'm going to go ballistic." Greg lowered his voice and then asked, "Just out of curiosity, since you moved things around, I couldn't find it. Where exactly is it?"

I didn't have the heart to tell him that Maddy and I had mixed things up so much that we didn't know ourselves, which was exactly the way I wanted it. "Are people really that ghoulish?"

Greg just laughed. "You wouldn't believe some of the things I've heard today. I had four customers offer to pay me something extra for my trouble if they could get the right table. I was pretty tempted to take money from all of them, and then put them wherever I wanted to."

It sounded so much like Greg's sense of humor that I was worried that he'd done exactly that. "You didn't though, right?"

"Eleanor, I said I was tempted, not that I'd actually do it." He paused, and after a momentary grin, he added, "You've got to admit it, though, it would be hilarious."

"I guess it might be, under different circumstances," I said, "But don't give in to the temptation." Almost as an afterthought, I said, "And don't tell Maddy what's going on, either. Who knows what she might do."

"Might do about what?" my sister asked as she came back in with a bin of dirty plates, glasses, tableware, and serving pans. Our staff was so close to the bone that we all took turns bussing tables whenever they needed it.

"I was a little worried how you might treat people who asked you if they could sit at the killer table," I said.

"You're too late to be concerned about that. I've already had three different parties ask me if they could sit there," Maddy said nonchalantly.

"What did you do about it?" I asked.

She looked at me as though I'd gotten amnesia for a second. "Eleanor, after we mopped and rearranged the dining room, how could either one of us possibly know for sure?"

I smiled and sighed a little from relief. "So, that's what you told them?"

She grinned at me. "Of course not. I told them they all had it. Who knows? I might have even been right once."

My worst fears were coming true right before my eyes. I asked, "You didn't charge them for the privilege, did you?"

Maddy looked as though the idea hadn't even occurred to her. She turned quickly to Greg and asked, "Why is my sister asking me that, Greg; is that what you did? If you did, that's absolutely brilliant. I must say, I'm impressed."

"I was tempted, but I didn't do it," Greg admitted.

"Excellent," Maddy responded with a wicked grin. "We can have a race, and whoever generates the most extra cash gets to keep it instead of putting it in our communal tip jar. How does that sound?"

I had to stop this before it got even worse. I wasn't sure how that might be, but when it came to this kind of stunt, my sister was a full-fledged genius. "I don't want either one of you doing that," I said.

"Is that my boss talking, or is it coming from my sister?" Maddy asked.

"That depends," I answered. "Honestly, it's probably a little bit of both." That approach was not going to work, and I knew it. "Please?" I added softly as I looked at her. "Would you do it for me?"

"You don't have to worry, Eleanor. Greg and I will behave ourselves," Maddy said. I was on edge, both from the murder and the reaction I was getting from my customer base, and my sister must have sensed something in my stress level to agree so quickly. Sure, folks had come out to the Slice, but I had to wonder what their motives really were. While it might not mean much to Maddy or Greg, it was very important to me.

I needed to lighten the mood. I couldn't have my staff picking up on my somber mood. I flipped my towel at them and said, "Go on, you two, shoo. You both need to get back to work."

Maddy grinned, then offered me a salute on her way out. Greg joined right in with one of his own as the two of them faded away back into the dining room, and I finally found my own smile again. I loved it when we could all lighten the mood a little, but I hoped Maddy hadn't taken Greg's idea to heart. Knowing her, it sounded exactly like something she would do if the mood struck her. In warning her not to do it, I was afraid I might have just given her another idea she could exploit, not so much for profit, but for her own personal entertainment.

I was still grumbling about the idea that many of our customers were at the Slice because of the murder, and not because of our offerings, when Bob Lemon came back into the kitchen. The attorney, and Maddy's boyfriend, was smiling as he came in, and I had to wonder what had made his day so happy.

"Maddy should be up front waiting on tables, Bob," I said absently as I finished another sub and put it on the conveyor.

"I know. I saw her when I came in," he said, still grinning at me as though he was some kind of goofy kid.

I was overworked, and I really didn't have time for any foolishness at the moment. "Is there something I can do for you, Bob?" I asked.

"Don't worry; you don't have to stop working, but I wanted to show you something if you've got a second," Bob said as he reached into his pocket.

"Okay, but make it quick," I replied, wiping my hands on the towel I always kept nearby while I worked in the kitchen. I hadn't meant to snap at him, but I didn't feel like apologizing at the moment. Besides, if my abrupt tone had bothered him, I was certain that he would have said something about it.

"That's okay. I can see that you're busy. Don't worry about it. It can wait," Bob said, clearly deflated by my behavior. So he'd picked up on my mood after all.

I stopped what I was doing and said as sincerely as I could manage, "I'm sorry. It's been a bad couple of days around here, but that's no excuse for me to take it out on you. What's up?"

"Do you really have the time?" Bob asked.

"I do," I said, hoping that whatever he had to show me wouldn't upset my world any more than it already was.

"Look at this," he said as he brought a ring box from his suit pocket. As he opened it, he said proudly, "I'm going to ask your sister to marry me as soon as you two take your afternoon break."

I looked at the engagement ring—a huge, beautiful diamond mounted on an intricate gold band—and then studied Bob. "Are you absolutely positive that you want to do that today?"

He sighed. "Why wouldn't I? I love her, and I know in my heart that she loves me."

How could I say something without shattering his feelings? Maybe I could talk him out of proposing before he actually got down on one knee. "She's been married four times; you know that, right?"

Bob snapped the box shut and put it in his pocket. "Eleanor, why do I have the feeling that you're not all that excited about the idea? Is it because you're afraid she'll quit working here for you once we're married?"

"What? Of course not. Why would she do that?"

"You're teasing, right? The real question is, why wouldn't she?" Bob asked, clearly confused by my question. "I can more than take care of her. Maddy won't ever have to work again once we're married."

"She doesn't *have* to work now," I said, not really sure if it were true or not. I didn't know much about my sister's finances, but I knew that at least one of her husbands had been rich. She might be living on what I could pay her, or she might have enough money in her checking account to buy the place outright if she wanted. "I'd like to think that she likes being here. I know I love having her in my life every day."

"I'm sorry," Bob said as he ran a hand through his hair. "This was a mistake. This didn't go anything at all like the way I'd planned."

"And that's my fault how, exactly?" I asked. I might have been lashing out a little now, but he was talking about taking my sister away from me. Okay, I knew how irrational that sounded even as the words popped into my head, but it was how I felt.

Bob didn't say anything as he left the kitchen rather abruptly, and I wished I would have forgotten about trying to spare his feelings and instead shared the conversation I'd had with Maddy about marriage. But it was too late. If he asked her to marry him, I had a feeling that my sister would hurt his feelings a lot more than I just had.

Chapter 10

"What just happened?" Maddy asked thirty seconds later when she burst back into the kitchen.

"Hey, I'm working as fast as I can," I said. "I can't force anything to cook any faster than it is now, no matter how much I wish I could."

She frowned at me, and then said, "I'm talking about Bob. What did you say to him, Eleanor? He was so excited when he got here, but after he left you, the poor man tore out of the restaurant so fast he almost knocked a pair of nuns over on his rush to escape. I have to believe that it was something you said to him. Please tell me this is just my imagination, and that I'm wrong."

"You're wrong," I said.

"Funny, but I don't believe you," Maddy replied.

I'd dug myself into a pretty deep hole, and I had a feeling that I wouldn't be able to climb out of it. "If you don't trust my answers, then why ask the questions?"

"Eleanor?" Maddy asked in that voice she used when she was being deadly serious, instead of her normally jovial mood. "Tell me what just happened, and start from the second Bob walked into the kitchen."

She wasn't going to drop it; that much was clear. "He caught me at a bad time, okay? I'm sorry."

Maddy studied me critically before she spoke again. "There's something else that you're not telling me. You might as well come clean, Sis. You know that I'll get it out of you sooner or later."

I was now firmly between a rock and a hard place. If I told her the truth, she'd know that Bob was about to propose, and that wasn't fair to either one of them. On the other hand, if I lied to her, she'd see right through it. I could lie when I was backed into a corner to just about anybody, but Maddy could almost always tell when I was even shading the truth a little.

"Talk to Bob," I said. "You need to hear it from him, not me."

She wouldn't do it, though. "Trust me, I will, but right now I'm talking to you."

I just couldn't bring myself to do it, though. I turned back to my work as I said, "Maddy, I'd tell you if I could, but I can't. You need to just drop it, okay? It's not my place to say anything. Trust me on this."

She frowned, took off her apron, and then tossed it onto the counter. "I'll be back a little later."

She was honestly deserting us when we needed her? "Where are you going? Did you forget that we've got a full house out there?"

Maddy shook her head. "I know, but I won't be long. Greg can handle it until I get back."

After she left, I looked out through the door. We were jammed, and I knew just how upset Maddy must have been with my refusal to tell her what Bob and I had talked about. I didn't like that she'd deserted her post, but I couldn't exactly blame her for doing it. If I'd been in her shoes, I most likely would have done the same thing.

I took the next pizza out from the line, slid it onto a platter, cut it, and then carried it out front myself.

As I delivered to a table, Greg came over and asked, "Where did Maddy go? It's crazy here right now, and we really need her."

"Sorry. She had to run an errand," I said.

"You don't understand. I can't handle this alone," Greg said, and for a second, I had a seizing fear in my chest that he would walk out, too.

When he didn't, I took a deep breath and then said, "You take the orders, fill the drinks, and run the register, and I'll bring the food out and deliver it as it's ready. It might not be perfect, but it will do until Maddy gets back."

"If she comes back at all," I thought to myself.

Greg and I managed to limp through, working that system for the fifteen minutes that Maddy was gone, but we were both relieved when she came back to the Slice.

"I'm sorry," I said the second I saw her.

"For what, exactly?" my sister asked as she made her way back to the kitchen to retrieve her apron.

"For the way I treated Bob," I added.

"And?" Maddy asked.

"For not telling you what the two of us discussed," I finished. "You did find Bob, didn't you?"

Maddy didn't look at all happy when she explained, "Oh, I found him all right, for all the good it did me. He wouldn't say a word, and when I pressed him about what happened in the kitchen with you, all he would say was that there was nothing to talk about anymore, that he'd changed his mind. What did he change his mind about, Eleanor?"

I didn't have the heart to tell her now. "Maddy, I still can't say. I'm so sorry."

"I am, too," she said a little coolly. "Like you said before, we're busy out there, so I'd better get back to work."

The second Maddy left the kitchen, I grabbed the phone and called Bob Lemon's telephone number.

Instead of his secretary picking up, Bob answered the phone himself. I could have made a crack then, but it clearly wasn't the time. "Bob, Maddy said you changed your mind about proposing. Was it because of what I said? I'm sorry; I was wrong to butt in like that."

"Did you tell her I was going to propose?" Bob asked, the ominous tone strong in his voice.

What an odd day this was turning out to be. "No, of course not. She said she found you, and you said you changed your mind. Was she lying to me?"

After a momentary pause, Bob admitted, "I told her I changed my mind, but I didn't tell her what it was about, and I assumed you wouldn't, either."

"I didn't say a word to her about it, but that doesn't mean I won't. I'm one of your biggest fans, Bob, but she's my sister, first and foremost. If you don't tell her right now, I will. I won't have her angry at me for something I didn't do."

"I think you've done plenty already, don't you? I was surprised, and more than a little hurt, by your reaction, Eleanor. I thought you liked me."

"I do. I'm just not sure Maddy wants to get married again to anyone, even you," I blurted out.

"Ever?" Bob asked softly.

"I'm sorry," I said, "but that's what she told me."

He hesitated, and then asked, "Is there any chance that was a long time ago?"

It nearly killed me to tell him, but I admitted, "We were just talking about it this morning."

Bob's voice was quite somber as he said almost wistfully, "I knew she teased a great deal about being finished with matrimony, but I never took her seriously. Perhaps I should have." His voice nearly started to break, but he quickly put it back together. "Eleanor, maybe I should thank you instead of being angry with you. After all, you very well may have saved me a great deal of embarrassment."

"Bob," I said, "If you have any sense at all, you need to ignore me. Do what's in your heart; don't base your actions on anything

I say. If you want to marry my sister, you have my blessing to ask her. If you've really changed your mind, that's fine, too, but she has the right to know that you were at least considering it."

Bob sighed heavily. "I'm not at all sure what I'm going to do."

"I truly am sorry, but I can't keep this secret for you forever," I said.

"Do what you must," he answered, and then hung up on me.

It appeared that now I was the one in trouble.

By the time we took our dinner break, things had still not warmed up between Maddy and me, and I felt terrible about it. I kept thinking that if Maddy had been exaggerating and had really been interested in marrying Bob, I'd just blown it for them both, and that was something that I just couldn't live with. I knew that if Bob didn't propose soon despite my reaction to the idea, I'd have to tell Maddy what had happened and leave the next step up to her. Contrary to what she might believe, I didn't take any joy in messing with her love life, but I'd still managed to foul it up royally.

"Do you want to grab lunch?" I asked Maddy tentatively as I joined her up front. Greg had wisely taken off at the first opportunity, and I didn't blame him a bit. He must have sensed the storm clouds gathering, and had decided to go for some shelter of his own.

"No, thanks," she said as she refused to make eye contact with me. "I'm not all that hungry. You go ahead, though."

It was a noteworthy event when Maddy didn't want to eat out. I was afraid that I'd done as much damage as I'd imagined. "I said I was sorry," I repeated.

She pretended to be busy wiping a table down, though it was as clean as it had ever been since I'd owned it. In fact, I was worried that she might wear through the varnish if she didn't stop soon. "It's fine, Eleanor. I'm sure you have your reasons not to tell me what's going on."

It was pretty clear that she'd made up her mind. I grabbed my jacket and headed for the door. Before I walked out, I paused and asked one last time, "You're really not coming?"

"I'm really not," she said.

I knew how strong her stubborn streak was, since I had one myself. "Let me have your key, then," I asked as I held out my hand.

"You're firing me because I won't eat with you?" Maddy asked seriously.

"Of course not. I need a copy myself, remember? If you're going to stay here, I'll run over to Slick's and have him make me a duplicate. I can't bring myself to use the one Benet had. It shouldn't take long."

"Fine," Maddy said. "That's all right, then." She took her key off her ring, but instead of handing it directly to me, she put it on the table she'd just been polishing.

I almost said, "You missed a spot," as I picked up the key, but I knew better. This would not be fixed by a joke, and would most likely make matters worse. I walked outside, and as I locked the door behind me, my sister turned her back to me. I had to fix this, and as soon as I got a new key made, I was going to track Bob Lemon down and beat some sense into him.

As Slick made me a duplicate key, he asked, "I normally wouldn't ask you this, but is something wrong, Eleanor? I mean besides the murder in your pizza place and all. You look troubled."

"I stuck my nose somewhere that it didn't belong, and it got nipped off," I admitted.

Slick nodded. He was in his fifties, bald as a cue ball, but he did sport a pretty magnificent mustache. We'd been friends for a long time, and he and my late husband, Joe, had been great pals as well.

"Don't beat yourself up too much about it. It happens to me all of the time," he said as the key machine started to automatically cut a duplicate.

"How do you fix it?" I asked, honestly curious. "I could use some good advice."

"Usually, I just tell Nancy that I was wrong. That normally works for me," he said with a grin.

"Even if you don't think you are?"

"Especially then," Slick admitted. "It makes life a lot more pleasant all the way around, and what does it cost me? It doesn't hurt anyone to eat a little crow every now and then. As a matter of fact, it could even be considered healthy by some. I know it's helped keep my marriage going, even after all these years."

The key was finished, and Slick took it out of the clamp, then buffed it on a wheel attached to the cutting machine. He held both keys up to the light back to back, and then nodded. "That should do it, but if you have any problems, bring it back and I'll cut you another one on the house."

As I paid for the key, I asked, "I'm happy to pay for the advice, too. How much do you think would be fair?"

"What a coincidence. We're running a special today," he answered with a grin. "You buy a key, and you get the advice thrown in for free."

"I've got to say, that's the best deal I've had all day," I answered with a smile, despite my mood. Slick had a way of doing that, and I knew that Nancy was a lucky woman to have this man in her life.

I had the key. Now it was time to go attorney hunting. I found Bob on a picnic table in front of his law office eating a sandwich. Why had he waited so long to eat? Had he planned to wait for Maddy? If so, he was in for a long wait. The lawyer didn't look all that pleased to see me, but I couldn't let that stop me.

"Got a second, Bob?" I asked as I sat down, not caring that much if I was welcome or not.

He shook his head as he dropped the sandwich on the wrapper. "This is not how I'd hoped my afternoon would turn out."

He looked at me for a second, and then asked, "What is it with you two? Don't either one of you ever take no for an answer?"

"Not when it's important," I said. "I owe you an apology, a real one, and I need you to accept it."

He frowned at the table in front of him as though it had done him a grave disservice. "You have nothing to apologize for, Eleanor. I asked you a question, and you gave me your honest opinion. I can't expect anything more than that."

Boy, he was as stubborn as my sister. Maybe they were the perfect match after all. "That's just it. It wasn't how I really felt," I said. "You caught me at a bad moment, and I lashed out at you. I had no business treating you that way, and that's what I want you to forgive me for."

"You can rest easy, then. You're forgiven," he said after a moment, but he still wouldn't make eye contact.

"Not until you say it like you mean it," I replied as I touched his hand lightly.

Bob looked up, stared at me a few seconds, and then let out a sigh of relief. "Fine. I forgive you."

"Then you'll propose to my sister?" I asked.

"Not a chance," he said, shaking his head.

"I thought you forgave me."

"I did," Bob said, "But that doesn't mean you weren't right. Do you honestly think you're the only one Maddy ever told that she didn't want to get married again? I heard her say it a dozen times, but deep in my heart, I never believed her."

"Bob, she may not even know that she's ready," I said. "I honestly don't think she'll have an answer until you ask."

He wadded up the rest of his sandwich and threw it into paper bag in front of him. "It really puts me out there on a limb, doesn't it?"

"I don't mean to get all mushy on you, but isn't that what love is? It's taking that leap of faith that makes you feel alive."

"Wow, a pizza maker and a philosopher," he said, adding a smile that I'd missed. Maybe he really had forgiven me. "I didn't know I'd be getting two such diverse talents for the price of one."

"What can I say? I charge for the pizza, but giving advice is my true passion." I laughed as I said it, and Bob smiled a little again, this one warmer than before.

As the attorney stood, he said, "Thanks for coming over here and apologizing, Eleanor. I really do appreciate it."

I felt my heart sink when I realized that he was serious about changing his mind about the proposal. I may have just cost my sister her last real chance at happiness, and I didn't know how I'd ever be able to forgive myself. "So, you're really not going to ask her now?"

"I can't do it."

"Bob, please," I said.

With a broad grin, he said, "Relax, Eleanor. What I can't do is not at least take my chances and try." Bob tossed his sandwich bag into a nearby trash can, and then added, "As a matter of fact, if you know where she is, I'm going to go propose right now." Bob shrugged a little as he added, "After all, what do I have to lose but a little bit of pride? The chance at happiness is worth the risk, wouldn't you agree?"

"I couldn't agree with you more. That's the spirit," I said. "No matter what happens, at least you can be sure that I'm on your side."

Bob and I walked back to the Slice together, but he was pretty focused on preparing what he wanted to say. I tagged dutifully along in silence, and when we got to the front window, I could see Maddy sitting at a table eating lunch. She'd made herself some kind of sub, and I remembered that I hadn't eaten yet.

"I'm going to let you in, and then I'm going to take off again so you two can be alone," I promised.

He hung back just out of sight. "Eleanor, don't disappear on my account. You can hang around, if you'd like," Bob said. "After how deeply you're involved in this, it's only fair that you get to hear the proposal, too."

I would have loved to stay, but I wasn't sure how my sister would feel about an audience. "Thanks, but you two deserve to have some privacy."

I started to unlock the door, but to my surprise, Bob stayed back. Was it possible that he was already getting cold feet? "Aren't you going in?"

"Give me a second to work up my nerve," Bob said with a nervous smile. "I'll be right there."

"Don't take too long," I said. "We're opening soon."

"Don't worry."

Maddy looked up at me as I closed, but didn't lock, the door behind me after I walked into the Slice.

"You're early," she said to me in a flat voice.

"As a matter of fact, I'm not really even back yet. Bob is standing outside. He wants to come in and talk to you."

She looked less than elated by the news. "I was under the distinct impression that we were finished talking for the day."

I hoped that my sister's stubborn streak wouldn't sabotage her chance at a happy life. "You need to keep an open mind to whatever he says and hear him out, Maddy," I said.

She studied me for a second, and then nodded. "Go on. You might as well tell him to come in."

I grinned at her, and then turned back to Bob and gave him a thumbs-up sign. "It's all clear."

As the attorney walked in, I lingered for a second and whispered, "Good luck," before I left and locked the door behind me.

If he heard me at all, he didn't show it.

As I left the Slice to them, part of me was tempted to stand nearby and watch them from outside the window, but I decided not to do it. If Maddy spotted me snooping, I'd never hear the end of it, and besides, I'd meant what I'd said. They deserved to have this time alone, and I was going to give it to them.

I didn't feel like driving anywhere, so I walked down to Paul's Pastries to see if there was any chance that he was still open this late. If he was, I might just see if any of his treats caught my eye. That was a lie; they all garnered my attention, but I was trying to be a little more selective in the goodies I ate, since my jeans weren't exactly getting any looser as I got older.

Paul, a tall and thin handsome young man I was proud to count as a real friend, smiled at me as I walked in. "Hey, Eleanor. It's nice to see you. What's going on? Is your sweet tooth calling my name?"

"It's so loud I can barely rest at night," I answered with a grin.

"What can I tease you with today?" Paul asked as he waved a hand toward his display. "We don't have a great selection at this time of day, but everything we do have is good."

"You don't have to sell me on how great your things taste," I said. I studied the case, and found myself being torn between a peanut-crusted donut and one that was covered in white powdered sugar. They both looked good enough to be featured in a catalogue. "I'll take both of those," I said decisively.

"Would you like to eat them here, or do you need them to go? Honestly, I could use the company, if you have the time to hang around a little."

"I'd be delighted to stay," I said. I was in no hurry to get back to the Slice, not with the conversation that must be going on at the moment between Bob and my sister. "Throw a chocolate milk in, too, would you?"

"I'll do better than that," Paul said with a smile. "If you don't mind, I think I'll join you."

That was indeed a rare occurrence, and I wondered at times if Paul ever sampled his offerings, given how thin and fit he was. If our positions were reversed, I doubted I'd be able to get out through the front door after a month of being around all of those baked treats.

"I'd love it if you could," I said, meaning it.

Paul grabbed a coffee and a plain cake donut for himself, and then brought the full tray to the table I'd selected by the window.

"Here you go," he said as he served me, and then sat down across the table from me.

After the first bite, Paul said, "I was sorry to hear about Benet. I wasn't a fan of the man, but at least he wasn't afraid to let people know where he stood. I can't believe someone killed him at the Slice."

"Me, either," I said. "He really wasn't easy to get along with at all, was he?"

Paul shook his head. "I knew him for three minutes and my blood pressure spiked higher than it should have been. I can't imagine being in his life on a daily basis. Eleanor, do you have any idea who might have killed him?"

"The police are investigating the case," I said, trying to sound as nonchalant as I could.

Paul just laughed. "I don't doubt it, but I'm willing to bet that you are, too. Come on, you can trust me. How can you not look into this? Your place and your reputation are both on the line."

"Maddy and I are asking around," I admitted.

"Do you have any good suspects yet?"

It was clear that Paul honestly wanted to hear about it and wasn't just being polite. "Well, so far we've talked to his wife, his assistant, and his TV producer," I said. "There's bound to be more suspects than that, given the man's demeanor, but Maddy and I are still checking them out."

"Did he have any ties to Timber Ridge?" Paul asked as he took another sip of coffee. His donut, for the most part, still lay untouched on the tray. How could he not devour it? It was taking every ounce of self-control that I had not to scarf my donuts down, they were so tasty.

I honestly didn't know how to answer that at this point. "We have our suspicions, but there's nothing we can prove yet."

"You will. I have faith in you two."

"I hope it's warranted," I said as I broke down and took a healthy bite of the peanut donut. "These are amazing."

"They should be," Paul said with a bit of a wicked expression on his face. "I stole the recipe from The Charlotte Donut Explosion."

"Don't they mind?" I asked with a grin.

"They might if they knew about it, but I did it fair and square. I must have eaten twelve dozen donuts before I figured out what made theirs so special."

"Whatever the reason, you may have even surpassed them," I said as I polished the peanut donut off. "They're almost too good to eat."

"But not quite, right?" he asked as he took a sip of coffee.

"A picture might be worth a thousand words, but one bite of your treats is worth a thousand pictures," I said. I took a bite of the powdered one, and though it was good, I wished that I'd saved the peanut one for last. I made a mental note for next time, knowing that no matter how much I wished that I had more willpower, I'd be back.

"Hang on," Paul said when I looked up at him. "You've got a little powdered sugar on your nose."

I brushed my nose, and then asked, "Did I get it?"

The baker shook his head as he reached out a napkin and brushed it away. As he did, I looked into his eyes and saw them beaming, but a movement at the window distracted me.

When I looked up from the tray, I saw David Quinton hurrying away from us.

Without meaning to, it appeared that I'd just caused myself another problem that I had to fix fast before it blew up in my face.

Chapter 11

"David, wait up," I called out as he hurried away from Paul's shop. I had to run to catch him, and I must have looked like a fool chasing after the man, but I didn't care.

"David," I said, nearly out of breath as I grabbed his arm. "Didn't you hear me?"

"Hello, Eleanor," he said. "Sorry about that. I was thinking about something else."

I had to give David credit for being such a terrible liar. After all, I wanted to be able to read when he was angry or hurt, not be fooled by a disguise he showed the world. I spun him around to face me, and then I said with every ounce of conviction that I possessed, "I don't know what that must have looked like just now, but I had a little powdered sugar on my nose, and Paul got it off for me. That's the sum total of it. Nothing happened."

"You don't owe me any explanations," he said. "We never said that we were exclusive." I could tell that he was hurt, and I hated being the cause of it.

I couldn't think of a thing to say, so instead, I kissed him, as soundly as I knew how, not caring who might see.

When we finally pulled away, an older man standing nearby began applauding, and I felt my face redden slightly.

"Okay, now I believe you," David said with a crooked little

smile. "I'm sorry if I overreacted, but you've got to admit that Paul is a handsome young man."

"I never denied it," I replied, and before David could react, I hugged him. "You're not so bad yourself, mister, and you've got one big advantage over him."

"What's that?" David asked.

"You're the one I'm dating," I answered. "Just you, and nobody else."

"That's a good point."

I don't know what possessed me to say it, but I added, "Trust me, if I wanted to be with Paul, I would be."

I realized how it must have sounded, but before I could correct it, David just laughed. "My, aren't we full of ourselves today. Eating powdered donuts must make you feel invincible."

"You know what I meant," I said.

"I understand," David said. "I'm just teasing you. Listen, I'd love to stay and chat, but I'm late for a meeting. Sorry about the way I reacted just then."

"A little jealousy isn't necessarily all that bad," I said. "But you don't have anything to worry about."

"Neither do you," David said, the smile on his face deep and wide.

I was feeling pretty good about things with him when Bob Lemon nearly knocked me down near the Slice in his rush to get past me.

"What just happened?" I asked, afraid I already knew the answer. It appeared that one of my worst fears had just been realized. "Did she say no?"

"She has to think about it," Bob said, clearly unhappy with the result. "I guess that's better than nothing."

I smiled and hugged him. "Are you kidding? That's a major victory, if you ask me. My sister must really care about you. You know that, don't you?"

"I do," Bob admitted. "I just hope she'll say yes, and soon."

"If it helps, I'm rooting for you," I said.

"I appreciate that," he said, "but you're not the sister I need to win," he added as he hurried off.

When I walked back into the Slice, I found Maddy in the kitchen furiously chopping vegetables, even though we had plenty for the rest of the day.

"What's up, Sis?" I asked as innocently as I could manage.

"Don't play dumb with me," Maddy said as her gaze never left the cutting board. "Bob told me you knew about the proposal all along."

At least I didn't have to keep that secret any longer. "Do you understand why I couldn't tell you?"

"I don't know that I do, actually," Maddy said as she continued to chop. "A little warning might have gone a long way. I told him I had to think about it, in case you're wondering."

"I heard."

"He couldn't wait to call you, could he?" she asked, giving the cutting board another serious whack.

"As a matter of fact, I just saw him outside," I admitted.

"You weren't watching us, were you?"

"No," I said, glad I could admit that honestly. "I was at Paul's getting into a mess of my own at the time."

That got Maddy's attention. "Anything you'd care to share with me?"

"Maybe later," I said as I moved closer and took the knife from her. "I believe that we've got enough for tonight."

She looked down at the pile, and then grinned at me. "Tomorrow, too, I'd wager. Sorry about that."

"Hey, I understand completely. Cooking helps, doesn't it?"

She frowned at me as she said, "I wish. I'm no closer to an answer now than I was when he asked."

I put my arm around Maddy's shoulder. "You've got time, don't you? He didn't give you a deadline or anything, did he?"

"No, Bob is too sweet a man to try to do something like that. He'd never try to rush me. I'm just not sure when I might have an answer for him. I honestly have no idea what I want, and I can't tell you how frustrating it is for me. You know me, Eleanor. I pride myself on being decisive, and yet I can't make up my mind about the most important question I've been asked in a long time."

"Don't worry. You'll find the right answer. I have faith in you," I said.

"I'm glad at least one of us does." She glanced at the clock and said, "It's nearly time to open. Did you get enough to eat at Paul's, or should I make you something before the crowds hit?"

"I'm good," I said. "Let's go face the day. Oh, before I forget, here's your key." I handed it to her, and she took it gratefully and returned it to its rightful place on her key ring.

As she did it, she looked at me and said, "Eleanor, no matter what I say to Bob's proposal, I'm here as long as you want me. Okay?"

I hugged my sister, and then said, "That's good to hear."

After we broke apart, Maddy said, "While I'm thinking, I could really use a distraction, and investigating Benet's murder might be the perfect solution. What are our plans on how to keep digging into it?"

"Well, we've spoken to the three people closest to Benet that were in town, but I'm not entirely certain that Cindy has told us the complete truth up to now."

"I can't see her lying to us," Maddy said with a frown. "Why would she? We're just trying to help."

I thought about that, and then said, "She might do it if she was hiding something."

"Like what?"

"That I wish I knew," I said. "There was something between Cindy and Benet, but I can't for the life of me figure out what it might have been."

"Then maybe we should tackle her first," Maddy said as she glanced at the kitchen clock. "I'll go open the front door."

She came back ten seconds later.

"That was fast," I said.

"I never opened it," Maddy admitted.

"Any reason in particular why not?" I asked.

"Cindy's outside waiting to get in, so I thought you might want to talk to her yourself before things get crazy for our evening shift. You two have a closer connection than I do with her, so you might have better luck if you speak with her alone. Now might be the perfect opportunity to question her."

"That's a great idea," I said. "Let's go."

There were no other customers waiting outside, so I let Cindy in and locked the door behind her. She asked, "Are you open yet? I don't want to interfere."

I looked at my watch and lied, "We've got a minute before we let the masses in. Come on back into the kitchen where we can talk."

Cindy agreed, not noticing that I'd shaved a bit off the time. Maddy smiled at me, and out of Cindy's sight, my sister gave me a thumbs-up.

As Cindy and I walked back into the kitchen, I saw Greg standing just outside. Behind him, Josh Hurley was waiting as well.

"I'll go let them in," Maddy said, and then looked right at me as she added, "We've still got a few minutes before we open, right?"

"Right," I said, happy that she'd bought me a little time.

Cindy and I went back into the kitchen, and she took one of the barstools I kept there for the rare times I allowed visitors in my kitchen.

"How are you holding up?" I asked her as I set my kitchen in order to prepare for our first customers of the evening. "Have you decided when you're going to have your grand opening at the bookstore?"

"Do you mean the reopening?" she asked, a little crestfallen.

"Cheer up. That's the joy of owning your own business," I told her. "You can call it whatever you want to."

"I suppose," she said. "To tell you the truth, after what happened yesterday, some of the bloom is off the rose, if you know what I mean."

"You just have to weather the storm," I said, not meaning to give her yet another pep talk. I had questions to ask Cindy, but I had a difficult time not trying to buck up her spirits. After all, we were more alike than different, and I suppose part of it was that I wanted to help her succeed. I couldn't focus on that now, though. I had to ask her a tough question that had been hounding me since we'd spoken the day before.

"Cindy, I hate to ask you this, but I need to know what you were talking about yesterday when we spoke."

"What do you mean?" she asked. Was she that dense, or was she just playing with me? I couldn't imagine that she didn't know exactly what I was talking about.

"When I asked you if you'd met Benet before, you said not really, and when I pushed you, all you'd tell me was that it was complicated." It was time to lay my cards on the table. "Cindy, the author you brought in for a book signing was murdered in my pizzeria. I know you think it reflects badly on you, but how do you think my customers must feel? If I don't solve this case, and soon, it's going to haunt me to the point where it may kill my business. Maddy and I are going to investigate, but to do that, I need your help. You have to be honest with me. I feel as though I've been of some help to you lately, and all I'm asking is that you do the same for me in return."

I shouldn't have been so forceful, but I was afraid that it might be the only way I could get through to her.

After a moment, Cindy finally nodded. "Okay, you deserve

that much, at least. All I ask is that you don't tell anyone what I'm about to tell you."

"If I can't say anything to Maddy, don't tell me at all," I said. I didn't even have to think about it. Maddy was so much more than my sister, no matter how deeply that bond went. Sure, she was my employee, but she was also my coconspirator; most of all, she was my best friend.

Cindy chewed her bottom lip for a second, and then reluctantly nodded. "Okay, you can tell Maddy, but that's it."

"I can probably do that unless it's vital information needed to catch a killer," I said, meaning it. If what she told me became pertinent to the case, I'd have to reserve the right to break my word to her. Catching a murderer took precedence over keeping someone's secret, no matter what the fallout might be.

Cindy nodded absently, and then she explained, "Benet contacted me six months ago, if you can imagine that."

"He came to Timber Ridge?" I asked, incredulous that no one in town knew that the chef had been here before now.

"No, he did it online," Cindy explained. "I got an e-mail from him one day out of the blue. He said he heard about my plans to open a bookstore and asked if there was anything he could do to help. I told him that having him there when I cut the ribbon would mean a great deal to me, but he claimed to have a scheduling conflict and said that he couldn't make it."

"And that ended your contact with him?" I asked.

"No, it was just the icebreaker. After that, we usually e-mailed back and forth once a week. He told me he was fascinated with what it took to open a bookstore, and then he gave me a glimpse into what his life was like."

I remembered how Benet had acted around Cindy when he'd come to town, and it just didn't jibe. "He was rude to you when he got here, though. There wasn't anything nice about him when he walked into your store. I was there, remember?"

"Hang on, I'm getting to that," Cindy said, looking worried as she continued to tell me the story. "Two months ago, we had a falling out online, and he told me not to e-mail him anymore. I was upset, especially since I didn't know what I'd done to cause it, but he never answered any more of my queries, and I finally stopped trying to get in touch with him altogether. As a matter of fact, I'd nearly forgotten all about him when he got in touch with me again."

"What made him change his mind?" I asked. I knew that time was getting away from us, but these answers might help me find the man's killer. If that meant that folks would be a little late getting their pizza, so be it.

"I don't know what happened, and that's the truth," she said. "I was shocked when I got the call from Oliver. I was told in no uncertain terms that I was not to speak to Benet, or anyone else, about our earlier e-mail exchanges, and to pretend that the chef and I had never met. If I violated that agreement, he would walk out of my shop forever."

"So you agreed," I said.

"Sure, why wouldn't I? I needed him as a draw, and he needed a venue to launch his book. It seemed to make perfect sense at the time. But then . . ."

She stopped, as though she were afraid to add any more to it. I couldn't have that, though. "What happened?"

"My mother found out that Benet was coming to town, and she started acting so strangely, it was as though I didn't even know her."

"In what way?" I asked.

Cindy shook her head as she said, "It's hard to explain. She seemed troubled by Benet's visit, but on the day he arrived, she was the first one to greet him at the hotel. When he came to the shop, he acted as though he actually might have been afraid of her. Can you honestly imagine my mother intimidating anyone? I know that I can't."

Cindy's mother, Janet, was the calmest and most soft-spoken

person I'd ever met in my life. Not only that, but she was barely five feet tall, and probably didn't weigh a hundred pounds soaking wet. The thought of her menacing anyone was beyond me, but there were more ways to do it than to threaten someone physically. How had she managed it, though?

"Would you mind if I spoke with her about what happened that day?"

"As a matter of fact, I do," Cindy said emphatically. "Leave my mother out of this. She isn't a part of what happened to the man."

"How can you say that with any real conviction?" I asked as the kitchen door opened.

Maddy was there, with an apologetic look on her face. "I'm sorry, but the group that reserved most of the dining room for right now is here. We have about forty hungry customers hoping to get served an early dinner, if it's not too much trouble."

"What group?" I asked. "I don't remember anything about anybody in particular coming by."

Maddy looked sheepish as she admitted, "That's probably because I forgot to tell you. Sorry about that."

"It's fine," I said, just wanting the distraction to be over. "What's the name of the group?"

"It's the Senior Juniors again," Maddy said.

I remembered them. They'd chosen our restaurant six months before, and they must have liked what we served, since they were back again for round two. The group got its name because it was a collection of senior citizens who were named for their fathers, or the women who had married them. It was the oddest thing to bind a group of people together that I'd ever heard of, but I hadn't minded when I'd put their money in the bank.

"Don't worry. I'll get started in a second," I said. "We're not done here."

Cindy shook her head. "Eleanor, you told me at least a dozen times that the customer always comes first, and I know you meant it. It's fine. We can talk later. After all, it's not like I'm going anywhere anytime soon."

"Do you promise we'll discuss this more?" I asked. I really didn't want to disappoint the group, but we weren't finished, not by a long shot.

"I promise. We'll talk tomorrow," Cindy said.

"Or maybe even tonight," I suggested.

"We'll see."

"But either tonight or tomorrow, right?" I asked.

"Absolutely," she answered as she headed for the kitchen door.

"I'm holding you to that," I said.

She just nodded as she escaped through the kitchen door.

After Cindy left, Maddy said, "I'm so sorry. I didn't have much choice. After all, I'm the one who booked them."

"Don't sweat it, Maddy. You did the right thing."

"Wow, you sounded pretty desperate to finish your conversation with Cindy. Did you learn anything good in the short amount of time you had?" my sister asked me before heading back into the dining room.

I just shrugged as I started working on pizza crusts. "I thought I had one puzzle solved, but a new one just showed up."

"That's good, though, right?" my sister asked.

"Why do you say that?"

"Well, at least we're not up against a dead end. If anything, we have too many suspects. That's got to be something."

I just shrugged. "Maybe, maybe not." I clapped my hands together, and then said, "It's time to start making pizzas. Do you happen to remember what they ordered?"

She rolled her eyes. "I haven't lost my mind. I wrote it down." Maddy patted her pockets, and then asked, "Now, where could that slip be? I know I had it here somewhere."

"We could always just guess," I said with a grin.

She pulled a note from her pocket. "It was right here all along. We need ten large cheese pizzas."

"It's not going to be much of a challenge, but maybe that's a good thing." As I got out more dough from the fridge, I suggested, "Why don't you give me a hand back here, and the guys can wait on our customers."

"Two Spencer women working side by side in the same kitchen?" Maddy asked. "What would Momma say?"

"She'd say it's about time, I bet," I said. "Besides, don't forget that I'm a Swift. You know that."

Maddy said, "You might have taken Joe's last name, but you're a Spencer by birth, and deep down you always will be, so don't try to deny it."

"I wouldn't do it, even if I could." I had been proud to be Joe's wife, but no less honored to be the daughter of my mother and father. As far as I was concerned, there was no reason in the world that I couldn't be both.

Maddy smiled. "Good. While we're getting busy making pizzas, why don't you tell me everything that Cindy had to say?"

"Why not?" I asked. We were both good enough at making pizzas that it didn't require our total attention while we were doing it. As we worked, I brought Maddy up-to-date on what Cindy had said, especially the fact that her mother, Janet, might be a little more involved than anyone realized just yet. "Remember," I added as I slid my first pizza on the oven's conveyor, "that's just between the three of us. Cindy made me promise for the both of us."

"I won't say a word," she vowed.

My sister could be a little flighty at times, but I knew that when she gave her word about something, you could take it to the bank.

I started making another pizza as Maddy slid hers onto the conveyor right behind mine. After a few more pizzas, there was no more room to put them on the line at the moment, so we parked them on the counter so they could wait their turn. We were pretty far ahead of things, and the first pizza came out less than a minute later.

I prepped it to serve, and then asked, "Do you mind shifting gears again and helping the guys out in front?"

Maddy smiled at me. "You know me, Eleanor, I'm the Jill-of-all-trades. I can handle anything that needs to be done around here, too." As my sister took the pizza from me, she asked, "Are we going after Janet after work, or would it be better if we waited until the morning?"

"I don't like to think of it like we're going after anyone," I said. "I just want to ask her some questions."

"Because that's what we do," Maddy replied.

"Some days, it feels like that's *all* we do," I agreed.

"That's us. Ten hours of boredom followed by two minutes of excitement."

"Does our downtime ever last that long?" I asked.

"Honestly, when things are slow, it feels like it's two years sometimes," Maddy said as she disappeared through the door with the pizza. The door opened briefly for one more second as she added, "If I get a vote, I say we try to talk to her tonight after work."

In my heart, I knew that Maddy was right.

It might be late to interrogate one of our new suspects, but time wasn't exactly in our favor at the moment.

The faster we found Benet's killer, the better it would be for A Slice of Delight.

Chapter 12

"I didn't think they'd ever leave," Maddy said as all four of us cleaned up the tables from the Senior Juniors. They'd acted like kids, not worrying too much about the mess they were making, and after they were gone and back on their bus, they left a monumental cleaning task for my crew. Greg and Josh didn't seem to mind, though, something that was a bit out of character for them.

"Okay you two, what's going on?" I asked as they each carried bins of dirty dishes into the kitchen.

"Us? Nothing at all," Greg said with a smile.

"That's right. We're happy all of the time, don't you think?" Josh added.

"Come on, come clean. I know you're both up to something," I said. I turned to my sister and asked, "Maddy, do you have any idea about what's going on?"

"Don't look at me. I don't have a clue," she confessed.

I stared at both young men in turn, but I didn't say a word. I knew that one of them would crack before I did. I was making bets in my mind which one would talk first when Greg was the one who folded.

"Okay, the folks who just left gave us a nice tip as they departed," Greg admitted. "We were planning on sharing it with you two, but we were waiting for the right moment."

"Now's as good a time as any," Maddy said as she looked around the nearly empty restaurant. "How much did you get?"

Greg nodded toward Josh, and both young men dug into their pockets and dumped out handfuls of spare change onto a table as they smiled.

"They're mostly pennies," Greg added, and the two of them started laughing out loud.

"It's not all that funny to me," Maddy said.

"Oh, but it was," Josh said. "They acted like they were big spenders when they did it."

"They're probably on tight budgets," I said. I understood the way they felt, but I didn't like the idea that they were having fun at other peoples' expense. "It may have been the best that they could do with limited resources."

"You think we didn't think of that?" Josh asked. "If that was the case, we both would have been cool with it. We saw some of those bankrolls these guys were carrying around, though, and they could stuff a pillowcase between them, so that theory won't hold water. Eleanor, did you or Maddy happen to hear where the group is headed after this?"

"No, I thought this was just a day trip," I admitted.

Josh laughed. "They're going to spend three nights in Cherokee so they can gamble."

Greg said, "I guess we should just be glad we got them on their way to the casino and not coming back. We might not even have gotten that."

They collected the change and added it to the tip jar on the counter, counting it and laughing the entire time. I didn't get their sense of humor, but then again, sometimes they didn't get mine. As long as they were having fun, I didn't care.

"Is it okay if I come in?" David Quinton asked as he poked his head into the kitchen just as the main dinner hours were coming to a close.

"Of course you can," I said as I finished a sub and put it on the conveyor. It was a new offering with jalapeno peppers, spiced sausage, ham, and a sauce Maddy and I concocted one day when we were searching for something new and different. We called it a Sliced Screamer, and we served it with some fiery chips on the side. "What brings you here?"

"I just wanted to say hi," he confessed.

"Weren't you supposed to be working late tonight?" Since David had come back to town, he'd taken over managing the branch office of his company, and he often worked late, especially since I was tied up so much in the evenings. Our dates usually consisted of getting together after work and sharing a quick bite, but every now and then I left the restaurant in Maddy's hands and we had a real date.

Tonight wasn't supposed to be one of those, though.

"What can I say?" he said with a grin. "I missed you."

I gave him a quick kiss, and then said, "I miss you, too." A thought suddenly occurred to me. "I've got an idea. Why don't we have a mini date right now? I can make you anything you'd like for a late dinner, and we can eat back here."

"Eleanor, I didn't come by just so I could con you out of a free meal," David said with a grin.

"Who says it's free?" I asked, smiling back at him.

"Whatever you charge me, I'm sure it will be worth every penny," he said.

I couldn't help myself. I grinned as he mentioned one of the coins we'd just gotten so many of.

"Did I say something funny?" he asked.

"No. It's just a little pizza parlor humor." I explained to him what had happened earlier, and then asked him, "So, what do you say?"

He didn't even hesitate. "That sounds great to me, if you don't mind."

"I'd love to do it," I said. I rubbed my hands together, and then asked, "So, what do you feel like tonight?"

"What's that sub you were just making?" he asked.

"I call it the Sliced Screamer," I admitted.

After I told him what was on it, he shook his head as he said, "I'm not sure I'd like that. How about a pepperoni pizza with extra cheese on it, and a pair of sodas?"

Why not? "Going old school, huh? I like it."

As I kneaded the dough into the pan, I asked, "Are things finally slowing down at work? I know you inherited a real mess from your old boss."

"I really liked the guy," David said, "but if he were here right now, I'd kick his tin can all the way to Hickory."

"Is it really all that bad?"

David shrugged as he watched me work. "It was when I took over, but I'm finally getting everything in order again."

As I added sauce and the toppings, I asked, "Are you going to be bored once you've got it all squared away?"

"I doubt it," he said as he plucked a pepperoni slice from my hand and ate it.

"Hey, no more snacking," I said.

"Sorry. I missed lunch."

I suddenly felt bad about scolding him, but that was one of my kitchen rules. "Okay, I'll let it pass this time, but no more. Now, sit over there on the barstool and tell me how you're going to spend your time while I'm here working."

He took the seat, and then said, "I don't know where to even start. There's so much I want to do, but I haven't been able to with the mess my predecessor left me. There's plenty to keep me busy."

I slid our pizza onto the conveyor, and then took the other barstool and joined David at the counter. "Whew, that feels good."

"Seeing me, or getting off your feet?" he asked.

"Would it be bad if I said both?"

"No, it would be perfectly understandable," David answered. "I don't know how you do it, Eleanor. I'm not sure one day off a week is enough."

"We manage just fine, but then again, Maddy and I are both lucky enough to have understanding boyfriends." I almost told him then about Bob's proposal, but decided that if Maddy or Bob wanted anyone else to know, they'd tell him themselves. I certainly had no business telling anyone, not even David.

"Did I just say something wrong?" he asked. Could the man read me that well already? That could mean trouble for me if I ever had to tell him a little white lie.

I was saved from answering by Maddy's arrival back in the kitchen. "Do you have that large sausage and pepperoni pizza ready yet? They're getting impatient, so I promised them that I'd come back and check on their order." She looked at David and asked, "Are you still here?"

"No, I left a minute ago," he said with a smile.

Maddy looked at me and said, "He's hilarious, isn't he?"

"We all have our moments," I said. I glanced at the conveyor and said to Maddy, "They're going to have to wait one more minute until it's ready."

"You could always just reach in and pull it out early," Maddy said. "I do that sometimes myself."

"You shouldn't," I said. "Especially with pizzas. They need the entire time to cook; though you might get away with pulling a sub out of the oven a little early, I wouldn't recommend it."

"No one's complained yet," Maddy said.

I didn't want to have that particular conversation with Maddy with David sitting right there, and bless his heart, he must have sensed it.

"If you two will excuse me, I need to go wash up. Are we eating back here, or should I grab a table?"

I thought about eating in the kitchen, but I needed a bit of a break from it all. "Why don't you go grab the table closest to the kitchen, and I'll be out as soon as our pizza's ready."

After David was gone, I said, "Maddy, I'm serious about this. Just because no one has complained doesn't mean they haven't noticed. We can't afford to lose any customers over this. I'd rather they have to wait three minutes for something good than get something second-rate right on time."

"No need to keep drilling me about it. I understand," Maddy said. "I won't do it again, scout's honor."

"You and I both know that you were never a scout," I said with a smile.

She protested, "Hey, is it my fault they wouldn't take me?"

"That's not what Mom said," I answered.

"Who are you going to believe, our dearly departed mother, or your dear, sweet, trustworthy sister who's standing right in front of you?" She didn't even wait for me to answer. "Okay, scrub that. I'll do better from now on, Eleanor. I promise."

"Good," I said. I hated being the boss with my sister, but she had a tendency to cut corners if she thought she could, and with my limited profit margins, I couldn't afford to give anyone a reason not to come back.

"Did you tell him?" Maddy asked as she motioned toward the front toward David.

"Tell who about what?" I asked, focusing on what I had to do next.

"I'm talking about Bob's proposal," Maddy answered, as though I were slow on the uptake.

"I didn't say anything to him about it," I confessed. "I figured that was your right; if you want folks to know, you can tell them yourself."

Maddy nodded. "That's good. Thanks. I don't want the word to get out before I actually make my decision. He won't be mad when he finds out, will he?"

"David? I don't see why he would. After all, it doesn't exactly involve him, does it?"

Maddy was clearly surprised by my reaction. "Seriously? I'd think the possibility of his girlfriend's sister getting hitched might matter just a little bit to him, but maybe that's just me."

"When the time is right, do you want to tell him yourself?" I asked, just as David walked back in.

"Tell him what? Are you two talking about me again?"

"I thought you were going to wait at the table," I said.

"I got hungry," he admitted. "But I still want to know what you two were saying about me."

"Wow, what an ego you must have," Maddy said to him with a smile. "My pizza's next in line, right?" she asked as she turned back to me. "Is it ready yet, or should I come back in a minute?"

The pizza she'd been waiting for finally slid out on the conveyor, golden brown, bubbly cheese on top and perfectly done crust all the way around.

"You're all set to go," I said as I plated the pizza and cut it.

After Maddy left to deliver it, David said, "How about ours? We're next, right?"

I glanced inside the oven. "Right after the sub I made, remember? Down, boy. It's going to be another four minutes before ours is ready."

David nodded, and then asked, "So, are you?"

"Am I what?" I asked, though I knew perfectly well what he was asking.

"Are you going to tell me what you two were talking about just then? I ordinarily wouldn't ask, but since I suspect it's about me, I thought it might matter."

I wasn't exactly sure how to handle it. "Maddy has a secret, but until she gives me the green light to say anything, I don't feel right about telling anyone else. Does that make any sense at all to you?"

"Sure it does," David said as he took his seat on the barstool again. "I'd hate to be the cause of a rift between the two of you. When she's ready for me to know, you can tell me, but until then, I'm fine with not hearing what it's about."

I walked over and gave him a kiss.

"What was that for?" he asked. "Not that I'm complaining."

"For changing into a man I could really get used to having around here," I said.

"In that case, you're most welcome."

He glanced at the conveyor's output end and asked, "Is that thing ready yet? Maybe there's something wrong with the conveyor belt."

I laughed. "You're as bad as Maddy sometimes."

"I'll take that as a good thing," he said.

"The interpretation is entirely up to you," I answered as the sub sandwich slid out. I plated it, cut it once, and prepped it to be served.

Greg came back at that exact moment and collected it, as though he somehow knew that it was ready. It was a knack that most of my people acquired over the years. They could judge the time it took something to run through the oven nearly as well as I could.

"Hey, David," Greg said as he grabbed the sub and left.

"Hey," David said to the closing door.

"You've got to be quick around here," I said with a smile.

"So I see."

After our pizza came out, I prepped it to serve, and then slid it in front of David. "We can eat back here, if you'd rather."

"You don't mind?" he asked. It was pretty clear that was his preference.

"No, it's fine with me."

"Let's do that, then."

"Fine," I agreed. "You can set the table. There are plates over there, glasses here, and tableware if you need any."

"For pizza? You're kidding, right?"

"Hey, everybody's different," I said as I retrieved two sodas from our kitchen fridge. Maddy and I liked to keep some chilled there so we didn't have to go up front if we were eating during business hours.

David took a slice, and then had a quick bite. "Man, that's good."

"You approve?" I asked, and then took a bite of my own.

"You bet I do."

As we ate, I had to stop now and then to take care of business, but David didn't seem to mind. Why should he? He had a hot pizza in front of him, plenty of soda to drink, and my sparkling conversation.

The only problem might be ever getting him to leave.

After we finished eating, David stood and reached for his wallet. "That was good enough to pay for."

"Put that away, silly. I'm not going to charge you when I feed you. This was a date, remember? There's got to be some advantage to dating me."

He smiled. "Oh, that's just one part of it. Since everything's on the house, I'll be back in an hour when you close up for another bite."

"Okay, maybe I should clarify that," I said, matching his smile with one of my own. "I won't charge you once a week, but the rest of the time, you're running a tab."

"Sounds fair to me. May I have permission to kiss the chef?"

My smile must have faltered a little as he said it. "Eleanor, I'm so sorry. That was a colossally bad choice of words."

I'd just managed to forget about Chef Benet's murder, but his slip of the tongue brought it all back to me. "It's fine," I said as I gave him a quick peck.

He knew better than to apologize again, instead making a quick exit.

I knew that no matter how much I wanted to just wish it all

away, there was no getting around the fact that it was time to step up our investigation of Benet's death. I wasn't at all sure how long most of our suspects would be available, but Maddy and I needed to make the most of it while they were around. We needed to talk to Janet first, but after we were finished with her, it was time to tackle the out-of-towners again.

I decided to focus on one thing at a time, though, and at the moment, I needed to think about pizza.

At least that was how I felt until an unwanted visitor came into the Slice and took that option away.

"I don't suppose you're here to grab a slice of pizza or to see your son," I said as the police chief walked in.

"Sorry, it's about Benet's murder."

"I was afraid of that," I said. "What about it?"

"I need to know the last time you saw him," the police chief said.

"Do you mean before I found him pinned to one of my chairs like some kind of bug?"

Kevin Hurley nodded. "Sorry, I should have known that I needed to be more exact in my wording to you. Your sister said the exact same thing, as a matter of fact."

Good for Maddy. "I guess neither one of us likes being considered a suspect in a murder case."

"Who said you were a suspect?" Chief Hurley asked.

"Come on, neither one of us is that stupid. Maddy and I found his body in our dining room, and we weren't big fans of the man, either. It's not a big step thinking we might be in your sights."

The police chief sighed, and then leaned against the wall. "Eleanor, I might have suspected you in the past, but I don't think you or your sister killed Benet."

That was a revelation to me. "Are you kidding? Why not?"

He smiled wryly, and I saw a shadow of that boy from high school a long time ago that I'd fallen for. "Are you trying to talk me into something here?"

"No, sir. We didn't do it. You have my word on it."

The police chief said, "So, tell me. When did you see him? How many times, where, and under what circumstances since he came to town?"

"That's a lot of questions all at once," I said. "Any chance you might answer one or two of mine after we're finished?" I needed information, and I had no other way of getting anything about the official police investigation without Kevin Hurley's help.

"Eleanor, we're not playing Twenty Questions here."

"I'm not asking you to give away state secrets," I said. "Would you at least keep an open mind and think about it?"

"Okay, I'll consider your questions after we're finished here, but I'm not making any promises."

"That's good enough for me." I thought about it a few seconds, and then said, "Let's see. The first time that I saw him was at the bookstore, where he had a temper tantrum and antagonized his producer, his wife, and his assistant in the span of about three minutes."

Chief Hurley nodded, and then asked, "What about Cindy or her mother, Janet?"

That was interesting. "Do you think one of them might have done it? As far as I know, Janet wasn't even nearby when Benet arrived. At least I didn't remember seeing her there."

"Cindy was around, though, wasn't she?"

"She was," I admitted. "She admitted to me that she was worried that Benet wouldn't follow through with the demonstration and the signing, and she thought it might ruin her."

Hurley jotted something down in his notebook, and then said, "So, she had a motive to kill him if he'd gone back on his word."

I shook my head. "No way. Cindy wouldn't gain anything by doing that, and besides, you've known her as long as I have. That girl doesn't have the least bit of a temper as far as I know. It couldn't have been easy being raised without a father, and a lot of kids might have turned out bad under the circumstances, but Cindy never did, as far as I know."

"That's right, as far as you know," the chief said.

"What does that mean?" I asked him. "Does she have a police record?"

"No," the chief of police admitted, "but there were stories that she burned down the Johnson barn when she was a kid."

"I still don't believe it," I said, "and you should know better yourself than to listen to those lies."

"I'm just trying to get the facts straight," he said. The way he sighed, it sounded as though the police chief had the weight of the world on his shoulders, and I didn't envy him his job one bit.

"I can't see Cindy killing Chef Benet," I said flatly.

The chief kind of shrugged, and then asked, "And you didn't see Benet fighting with anyone else?"

"That's right," I said quickly, and then hesitated. "Wait a second, it's not, but it doesn't matter. It didn't mean anything."

"What didn't?" Kevin asked, his interest clearly perking up.

"He and Paul were arguing about the proper way to make pastry when I found Benet at the bakery."

"Were they having a nice discussion, or was there yelling involved?"

I knew that I was burying Paul with my account of things, something I didn't want to do. "I think it was just two professionals with different points of view."

"Were they yelling?" Kevin repeated.

"Yes," I admitted.

"I'll talk to him," the chief of police said as he jotted that down as well.

"Tell him that I'm sorry I threw him under the bus when you do," I replied.

"Eleanor, you didn't throw him anywhere. I'll talk to Paul next, and most likely, I'll be able to rule him out as a suspect. After all, he was probably still at the bakery when Benet was murdered. I need an exact time when you left him alone in the dining room."

I thought about it, and then told him, "At two o'clock, he was alive."

Kevin nodded. "Okay, that makes sense. My medical examiner told me Benet was murdered between two and three, as near as he can tell."

Maddy and I had already figured that one out for ourselves. "This might be a stupid question, but are you sure the knife is what killed him?"

The police chief looked amused by my question. "Well, I can tell you for sure that he wasn't electrocuted."

"He could have been poisoned, though," I said.

"Why would someone take a chance on being seen knifing the man if they'd already poisoned him?" the chief asked.

"I don't know," I admitted. "When a chef is murdered, doesn't poison come to mind first thing?"

Chief Hurley shook his head. "Not when one of your blades is driven all the way through him."

I shrugged. "I just thought you might want to be thorough. After all, enough people wanted the man dead. Who's to say there was just one murderer and one attempt on the man's life?"

Chief Hurley bit his lip, and then grabbed his radio. "Tell the M.E. I need to see him. Yes, right now."

He put his radio back on his belt, and then said, "It's probably a wild goose chase, but I'll ask him if he ran a toxicology screen."

"It was just a thought," I said.

"I'm not sure I'm all that thrilled with the way your mind works, if that's the kind of things you're thinking about," he said.

I shrugged. "Maybe Maddy's mystery novels are finally starting to rub off on me. Have you been able to eliminate any of the suspects?"

I wasn't sure Chief Hurley even realized that I was pumping him for information, but while he was in a talkative mood, I was going to take advantage of it. "No, everyone was in and out of that bookstore so much, even Cindy could have done it."

"You don't think that, though, do you?" I thought about what we'd been talking about, and wondered if her previous relationship with Benet may have had more to it than she'd told me.

"At this point, I don't know what to think," he said. "I'm still collecting information."

And here I was, holding some out on him. I couldn't keep what I knew from the chief of police any longer, even if it meant pointing him in Cindy's direction.

"Did she tell you that she and Benet had an online relationship before he came to town?" I asked softly.

It appeared that Kevin thought I was teasing him at first, but then he saw the look on my face. "Are you serious?"

"They weren't doing anything icky," I said, "but they chatted a lot online."

"I need to see her computer, then," the chief answered, suddenly losing all interest in talking to me.

"I'm sure that it doesn't mean anything," I said, but it was too late.

He was already gone.

Good job, Eleanor. You just put the chief of police on the trails of two friends.

I didn't know if I'd thrown them under the bus, but I surely hadn't done them any favors. Then again, if Chief Hurley found out some other way, it might be even worse for them. Maybe he was right. Maybe it was better to get everything out into the light, examine it, and then see what merited a closer look.

I was still wondering if I'd done the right thing when Maddy came back to pick up a pizza.

"What did you say to Hurley?" she asked as she grabbed the pie.

With a sick feeling in the pit of my stomach, I told her everything we'd discussed.

Maddy whistled softly to herself. "Wow, you didn't tell him anything about me, did you?"

"Of course not," I answered.

"Okay. Just remind me to stay on your good side."

I started to throw a towel at her, but then changed my mind.

"Deliver that pizza," I said, "and let's start wrapping up around here. We need to talk to Janet, and then we need to get our rest."

"Any reason in particular?" she asked.

"You bet. We have a big day tomorrow."

"Yeah? What did you have in mind?"

"I think it's time we start asking some hard questions, and I want to start with Jessie, Oliver, and Patrice."

Chapter 13

"Hi, Janet. It's Eleanor and Maddy from the Slice. Can we come in? We brought you a pizza." I'd had the idea at the last second before we left the pizzeria to make something for Janet to help get us inside. I knew Janet loved a thin-crust pepperoni pizza late at night, since she ordered one about once a month from us.

"I didn't order anything," Janet said, looking a little shaky and confused as she opened the door. From her red eyes, I had a feeling that she'd been crying for some time. It was no wonder, given all that had happened lately.

"We had a customer who changed his mind, but he'd already paid for it," Maddy lied. "Of course we thought of you. It just came out of the oven, so if you want it, it's all yours, on the house."

"It's sweet of you to think of me," she said as she looked at the box, "but I couldn't. I'm too upset right now."

"You still have to eat, don't you?" I asked. It was important that we speak with her now. I knew that, and I hoped that my sister did as well.

"I suppose you might as well come in," she said, but I could tell that whatever was upsetting her was weighing heavily on her mind.

I'd had my fill of pizza, but I wasn't about to let that stop me.

It was most likely the warmest invitation we were going to get. "We'd love to," I said as I took off my coat, and Maddy did the same as we stepped inside. The weather had taken a sudden cool turn, and it was nice to be able to wear a jacket again.

"We might as well eat in the dining room," Janet suggested.

Maddy nodded as she held up a two-liter bottle of cola we'd brought along as well. "We brought soda, too."

"That's nice," Janet said, glancing at the front door every now and then. Was she waiting for someone to show up, or was there somewhere she needed to be?

"We could use some cups, plates, and napkins, too, if you wouldn't mind," I said.

After we were set up, we all shared in the pizza. There were times when thin-crust pizza was my favorite, but usually I liked the thicker, traditional crust. I'd made Chicago-style pizza, too, from time to time. I loved pizza in all of its incarnations.

As we ate, I asked, "How's Cindy doing?"

"To be honest with you, she's an absolute wreck," Janet said, clutching a tissue in her hand as though it had magical properties. "The poor thing is afraid that her bookstore is doomed because of what happened. Cindy doesn't believe people will ever be able to forget what happened to that man who was murdered in your restaurant. I tried to reassure her that it wasn't true, but I wasn't sure. What do you think, Eleanor? Given enough time, they'll forget about it, won't they?"

It was a hard question to answer, though I'd weathered my own share of bad news over the years. "I've had a few mishaps in my restaurant, but folks still managed to find their way back," I said.

"I'm sorry. That was indelicate of me, wasn't it?" Janet asked. "I'm just not myself right now."

"It's okay. All I'm saying is that sometimes bad things happen, and people usually find a way to bounce back." I couldn't ignore her reddened eyes any longer. I touched her hand as I asked,

"Janet, are you okay? You've clearly been crying, and when you're not, you're staring at the front door."

"Don't worry about me. I'm fine," she said as she dabbed at her eyes with a tissue again.

"Forgive me for saying so, but you don't look fine to me," I answered softly. "It's about Benet and his relationship with Cindy, isn't it?"

Janet froze up when she heard my words. "What are you talking about, Eleanor? What exactly do you know?"

"You must have been shocked when he just showed up like that so unexpectedly," I said, taking a stab with my comment based on Oliver's information that Benet had come to town on family business, and then adding Cindy's own input that Benet had sought out a relationship with her for reasons that logically didn't make all that much sense. Everything clicked at that moment, and when I added Cindy's lack of a father and Janet's own tears into the mix, I suddenly suspected exactly why she was reacting the way she was.

"Benet was Cindy's father, wasn't he?" I asked.

And that's when Janet fainted.

"Where did that come from?" Maddy asked me as she reached over to keep Janet from falling out of her chair. As we eased the poor woman to the floor so she wouldn't fall off her seat and hurt herself, my sister asked, "Why didn't you tell me what was going on? A little warning would have been greatly appreciated."

"Sorry, but it just occurred to me," I said. As I looked at Janet, I saw that there was no color in her cheeks. "Is she okay?"

Maddy felt for a pulse. "She's fine. The shock of it must have sent her over the edge. It looks as though it's true, though, doesn't it?"

"It all added up in my mind, but I still wasn't positive even as I said it."

Maddy looked at the prone woman, and then said, "By the way she reacted, I'm guessing you were right."

"What happened?" Janet asked as she finally began to stir. When she realized that Maddy and I were kneeling beside her, she managed to shake if off and sit up on her own.

"You fainted," I said. "How are you feeling?"

"How do you think I feel? I'm devastated," Janet admitted. "I thought I'd take that secret to the grave with me, but when Tony showed up at the bookstore out of the blue, I thought I was going to die."

"So, you didn't know that your Tony was Antonio Benet," I said. "Didn't you recognize his name or his face on television?"

"I only knew him as Tony B," Janet admitted. "I'm ashamed to say that I didn't know him all that well when we were together, if you can call it that. What it boils down to is that we had a torrid weekend fling. It's not easy for me to admit that even now, and I didn't know that I was pregnant until he was gone. I was a senior in college working at a summer camp in the mountains, and I'd just broken up with my boyfriend. Tony came to visit one of the other counselors, and one thing led to another." She seemed to be reliving it as she told me. "After I learned that I was pregnant, I didn't come home for a year."

"Where did you go?" I asked. This woman, someone I thought I knew, had lived a whole other life that I didn't know about.

"My aunt and uncle took me in." She took a deep breath, and then added, "Could I possibly get a glass of water, please?"

Maddy got up to get one, but before she did, she said, "Don't say a word until I get back."

"Eleanor, could you help me to my chair while she's doing that?" Janet asked.

I did, and Maddy quickly came back with the water. After taking a sip, Janet continued with her story. "I stayed away until Cindy was three months old, and then I came back home as a 'widow.' It was the only way my father would let me back in my parents' lives, and I needed them desperately. I made one mistake, and it nearly cost me their love. But I wouldn't have changed anything even if I could," she admitted. "After all, I got Cindy, and she worth every bit of it."

I felt bad about pressing her. It was clear that she'd already gone through a great deal, but it was time to get some answers to my questions. "I have to ask. Didn't you recognize Tony when Cindy started talking to him? At the very least, you must have seen one of his book covers."

Janet just shrugged. "You've met the man, but picture him in his early twenties. The Tony I knew barely weighed a hundred and fifty pounds soaking wet, and his hair was jet black. When I first saw Benet's picture, something must have stirred in me, but I didn't consciously realize that it was my old boyfriend at the time."

"When did you know for sure, then?" Maddy asked her.

"The day of the signing," Janet replied. "He found a way to get me alone, and the second he said my camp nickname, I knew who he was."

"You must have been in shock," Maddy said.

"I couldn't believe it. He'd been worming his way into Cindy's life through the Internet, while I had no idea that he even knew who we were." She cried for a moment, and then quickly brought herself back under control. As Janet dried her eyes once again, she added, "All he had to do was ask me, and I would have allowed him to see her. She was his daughter, for goodness sakes. I'm not some kind of monster."

"Are you saying that you weren't angry with him?" I asked. I could think of half a dozen reasons Janet wouldn't mind seeing Benet dead, and I had a hard time believing that she would just roll over like that.

"How would that be fair to anyone? Tony never even knew about Cindy. How could I blame him for anything? We talked about it like adults, and I agreed not to stand in his way if he wanted a relationship with his daughter. Besides, she's a grown woman. I couldn't very well stop her, if she set her mind to it. She's a legitimate widow herself, not some pretend one like me."

I had a sudden thought. "Does Cindy know that Benet was her father?"

"I told her an hour ago," Janet admitted.

"How did she take it?"

"She didn't believe it at first, and then she stormed out of here as though she were on fire. I don't know where she went, or if she's even going to come back. I've botched the whole thing, and I don't know what to do about it. When you two showed up, I kept thinking that Cindy would come back any second. That's why I kept watching the door. Now I'm wondering if she'll ever be coming back at all. She's too impulsive, just like me."

The tears began again in earnest, and as Maddy and I did our best to comfort her, I couldn't help wondering if Janet's demeanor was because of her lost daughter, or what she might have done to protect her. What if Janet was lying about what her true reaction had been when she'd discovered that Cindy's father was right there in the bookstore? What if she had no intention of letting Benet into her daughter's life? Would she kill him to keep that from happening? Parents had committed murder without flinching to protect their children before, and we had only Janet's word that it had happened the way she'd told us.

"Find her for me," Janet pled through the tears. "I can't stand thinking she's out there somewhere all alone."

"We'll try," Maddy said, much to my surprise. Most folks thought I was the soft touch of the family, but my sister showed time and time again that she cared at least as much about people as I did.

Once we were outside, I asked, "What made you volunteer us like that?"

"Think about it, Sis," Maddy said as we made our way to my

car. "If we can find Cindy before her mother can get to her, we can at least confirm some of Janet's story."

I looked at Maddy. "Then you don't believe her completely either, do you?"

"There's something a little too altruistic about the way she says she reacted for my taste," Maddy said.

"Okay then, we'll look for Cindy," I agreed.

"Any idea where she might be?"

"Actually, I believe I've got a pretty good one," I said.

We drove back toward the promenade, and Maddy looked at me oddly. "Where exactly are we going, Eleanor?"

"The bookstore," I said. "That's where she's been spending all of her time lately, and just think about it. Where would you go if your world were suddenly collapsing?"

"Either my place, or yours," Maddy replied quickly.

I touched her arm lightly. "That is so sweet."

"Hey, we're all we've got," she said.

"What about Bob?"

"He'd be fourth on the list, right after the Slice," Maddy admitted, "But is it wrong that I didn't even think of him for the top spot? What does that say about our relationship?"

"It's not right or wrong," I said, though I wasn't sure that I believed it myself. Was it a slip of the tongue, or had Maddy actually forgotten about her boyfriend until I'd brought his name up?

We got to the promenade, and after parking in the visitor's lot up front, we walked to the lone shop with its lights blazing.

It appeared that the owner of the Bookmark was exactly where I'd predicted that she'd be.

"Cindy, it's Eleanor and Maddy. Open up." I knocked on the door, but at first, I didn't see any activity inside. Could she have left her lights blazing and forgotten all about it?

"Maybe she's not here," Maddy said.

"Hang on. What was that?" I saw movement in the back through her window, but if it was Cindy, she made no effort to come let us in, and we couldn't exactly have a conversation with her from the walkway if she didn't want to talk to us. "Did you see it, too?"

Maddy touched my shoulder. "I did, but she clearly has no interest in talking to us, at least not right now. She's not coming out, Eleanor, and we can't make her, unless you want to break her window with a rock."

"No, thanks. I've gone through that before, and it's not a good thing to have happen to you. I've got one more idea, and then we can go if it doesn't work."

I knocked once more, and then said loudly, "We've talked to your mom, and we know that Benet was your father. We can help."

For a second I thought it wasn't going to work, and then I saw her head peek out slowly. "She actually told you about him?" Cindy asked, starting toward the door with fire in her eyes.

"She didn't want to, but I kind of implied that I already knew that it was true," I admitted.

Cindy shook her head. "How could you possibly know that, Eleanor? I didn't have a clue myself, and dear old Mom never let on all these years."

I didn't like doing this with a wall of glass between us, but I didn't really have any choice. "I put it together from what I learned from several different people, including you."

"So, I'm the last one to know?" She was legitimately angry now.

"No. I figured it out, but I doubt anyone knows but the three of us." It was time to push her a little harder about meeting face-to-face. "Could we come in and talk? I'm getting tired of yelling through the glass."

Cindy debated it, and then finally unlatched the door. "You might as well. I can't believe this is happening. All this time I thought my father was dead, and now I find out that he was actually in my shop and didn't even tell me."

"It was probably hard on him, too," I said, not really wanting to make excuses for a man I hadn't liked from the first second we'd met.

Maddy added, "Your mother just told us that Benet didn't know himself until recently. I'm guessing it was about the time he contacted you through your e-mail account."

Cindy seemed to slump down even farther. "I can't hate him then, can I? It's *all* my mother's fault."

"Hang on a second," I said. "You shouldn't jump to conclusions before you at least hear her side of things."

"Eleanor, how can you say that? I thought we were friends."

"We are," I said quickly, realizing that I didn't have long to make my point. "This isn't going to be easy to hear, but you need to listen to me. Your mother had a fling with your father, and he was gone out of her life before she even knew that she was pregnant. She's done her best by you over the years, and you know it. You can't blame her for something that wasn't her fault."

Cindy didn't care for that one bit. "I don't want anyone justifying her actions or her motives for what she did. She could have found him if she'd really wanted to. I deserved the chance to get to know my father."

How could I argue with something as illogical as that? I was searching for the right words when Maddy said, "But you did get to, at least a little bit. You told me the two of you chatted online quite a bit before he came to town."

"Are you saying that's the same as getting to know the man face-to-face?" Cindy asked her.

"No, of course not. All I'm saying is that something is better than nothing, ten out of ten times."

The air seemed to go right out of her with that. As she slumped back against the counter, Cindy said, "All I know is that I deserved better than I got."

"No one's denying that, but your mother's very worried about you," I said. "She's really torn up about this."

Cindy shook her head, and I could see that she was fighting

back her tears as she said, "I'm the one who's hurting right now, not her."

"Cindy, you know in your heart that's not true, don't you?" I asked.

She shook her head. "I don't know what to think right now, Eleanor. I'm just so confused."

"You could always come stay with me until you figure things out," I said, realizing too late that I'd done it again. Maddy had scolded me for inviting Patrice Benet into my home, and now I was doing it with Cindy. Was I that lonely that I needed the company of murder suspects to make my life a little more complete? No, it was my compassion for them that had driven me to make the offers, and I stood by what I'd offered.

Her sigh was heavy as she said, "Thanks, but I guess I'd just be delaying the inevitable. I need to go home and settle this with my mother tonight."

"You really just learned about Benet tonight?" I asked. "Didn't you suspect anything before?"

Cindy shrugged. "I just had a feeling that Mom knew him from somewhere, because when the two of them went in the back to talk, there was some real tension in the air, but I thought it had to be about the signing. When she told me tonight that he was my dad, I couldn't believe it. To be honest with you, I'm still not even sure it's true. We can both be too impulsive when it comes to our infatuations."

"I wish there was something we could say or do," Maddy said.

As she stood, Cindy said, "Thanks for the thought, but there's nothing anyone can do now. I have to work this out on my own, and the sooner I do it, the better."

After the lights were off and the place was locked up tight, we followed her outside.

Cindy said, "Thanks for listening to me rant and rave."

"Given the circumstances," Maddy said, "I think you had it coming."

"Yeah, maybe you're right," Cindy said with the ghost of a smile that was there briefly, and then vanished. "Good night."

"Good night," we said as we watched her walk away.

"Should we call Janet and warn her that Cindy's coming home?" I asked.

"No, let's let it be a happy surprise," Maddy said. "I'd say that Janet is entitled to that, don't you?"

"You're probably right," I said. "Is there anything else we can do tonight to further our investigation?"

Maddy looked a little uncomfortable as she glanced at her watch. "I'd love to, but I'm supposed to see Bob. We need to talk. Aren't you getting together with David?"

"No, our little impromptu dinner was all the time he had for me tonight," I admitted. "Don't worry about me. I'll find something to do."

"You're not doing any more digging on your own, are you?" Maddy asked me.

"Why, are you afraid of missing out on the excitement?"

"No, I'm what I'm afraid of is that you'll do something foolish and risky," my sister said.

"And something might happen to me?" I asked.

"Sure, that's true," she answered with a grin. "But honestly, I don't want to miss out on the fun myself."

We laughed as we went our separate ways. I wondered if tonight was when Maddy would have an answer for Bob. I also thought about how it would be at Cindy and Janet's house tonight. The two women had a great many feelings to work through.

But most of all, I had to wonder how there could be so many people in Benet's life that might have delighted in seeing the man dead. I thought about calling Kevin Hurley with the news of what we'd uncovered about Cindy's father, but I decided that was one family secret I was going to keep, at least for one night.

Chapter 14

"So, how did it go last night? Did you say yes?" I asked Maddy as I picked her up bright and early the next morning at her apartment. We'd agreed to carpool so we could do a little more investigating before we had to get to the pizzeria to prepare for another day's work, and I'd volunteered to drive.

"Say yes to what?" she asked as she stared at me, clearly a little confused by my question.

"To his proposal," I said.

"Of course not," she answered, clearly a little miffed that I'd even asked her about it.

I swear, I had never known my sister to drag her feet like she was doing. "Well, how much time do you need? It's not like you haven't agreed to marry men four times before. I wouldn't think you'd need all that much practice saying yes."

"Eleanor, you're as bad as he is," Maddy said, sipping the coffee I'd made for us. "I need more time before I make that kind of commitment again."

"Is Bob pressing you for an answer?"

"No; not with words, at any rate. Do you know how it is when you're expecting a telephone call, so every time the phone rings, you nearly jump out of your skin? That's how it is being with Bob. If I dare start any sentence with any inflection at all, he looks at me as though I'm about to make a prediction about the end of the world. It's kind of unnerving."

"Then tell him that," I said. "Cut the guy a little slack. He did ask you a pretty important question that could change the rest of both your lives."

"I told him that I'd think about it. What more can he ask? I have a feeling that he'd be happier with a delayed yes than a quick no."

That was an interesting thing to say. "Does that mean you think that you'll eventually decide to marry him?"

She stared at the window a second, and then said, "At this point, it depends on what hour of the day you ask me the question. Could we please talk about something a little more appealing, say like murder?"

"I get it. Let's talk about the case." I looked at my watch, and then added, "We're due to talk to Oliver and Jessie in the hotel dining room, but we're cutting it close. They've agreed to speak with us about Benet, but I got the feeling that they weren't about to give us all that much time."

"I'm kind of curious about why they'd talk to us at all," Maddy asked. "It's not like there's anything to gain by speaking to us."

"Well, I may have overstated our role in the police chief's investigation of the murder," I admitted with a grin.

"If you said we had any role at all, we both know that you'd be lying," Maddy answered, laughing.

"Hey, it's not my fault if they misinterpreted my intent. I implied that convincing us of their innocence would go a long way in making Kevin Hurley less suspicious of them."

"And why would they believe that?"

I grinned at my sister. "It might have something to do with the fact that I said outright that convincing us of their innocence would go a long way in making Kevin Hurley less suspicious of them."

"There's nothing like subtlety, is there?" Maddy asked.

"Hey, it was the only way I could get them to agree to this meeting at all."

As we drove to the hotel, Maddy asked, "What's going to happen when Kevin finds out what you said?"

I shrugged. "We'll worry about that when and if it ever comes up. Chances are, he won't ever hear that I said it. Besides, it's not like it's on tape. I can always say that they misunderstood."

"You can," Maddy said with a slight smile. "But will you?"

I glanced over at her. "You don't disapprove of what I did, do you?"

She laughed. "Are you kidding? Not at all. I just want to be sure you're ready for the heat that might come your way."

"I'm wearing my fireproof undies today, so I should be good."

We found Jessie and Oliver having an intense conversation in the dining room of the hotel when we got there, and I wanted to hang back to see if I could learn what it was about, but they spotted us before we could get close enough to eavesdrop. Their conversation died at that instant, and Maddy and I walked over and joined them at their table.

"Thanks for meeting us," I said as we sat down.

"It didn't sound as though we had much choice," Oliver replied.

"Now, Oliver, be nice," Jessie said, and then turned to me. "Would you two like something to eat? It's on my expense account, so help yourself."

Maddy said, "That's kind of you," before I could refuse the offering. I didn't want Jessie to think she could buy us off with eggs and French toast.

"You're most welcome. If there's anything we can do to expedite things around here, we're happy to help out."

"That's good to hear," Maddy said. "We really appreciate it."

"First things first, then," I said, jumping in. "Let's get this out of the way right off the bat. We know that everyone around Chef

Benet had the opportunity to sneak away to the Slice and kill him. No one we've talked to so far has accounted for their time completely when the murder took place."

"Really? I can," Jessie said.

"Go on, we're listening," I said.

"I was on the phone with my network. I couldn't very well do that and kill the man, too."

"You were on the phone from two to three?" I asked. "That's one long conversation. I'm sure the police chief can confirm it with your telephone records, so you should be in the clear soon."

"Well, perhaps not the entire time," Jessie admitted. "There may have been some gaps between phone calls, but we were trying to figure out how to handle Benet's desertion."

"You weren't going to just let him go, then," I said.

"Not without a fight," Jessie admitted, and then must have realized how it had sounded. "I'm talking about a legal battle, not a physical confrontation, though."

"I don't know why you bothered fighting to keep him," Oliver said snidely, and Jessie sent a sharp look his way.

"Watch your tongue, Oliver," Jessie said.

"Why should I? You've made it abundantly clear that I'm not even being considered for my own show. It's time people learned the truth about what a fraud the man was." He looked at me and said, "Tony Benet could barely boil water without burning it. I'm the man behind his food, every last bite of it, down to the last recipe."

"Are you saying he couldn't cook at all?" I asked. I had a hard time believing that, especially after learning about his television shows and his cookbooks.

Maddy said, "That can't be true. I saw him make eggs Benedict on *Good Morning World* just two months ago."

"Of course he could cook," Jessie said.

"Okay, maybe I overstated it a little," Oliver said. "The man wasn't completely untrainable. I managed to teach him how to put on a good show, but the recipes are all mine."

"Even if that were true, and I'm not saying that it is, if it were, you signed them away to us," Jessie said. "Oliver, don't make me invoke your nondisclosure agreement." The last bit was said with real menace in her voice.

"So, there's some truth to this after all," I said to Jessie. "That would make you look pretty bad if it got out, wouldn't it?"

She just shrugged. "Who's to say how much of what Benet came up with was all his own? Most recipes are pretty basic. After all, how many ways are there to make meatloaf, or even bread?"

"You're just showing your ignorance, Jessie," Oliver said smugly. "There are more methods, not to mention ingredients, than you could ever imagine. That's what Tony lacked, when it boils down to it. He had the imagination of a tree stump. I was always the one with the vision, and the ability to boil it all down into a recipe."

"It must have been tough on you, then," I said, "seeing him get all the credit for your creations."

Oliver shrugged. "It wasn't as bad as all of that," he said. He must have realized just how bad he was making himself look. He added, "I could live with it, as long as I thought I had my own chance at a show one day."

Jessie kept shaking her head. "I told you before, we've talked about it at least a dozen times. You don't have that 'it' factor you need for television."

Oliver looked at the woman with real contempt as he said, "If you wanted to, you could put me on the air in a week. I coached Tony on how to cook. Why couldn't you find someone to teach me how to host a show?"

"That's easy. One is a skill, the other is a talent," Jessie said. "Sorry, but you've got the wrong one. I can find a hundred cooks to replace you in a heartbeat, but Benet was one of a kind."

"That is garbage, and you know it," Oliver said as he stood, threw his napkin on the table, and stormed off.

Jessie shook her head. "I meant what I said before, but even if I hadn't, he just killed any chance he ever had of being on television. Once word gets around that he broke our nondisclosure agreement, he won't have a chance of being on a public access station."

"Is what he said true?" I asked. "Was Oliver honestly the creative spirit behind the chef's work?"

Jessie shrugged. "Honestly, it never mattered much to any of us. Oliver is under the deluded impression that folks turned on Benet's show for his recipes, but how many people actually made what he demonstrated? They tuned in to be entertained, and as much as I hate to admit it, Benet was fun to watch when the camera was rolling. I know it doesn't seem like much, but I'm probably going to get fired now that he's gone. He was the last good show of mine that the network picked up, and I've had a few losers since then."

"So, are you saying you didn't have a motive to kill him?" I asked.

She looked at me as though I were crazy. "Are you kidding? Killing him would be cooking the goose that laid all those golden eggs. It just doesn't make sense." Her cell phone rang, and when she looked at who was calling her, she said, "Excuse me, this is one call that I have to take. I hope we were able to help." She answered the phone as she walked away.

As the waitress finally started to approach us, I said to Maddy, "There's no reason to stick around here anymore. She's not coming back."

"Are you kidding?" she asked as she smiled at the young woman. "We were invited to eat here on Jessie's tab. As far as I'm concerned, we owe it to ourselves to take advantage of it. Remember the wedding brunch we had here when Tammy Lynn Lake got married?"

"The bill for that wedding had to have outlived the actual marriage," I said, remembering how quickly the bride and groom had broken up.

"The food was out of this world, though," she said.

I was still reluctant to do it when Maddy told the waitress, "We were instructed to tell you that this is on Ms. Taylor's tab."

"Of course," the young woman said. Her name tag said that her name was Naomi. "May I start you off with some freshly squeezed orange juice?"

"You may, Naomi," Maddy said with a big grin. "I don't know about my sister, but I'd like to sample the breakfast bar."

"Absolutely." She turned to me and then asked, "And you, ma'am?"

I was about to refuse when I realized that I'd have to wait for Maddy to eat anyway, and there was no point being stubborn about it. "That sounds good. I'll have the same," I said.

"That's my girl," Maddy said. As the waitress left to get our juices, Maddy and I attacked the bar, sampling a little of just about everything.

After we'd had our fill, I said, "I'm not even sure I'll be able to work today after all of that. All I really want to do is go home and take a nap."

"It was great, wasn't it?" Maddy observed as she handed a tip of her own directly to the waitress.

"Oh, don't worry. It's already been taken care of," Naomi said.

"We just wanted to thank you ourselves," Maddy said.

"That's really generous of you," the waitress said, pocketing the offered bill.

On a lark, I asked the woman, "Did you happen to overhear what our breakfast companions were talking about before we showed up?"

"I'm sorry, but we're not allowed to discuss our diners, or their conversations they have here," Naomi answered quickly, and then, lowering her voice, she said, "As a matter of fact, they were discussing the best way to handle the two of you. There's something they were trying to hide from you, and they couldn't agree on exactly how to do it."

"Do you have any idea what it might be?" Maddy asked softly.

"They agreed that whatever they do, they have to keep you away from someone named Patrice. I'm sorry, that's all I got."

I dug a twenty of my own out of my wallet and added it Maddy's earlier offering.

"That's way too much," Naomi protested.

"Trust me, it was worth every penny."

As Maddy and I left, I said, "We need to talk to Patrice while Jessie and Oliver are busy. Jessie sounded as though she'd be on the phone for a while, and it sounded as though Oliver was going to go off somewhere and pout."

"Let's go pay her a little visit then," Maddy said. "You sure you're not too stuffed to do that?"

"Positive," I said. "I'm always ready to grill somebody."

The door to Patrice's suite was open as Maddy and I approached.

"What does that mean?" I asked Maddy softly.

"It looks like an open invitation to me," she replied. My sister was usually the brasher of the two of us, and before I could weigh the advantages of going inside, the decision was made for me as Maddy plowed on in ahead of me.

"Patrice? Are you here?" Maddy called out.

There was no answer at first, so Maddy started snooping around a little.

"What if we get caught up here in her room alone?" I asked. "How are we going to explain it?"

"I just want to do a little recon," Maddy said. She was heading for the bedroom when a voice called out from the balcony, "I thought I told you to keep my glass full, but look at this. I'm completely out of mimosas."

It was Patrice, and apparently she'd already started her day drinking. When she pivoted around, she saw us instead of the room service staff member she'd no doubt been expecting. "What are you two doing here? Everyone's deserted me, but I can't seem to shake either one of you at all."

"We came to chat," I said as brightly as I could manage. "Do you have a minute to talk?"

"A minute, an hour, a day, however long it takes until my drink is refreshed," Patrice said, slurring her words slightly. "Tell you what. Why don't one of you ladies scamper off and see what's happened to my mimosas, and I'll spend the time speaking with the other one?"

Maddy didn't look at all pleased by the arrangement since Patrice had designated her the unofficial bartender, but I offered a silent plea, and she nodded slightly. "I'll be right back," she said as I took a seat beside Patrice.

The balcony offered a lovely view of the mountains, and the upper reaches were shrouded somewhat in what was either fog or low cloud cover. Either way, it was a spectacular view.

"Again, I'm sorry for your loss," I said, the manners my parents had bred into me too strong to disregard.

Patrice looked at the view I cherished so much with clear distaste. "If you want the truth, I'm not certain I could call Tony's departure that much of a loss. The man couldn't keep his pants up, if you know what I mean. I should have realized long ago that he'd never change."

"Did he really cheat on you that often in the past?" I asked, trying to get some kind of corroboration that Janet's story had been true.

"He did it as long as I'd known him. After all, that's how we first met," she said, eyeing the bottom of her glass suspiciously, as though she expected it to magically fill itself up again without human intervention.

"How is that?" I asked.

"Oh, dear, naïve woman. He was with his first wife when he cheated on her with me."

My mother had always told Maddy and me that if a man cheats with you, one day he'll cheat on you, and I'd never had any reason to doubt the wisdom of her words. I didn't think that was a very good time to share that particular insight with Patrice, though. "Still, he was your husband."

"Yes, that's true. I never knew how bad 'for better or for worse' could be." She lifted the empty glass to her lips again, and seemed to discover its depleted state once more. "I begged him for a divorce a hundred times, but he wouldn't give me one. He said it would ruin his precious image. What did he care about that? One of his bimbos would have brought him down sooner or later, so why did I have to suffer in the meantime?"

"He couldn't make you stay married to him if you really wanted to leave him," I said. "If it wasn't for love, did you stay for the money, instead?"

Patrice surprised me by laughing at my question. "Dear woman, I have more money than Tony ever dreamed of earning with his little TV show and his quaint cookbooks. That's what first attracted him to me, I'm sure."

"So why didn't you just leave?" I would have never pressed her like that if she'd been sober, but I had a window to push her, and I was going to take full advantage of it.

For the first time since we'd been chatting, Patrice looked uncomfortable by my presence. "Let's just say that he knew about one of my dirty little secrets, and leave it at that."

It was clear she was done talking about her late husband, so it was time to shift subjects. "How about Oliver and Jessie? Why did they stay with him?"

Patrice waved a hand in the air. "They each had their reasons. Oliver would take whatever abuse Tony put him through, hoping that he might get a little credit someday for his own creations. The night before Tony was murdered, I heard my dear, sweet husband tell Oliver that he was nothing but a fry cook and that he'd never acknowledge poor old Ollie as anything else."

"How did he react to that?" I asked, fascinated by the revelation.

Patrice got a wicked little grin on her face. "He threatened to expose Tony, and when my husband just laughed at him, I thought Oliver was going to kill him right then and there."

"And Jessie?" I asked, hoping to wring every last bit of information out of her that I could. "Why would she kill him?"

"That's an easy one. If Tony left the show, it would be the same as killing Jessie's dreams and ambitions. She might feel there was nothing left for her to lose if he just walked away. My husband seemed to inspire hatred in people, not a particularly useful talent to have, but one of his very own. Everyone must be good at one thing in their lives, I suppose." Patrice pivoted in her chair, and then asked again, "Where did your sister go, all the way to Florida to squeeze the oranges herself?"

At that moment, Maddy arrived, but she was frowning.

Oliver was right behind her, and Jessie was one pace after that.

"You need to stop drinking, Patrice," Oliver said.

"Why should I? It helps ease the pain."

"Trust me," Jessie said, "I doubt you can feel anything right now. There won't be any more alcohol today." She turned to us and said, "She's normally not like this at all."

I'd seen her in her sober, and more timid, mode and I wasn't sure which I preferred. "She's been perfectly lovely," I said.

"I bet," Oliver answered. "Don't you two have a pizza place to run?"

I glanced at my watch and saw that we were indeed going to have to push things to be ready to open in time, and in all honesty, I doubted we'd get anything else from Patrice at the moment anyway, particularly not with her two self-appointed guardians hovering nearby.

"She's right," I said. "Come on, Maddy. We should go and leave them alone."

Maddy looked surprised by the move, but followed along.

"At least tell me you got something out of her," she said once we were alone in the elevator.

"Oh, yes. I'll bring you up to speed while we're driving to the Slice."

"Sounds like a plan to me," Maddy said. "I can't wait to hear everything."

Chapter 15

"What I want to know is, who *didn't* want to kill this guy?" Maddy asked me as we walked into the Slice and locked the door behind us. "I'm amazed he lasted as long as he did, to be honest with you."

As I began to pull out the ingredients to make our dough for the day, I said, "I know exactly what you mean. I never knew one man could inspire so much loathing in my life. Patrice called it his unique gift to the world."

My cell phone rang, and I wondered who it could be when I reached for it.

When I saw that it was Kevin Hurley, I almost didn't answer the chief's call.

"Hey," I said, against my better judgment.

"I'm outside," he said. "Let me in."

"Be right there," I said, and then hung up. There hadn't been a bit of nicety in his words, and I prepared myself for the worst.

"Who was it?" Maddy asked.

"Kevin Hurley wants to have a little chat," I said as I headed for the kitchen door.

"Then by all means, let's go talk to him," Maddy said, dropping her knife on the cutting board. It was from the same set as the one that had been used as a murder weapon, but they were the best knives that I could afford, so no matter what we thought about it, Maddy and I had to keep using them.

I wasn't at all certain that the chief of police would be frank in front of Maddy. "Maybe I should handle this on my own."

"Did he expressly say that I couldn't come?" Maddy asked.

"No," I admitted.

"Then I'm coming with you."

I knew better than to push it when she used that tone of voice with me. When Maddy made up her mind about something, it tended to stick.

Chief Hurley didn't look all that pleased to see us both approaching the front door, but it could have just been my imagination. He hadn't had it particularly easy over the past few years, and some of that was probably due directly to me. We'd had several clashes when it came to his son, Josh, and we'd butted heads more times than I could count about past murder cases I'd been dragged into against my will by circumstance.

"Come on in, Chief. We've got fresh coffee, if you're interested," I said, trying to be as nice as I could manage.

He smiled slightly. "Normally I would say no, but to be honest with you, that sounds great to me. I've been up since dawn."

"Come on back, then," I said. Maybe he'd been so abrupt because he was exhausted and not because he was miffed with me. I could only hope, anyway.

We all walked back into the kitchen together, and I poured him a cup.

I asked, "Do you mind if I work while we talk? I have to prep this dough, or nobody's going to be having pizza for lunch."

"Go right ahead," he said. I half expected him to pull out one of the barstools I kept there for company, but he just leaned against the wall as he took a long sip of coffee.

Maddy, at least for the moment, wasn't saying a word, which I took as a favorable sign. Instead, she went back to her task of cutting peppers into thin slices. If it hadn't been for the sound of the knife blade hitting the cutting board, I wouldn't even have known that she was there at all.

"First off, I had them check for poison," the chief said. "Like I thought, it was a dead end."

I tried to smile. "Hey, it was still worth a shot."

"I agree," he said. "I appreciate the input."

What was going on here? The chief of police was either in a spectacularly good mood, or he wanted something in return for his courtesy. Either way, I decided to push it while I had the chance. "Have you had any luck eliminating any suspects yet?"

He should have blown up about then if history was any indication, but he just shook his head. "Not yet. We have to work fast, too, because I can't keep these out-of-towners here much longer without probable cause." The chief took another sip of coffee, and then said, "Okay, let's lay our cards out on the table. I know you've both been digging into Benet's murder."

Maddy was about to speak when I warned her off with a quick shake of my head. If we started an argument with Kevin right now, our information sharing was about to end. Thankfully, Maddy caught my glance, and silently went back to her peppers. I started measuring flour as I admitted, "It's hard not to, when the poor man was murdered right out there," gesturing to our dining area as I said it.

"Don't take this the wrong way, Eleanor. I'm not saying that I blame you for doing it this time," Kevin said. He drained his coffee, and then asked, "As a matter of fact, I was kind of wondering if you'd uncovered anything yourselves."

I had to hide my look of surprise, and Maddy didn't even try.

Kevin Hurley shook his head when he saw my sister's grin. "I know, it must sound crazy to you, but my back's up against a wall, and I'm not dumb enough to not realize that folks around here confide in you and tell you things they keep from me."

"I'm sure it's nothing personal," I said, though that wasn't exactly true. Kevin had a way of threatening some people just by the way he spoke, and it was tough to be forthright when you were being intimidated.

He looked at me with those killer eyes of his, and I saw the old Kevin for just a second. "So, have you managed to uncover anything yet?"

I thought about keeping what I knew to myself, but I quickly dismissed the idea. I owed him the truth. It had to have been hard coming to me like that, and besides, if he found out later that I'd held out on him, he'd never trust me again. Frankly, there were times when I needed access to his information. The longer I thought about it, the harder it would be to tell him.

"Antonio Benet was Cindy Rankin's father," I said, blurting it out.

I don't know who was more surprised that I'd shared the information, Maddy or the police chief.

"How in the world could you possibly know that?" Kevin asked.

"Janet told us late last night," I admitted. "And Cindy backed it up."

"No offense, but why would they tell you that?" Kevin asked.

Maddy pointed her knife at me. "Tell him, Eleanor. The truth is, she only came clean when my sister said that she'd already figured it out herself."

Kevin looked at me with an impressed glance. "Wow. I didn't have a clue. How did you manage to put it all together?"

I really had no choice but to explain. "We were talking to Oliver Wills at one point, and he said that Benet was here on business, but when I pressed him on it, he said it was more like family business. Cindy had told me earlier that Benet reached out to her when he learned that she was opening a bookstore, even though the man, for all intents and purposes, was a thoughtless toad. He had to have had a reason, and coupled with Cindy's lack of a father, it all started to make sense."

"I don't know," Chief Hurley said as he shook his head. "It sounds kind of thin to me, to be honest with you."

"It worked, though," I said. "I was right."

He put the mug down on the counter, and then asked, "Is there anything else I need to know?"

I shook my head. "Everybody involved had a motive, and there's not an alibi among them, at least as far as we've been able to find out so far."

Chief Hurley nodded. "Thanks for that. If one of you will let me out, I need to have a talk with Cindy and Janet Rankin."

"I'd ask you not to tell them where you heard about it, but no one else knows," I said as my sister and I led him out into the dining room. I'd most likely just lost two friends, and I wasn't even certain that it had been for a good cause.

"I'll try to keep your name out of it, but I can't make any promises," he said.

"Thanks, I do appreciate it, but the second you ask the first question, we both know that I'm a goner."

"I see your point," Kevin said as we all walked to the front door together, "but do me a favor and don't call them and warn them that I'm coming. I want to get to them before they have time to come up with any stories."

"Just because Benet was Cindy's father doesn't necessarily mean that either one of them killed him," Maddy said.

"It doesn't mean they didn't, either." Kevin paused before leaving. "Listen, I know how hard this must have been for you, Eleanor. Thank you. I really do appreciate it."

"Trust me, I want Benet's killer caught, too," I said as I opened the door.

"Not as much as I do," he replied.

After Chief Hurley was gone, I locked the door, afraid of what Maddy was going to say to me once we were alone again. I'd betrayed a confidence, but in my mind, I really hadn't had a choice.

If either Cindy or Janet was a murderess, I needed to help catch them. And if they were both innocent of the crime, I'd just have to realize that the loss of their friendships was collateral damage in a bigger war.

Instead of badgering me, though, Maddy went straight to her station and started chopping veggies again.

I had to break the ice myself. "Listen, I know you don't approve of what I just did, but I didn't have any choice."

Maddy shook her head. "Stop jumping to conclusions, Eleanor, and relax. I'm not going to scold you. You're right. There was nothing else that you could do."

"You really understand?" I asked, the relief flooding through me.

"Of course I do," she said. "I almost blurted it out myself just before you did."

"You didn't, though, did you?"

Maddy shook her head. "No, I figured Kevin wouldn't approve our snooping."

"Ordinarily, I would say that you probably figured right," I said as I turned on the mixer and set the timer for the dough. "He was too nice today. I should have been on my guard more."

"Don't worry about it," Maddy said. "We'll find a way to make it right with Janet and Cindy when this is all over. It'll all work out in the end."

"I hope you're right," I said.

By the time Maddy, Greg, and I were ready to open the Slice at noon, I'd pushed to the back of my mind the fact that I'd told Chief Hurley about Cindy and Janet Rankin, but when I saw the mother and daughter standing outside as I approached the front door to unlock it, I knew that I'd have to deal with them sooner rather than later.

Instead of letting them in, I stepped outside after I unlocked the door and faced them both.

"I'm so sorry," I said quickly, hoping to take some of the steam out of them preemptively. "But I really didn't have any choice."

"There's always a choice, Eleanor," Janet said sternly. "You betrayed our trust."

"I never promised I wouldn't say anything," I reminded her.

"I never dreamed you'd blab it to the police, either," Janet said.

"Hang on one second," I said. "If you think about it, I just did you both a favor. You should be thanking me, instead of coming down here to scold me."

Cindy looked mad enough to spit. "Eleanor Swift, how in the world can you possibly say that?"

"Think about it," I said, keeping my voice steady and level. "The chief knows all about it now, so he'll investigate. It's out in the open, though, so nobody can hold this over your heads. The only way to kill a secret and the chance to be blackmailed is to put it all out there in the full light of day and let the chips fall where they may." I knew that I sounded like a cliché even as I'd said it, but I still hadn't been able to stop myself.

"Is that what you do with your own secrets?" Janet asked pointedly. "Because I don't recall you making any public declarations recently."

The thought of that really surprised me. "Janet, I don't have any secrets, and I haven't in a very long time."

"How can you be so sure about that?" she asked in a sinister way.

"I honestly don't know what you're talking about," I said. Was there a point she was trying to make, or was she just lashing out at me because of what I'd told the police?

"I imagine you'll be as shocked as everyone else when I expose you to the world, then," Janet said. As the mother and daughter turned away, Janet looked back and said, "Don't take it badly when it gets back to you, though. Honestly, you should just realize that I'm doing you the same kind of favor that you did for me today."

I had no idea what she was talking about, and as I turned to go back into the Slice, I saw that Greg and Maddy had followed me outside. It was pretty evident that they'd been standing there the entire time, and I hadn't had a clue that they'd witnessed the odd exchange.

"So what's the big secret, Eleanor?" Maddy asked with a grin.

"Yeah, I could use a little dirt to brighten my day," Greg added.

"I honestly don't know what she thinks she has on me," I admitted, still puzzled by her open threat.

"Now I'm even more curious than ever," Maddy said. "What are you going to do about it?"

I shrugged as I said, "I thought I'd open the doors to the public and make some pizza. How does that sound?"

Maddy frowned. "Do you mean to say that you're not even going to try to stop her?"

"You heard what she said," I replied as I walked past her and into the Slice. "Janet wasn't in any mood to be reasoned with. There's nothing I can do about the woman, so why not make some pizza?" I looked down the promenade and saw three college-aged students coming our way. "Unless I miss my guess, there are our first customers of the day."

We all walked inside, and I was thankful that I had the kitchen to myself. Janet's threat had disturbed me, not because I had anything to hide, but because a false rumor could kill a business quicker than the truth could.

I'd meant what I'd said, though. Whatever Janet said, there was nothing I could do to stop her from spreading things about me around town. In her mind, I'd broken her trust first, so she clearly felt justified doing whatever it took to get me back.

I just hoped it was a storm that I could weather, and prayed that it wouldn't sink me and my business forever.

* * *

I didn't think our lunch break would ever arrive, but finally it was time to close the Slice for an hour. I'd instituted the policy a while back, and hadn't regretted the loss of income at all. The freedom it gave us to get away from pizza for an hour was priceless, and Maddy and I usually took our break together, unless one of us had a particular errand to run or a boyfriend to meet. We were both free this break, but I didn't plan on using the time to eat. I had a plan, and if I knew my sister, she'd go right along with me. With Maddy, the more chance of getting caught doing something we shouldn't be doing, the better. I hoped Bob knew what he was getting himself into by proposing, but then again, that only mattered if Maddy said yes. I knew her better than anyone, including Bob, and I had no idea how she was going to answer him, or even when.

Maddy brought back a bin full of dirty dishes. "That's the last of it," she said, the relief clear in her voice. "I already let Greg go. I hope that's all right with you."

"It's fine," I said. We didn't need him for what I had in mind. "Do you feel like doing something dangerous and just skipping our lunch today?" I asked her.

"Do you even have to ask?" she replied with a smile.

"Don't you even want to know what it is I have in mind?" I asked.

"If you're in, then I'm in. You should know that by now. So, who are we going to kidnap? Or are we going to rob a bank, instead?"

"Actually, you're not that far off. I thought we might do a little breaking and entering," I said.

Maddy nodded. "Okay, it's not as risky as I thought, but that's fine. Who exactly are we going to burglarize?"

"I thought we might check out Benet's room and see if we can uncover any clues," I admitted.

"Don't you think they've moved his stuff out by now?"

"I don't think Patrice is thinking that clearly at the moment," I admitted, remembering how soused she'd been when I'd last seen her.

"Maybe not, but Jessie and Oliver seem to be on top of things."

"What's it going to hurt to take a look for ourselves?" I asked. "I'm willing to bet that Kevin Hurley and his crew are finished with the room, or he wouldn't have come calling over here this morning asking for my help."

Maddy grinned. "That whole thing was a little surreal, wasn't it?"

"I still can't believe it happened, but I'm not going to get used to us sharing information. I have a feeling this was a one-time thing."

"Well, you certainly made the most of it while you had the chance," Maddy said. "I know you hate the idea of dirty dishes just sitting around, but what do you say to leaving them and doing them later? We might not have all that much time to nose around if we finish everything up here."

I looked at the stack of dishes, and then realized that Maddy was right. If we did them now, we'd lose precious time investigating, and I wasn't sure how much of that we had to squander. "Sold," I said as I took off my apron and grabbed my car keys. "Let's go see what we can discover."

"I had no idea it would be that easy," Maddy said as her apron joined mine on the counter.

"You know how I get sometimes. Come on. I'll drive, and you can spend the time coming up with a way to get us into Benet's room."

Maddy laughed. "Trust me, it's not going to be all that hard. Steve Jenkins works the front desk over there, and that boy's got a crush on me a mile wide."

I knew Steve loved our pizza, and visited the Slice at least once a week, but I had no idea he had any romantic inklings towards my sister. While Maddy was younger than me, she was still a good fifteen years older than Steve, and he didn't look the type to go after older women.

"If you're sure," I said.

"Trust me. We're golden."

"Hey, Steve," Maddy said, offering the skinny young desk clerk the biggest smile she had in her arsenal. "How are you doing today?" Per my sister's request, I stayed off to one side so she could talk to the front desk clerk without me looming over them.

"I'm fine, Ms. Spencer," he said as he took a step backward, though there was a desk between them. "What can I do for you?"

"We need a favor," she said, lowering her voice a little and giving him a conspiratorial little wink.

Steve looked around as though he were being offered contraband. "What kind of favor did you need? I can't just give you a room, you know."

Maddy laughed. "It's nothing like that. We just need to get into a room for a few minutes."

"Is it your room?" he asked. "Because if it is, someone forgot to put your name on our registration sheet."

Maddy shrugged. "Not exactly, but it's okay. Nobody's going to mind," she said as she reached out and touched his hand lightly.

"Sorry, but I can't do that. I'd like to help, but if I did, I'd lose my job," Steve said as he pulled his hand away. Whatever hold Maddy might have had over the young man was clearly strictly confined to the restaurant.

"We need to see Antonio Benet's room," I said as I stepped forward.

"Why do you want to see *his* room?" Steve asked, clearly alarmed by our request. "The police just released it an hour ago. I'm sorry, but I can't help you."

"We won't take a thing," Maddy said. "I promise."

"That's not it," Steve said. "I couldn't give you the spare key to his room even if I wanted to."

"But you said the police already released it," I pushed.

"They did, but a man's up there right now packing everything away. He had a note from Mrs. Benet, so I thought it would be all right to give him the key and let him clear the room so we can rent it out again."

"What's the room number?" I asked, a new urgency in my voice. I hoped we weren't too late, since I had an idea of who was packing Benet's things but didn't know if the man up there was a legitimate representative of the widow.

"He's in room twenty-four," he said. "It's on the second floor."

I'd figured that out all on my own. "Thanks for the information. The next time you come in, your pizza's on the house."

"Thanks," Steve said. "I really appreciate that."

"I could have gotten the information on my own," Maddy said as we walked up the stairs.

"I know you could have," I said. Maddy was a lovely woman, but she might have overestimated her appeal to younger men, though I wasn't about to tell her that.

As I suspected, I saw Oliver Wills through the open door of Chef Benet's room.

What I hadn't expected to find was him cramming a batch of papers into a briefcase, and the chef's clothes and other belongings scattered all over the room's floor. Had he found the place that way, or had the chef's assistant been looking for something in particular before we'd arrived? I had to stop him, at least until I could uncover what he'd been looking for.

"What do you think you're doing?" I asked as I stepped inside, with Maddy close on my heels.

Chapter 16

"Oh, it's just you two," he said as he turned and looked at us. "Patrice asked me to collect her husband's things for her. She couldn't face coming back here."

That might have been true, but then why did he look so guilty as he explained it to us?

"Is that his briefcase?" I asked as I pointed to the leather satchel.

"Yes, of course it is," he said, and then tried to hide it from me.

I looked down at the embossed *OW* on the side. "Funny, I was under the impression that his initials were *AB*. Oliver, are you taking those papers for yourself, or are you going to give them to the widow?"

He looked at me as though I were a pesky gnat that was in serious need of swatting. "Okay, you caught me. Sure it's my briefcase, but why shouldn't I take them? They're the latest recipes I just finished creating for him, and they're not going to do him any good now, are they?"

"So, then, you're stealing from a dead man?" Maddy asked from across the room. I saw that she'd separated from us and was doing a little snooping of her own. Why had she given up that position of power, though, by commenting on Oliver's actions, thereby drawing his attention to her?

He looked over at her, and then said glumly, "You can't steal what belongs to you already."

"But didn't Benet already pay for them?" I asked, moving in closer so that I could touch the briefcase lightly. I had to get Oliver's attention back to me so Maddy could keep digging.

"You have no idea what you're talking about. He paid me peanuts for my treasures," Oliver said with open contempt for his former boss. "I gave him gold, and he somehow managed to spin it into straw."

"Kind of like a reverse Rumpelstiltskin," I said. There was a stack of cooking magazines on the side of the desk where Oliver had been searching, and I pretended to be clumsy when I knocked them to the floor. That should buy my sister a little extra time. "I don't know what's wrong with me today. I've never been so clumsy in my life."

I bent forward and began collecting them, but with my newly feigned clumsiness, I managed to scatter them even more across the floor.

Oliver put the briefcase down, though I noticed that he still kept it close to him, and then started to help me pick the magazines up. It took all I had not to peek at what Maddy was doing, but I didn't want to give Oliver any ideas, and I especially didn't want to point out that while he was helping me, my sister was doing as she pleased unsupervised.

I delayed it as long as I could, but Oliver and I finally managed to gather everything and replace it on the desk, despite my active attempts to keep him from doing it. "What are you two doing here, anyway?" he asked after he collected the briefcase again.

Fortunately, I'd been working on an answer to that question since we'd spotted Oliver there ahead of us. "We were here on a pizza delivery, so we thought we'd swing by and see if anyone had taken care of the chef's belongings. It was pretty clear that Patrice was in no shape to do it, and we wanted to give her a hand."

"She *has* been drinking a lot since we first heard the news," Oliver admitted. "I'm worried about her."

I searched his eyes to try to see if there was something deeper there when he spoke of Benet's widow, but I didn't see anything. That didn't mean that he wasn't hiding something, but it encouraged me to believe that they were just friends, and not something tawdrier. "Shouldn't you be with her right now, if that's the case?"

"Jessie's taking care of her while I do this," Oliver explained. "It looks like I'm not the only one who's going to be out of a job now."

"What do you mean by that?" I asked.

"Well, it's pretty clear that if Benet's not on the air, he doesn't really need an assistant, does he?" There was the hint of a slight smirk as he added, "He doesn't need an executive producer either, so Jessie's been scrambling, trying to come up with another show to pitch." He looked absolutely smug now.

"Do you think she'll actually change her mind about you?" I asked. I'd heard Jessie before, and I didn't believe it for a moment. Then again, if she had another use for Oliver, I could see her stringing him along until she got what she wanted. That didn't necessarily mean that she was a murderer, though, just a shark. From what I'd read, that made her good at her job, and nothing else.

"You'd be surprised. The last time I spoke with her, I have to admit that I was pretty persuasive. She's starting to come around," Oliver said with a grin.

"Well, good luck to you with that," I said as I hugged him. He'd been about to turn around to see what Maddy was up to, and I knew that I needed to stop him. I couldn't exactly see what she was getting, but it was small enough to fit into her purse. I'd have to find out later what she'd gotten. For now, I needed to keep distracting him.

"If you two will excuse me, I have more work to do here," he said as he extracted himself from my grip.

"The more the merrier, I say. We'll stick around and lend a

hand," I said. I looked over at my sister, and whatever she'd been trying to retrieve was most likely in her possession now. "Isn't that right, Sis?"

Maddy nodded and offered Oliver a big, if insincere, smile. "We have at least half an hour to help you before we open the Slice back up for our dinner crowd."

"Thank you, but I really do need to do this myself. Thanks for the offer, but I'm kind of pressed for time right now."

Maddy and I reluctantly let ourselves be led out of the hotel room, and Oliver closed the door firmly behind us. Not only that, but a second later, I actually heard him flip the bolt as well.

We got down the hallway before I asked Maddy, "What did you find?"

She looked around to be sure that Oliver hadn't followed us, and then pulled a crumpled envelope out of her pocket. "I don't know if it's important or not," she said as she handed it to me.

I took the envelope, covered in a grafitti of random scrawls and numbers, and pulled the letter from inside it. As I smoothed it out on my leg, I saw that it was from the network that Benet had claimed was hiring him.

But the contents of the letter told a much different story.

> *Dear Chef Antonio Benet,*
> *First of all, thank you for coming to us with your new idea for the proposed cooking series, Around the World with Dinner and Drinks. While we believe that this idea has some basic merit, we aren't sure that your proposal fully captures the essence of what one of our shows should be, so we are respectfully declining.*
> *We wish you continued success on your current show on your current network.*
> *Sincerely,*
> *Hiram J. Wannamaker*
> *CEO, Food Bites, Inc.*

Maddy had been reading over my shoulder. "That lying little sneak. He was just holding his own network up for more money, wasn't he? Benet had no intention of leaving."

I looked at the letter again, and saw that it had been dated six days before. "Maybe, but what if Benet thought the new show was in the bag when he told Jessie he was leaving? How hard would it have been for him to go back to her and tell her that he'd been wrong?"

"I've got a hunch that this was just confirmation of something he already knew," Maddy said. "Either way, it was information not everyone had access to, and he must have tried using it as leverage."

"I'm just glad we found it," I said. "Maybe we should go talk to Jessie and see if she knew that Benet was just bluffing."

"Don't forget: we have to deal with Patrice, too," Maddy said. "Is there one chance in ten that she's sober?"

"I'm afraid that might be asking for too much."

Maddy shook her head. "I understand getting lost in booze if you're torn up inside over losing someone you love, but honestly, she didn't seem all that upset by Benet's murder."

I remembered how dead inside I'd felt when I'd lost Joe, and I knew that I never wanted to feel that way again. "I can't really say. All I do know is that everybody handles it differently," I said.

Maddy grabbed my arm. "I didn't mean to say that. I was in no way comparing Joe to Chef Benet."

"I know that," I said as I tugged my arm away. "Don't worry about it. I'm fine."

"Then why are you crying?"

I reached up and brushed a cheek. Odd, I hadn't even realized that there were tears on my cheeks. "It's nothing."

"I upset you," Maddy said. "That's always something."

"Forget about it, okay? Let's just go talk to Jessie and Patrice."

Maddy nodded, accepting my offer to move on and forget this

exchange had ever happened. "You've got it. Any ideas on how we should approach them?"

I considered it a moment, and then said, "I think I'd like to split them up, if it's possible."

Maddy didn't answer until we made it all the way to my car. "I can come up with something, but there's something I need to know first. Do you have one in particular you'd like to tackle yourself?"

I'd thought about it, and I didn't have to give it another moment's consideration. "I want to take Jessie, if you don't mind."

She laughed. "Wow, it didn't take you long to pull that trigger, did it?"

"I'm sorry. If you want Jessie, I'll take Patrice."

She frowned. "No, I think we're better off doing it the way you suggested. You never know, maybe if I start drinking with her, she'll confide in me."

"Don't get too soused," I said. "We still have a full night's work at the Slice, and I need you sober."

"How sober?" she asked with a grin.

"Enough so I don't have to worry about you wielding knives in my kitchen."

"I'll do my best, but maybe you need to plan on doing some of the later prep work on the veggies yourself."

"I'll keep it in mind," I said.

By the time we got to the hotel, Maddy and I had worked out the basic framework of a plan.

"Are you good?" she asked.

"I'm fine," I replied. "The only problem is, I still don't know how we're going to separate them."

"There's only one way I know how to do it," Maddy said. "We're going to have to use the truth."

"You're right. I have to let Jessie know that I've got something she needs to see without letting Patrice overhear us," I said.

"That's what I'm thinking. Don't give her the letter too quickly, though. Milk it for what it's worth, and see if you can find out if she already knew about Benet's rejection before you show her the letter."

"Can I at least show her the envelope to tease her with it?" I said, joking.

Maddy groaned a little. "That thing is such a mess, I'm surprised you even kept it. Was there actually a grocery list scribbled somewhere on it?"

I nodded. "I figured it must have been part of some kind of recipe Benet was working out on his own. If we can believe Oliver, I doubt that it would taste very good."

"Well, at least it shows that he was trying. I have to give him credit for that."

"I'll give him that," I answered as we neared the door, "but that's all I'm going to give him."

Taking a deep breath, I knocked once, waited a minute, and then knocked again.

Jessie finally came to the door, and she tried to give us a smile, but for a split second I'd seen the tension she'd been feeling before she managed to hide it. "Ladies, what brings you two here again so soon?"

"We need to talk," I said to Jessie.

"Patrice and I have nothing more to say," Jessie replied.

"Funny, I thought you might want to discuss this," I said as I held the envelope up so she could see her competitor network's logo in the return address.

"What is that?" she asked as she reached out her hand for it.

I pulled it back, and then tucked it safely back into my pocket. "It's what we need to talk about."

"I'm sorry, but I can't leave Patrice alone," she said as she looked back at Benet's widow.

"I'll stay with her," Maddy volunteered. "She doesn't need to hear what her husband was up to before he was murdered.

There's no use putting the poor woman through anything more than we have to."

Jessie thought about it, and then nodded. "Let's take a walk, Eleanor. You've got five minutes, and then we're coming back here."

I agreed, but before Jessie would leave, she turned to Maddy. "Don't let her drink too much."

"Should she even be drinking at all?" Maddy asked in all seriousness.

"Honestly, no, but when I tried to get her to stop, she wouldn't. Just try to limit it, okay?"

"Okay," Maddy said.

After the door was closed, Jessie looked back at it. "Are you sure they'll be all right in there?"

"Maddy will take care of her," I said, though I wasn't absolutely certain I believed it. If Maddy thought she could get some valuable information from Patrice by plying her with more booze, I wouldn't put it past my sister.

"Now may I see that letter?" Jessie asked.

"Do you mean that you haven't read it already?" I asked.

"No, I never even knew it existed until you just showed it to me."

"What do you think it says?" I asked.

She shook her head. "Sorry, but I'm not playing that game with you."

I could be tough, too, though she hadn't seen it yet. "You might want to reconsider, if you really want to see what it says."

Jessie looked quietly angry, as though she were fighting to contain herself. "Eleanor, what game are you playing? Are you trying to see just how far you can push me? Because, if you are, I should warn you. I'm just about to my breaking point already, so it's not going to take much to push me over the edge."

"That was exactly what Benet was doing though, wasn't he? I'm guessing he made some kind of outrageous demand in order to be persuaded to stay with your show and not leave the network."

Jessie looked surprised by my statement. "How on earth could you possibly know that?"

"Just call it an educated guess," I said. "What did you tell him?"

"That we couldn't do it, no matter how much I would have loved getting another show on the channel."

"Didn't you think that he could handle it?" I asked.

"Trust me, nobody in the world had as high an opinion of Benet as he had of himself. The man thought he was much more talented than the evidence ever showed."

"And did you tell him that?"

Jessie frowned. "It's why we were arguing. I could have gotten him a raise, a small one anyway, but there was no way they were going to give him another show. He just didn't generate that much revenue for the network. The man was a B-list talent at best."

"And it's all about the money, isn't it?"

She sighed, and then said, "Eleanor, what business isn't? We have bottom lines just like everyone else, and if Benet lost another sponsor for his show, it wasn't all that certain that it was even going to stay on the air, let alone help him get a new show."

"How did he take the news when you told him?"

Jessie took a breath, and then said, "He was like a little boy losing his favorite toy. He pouted, threw a fit, and then refused to discuss it anymore. It's amazing, but that's how I managed to get along with him after everyone else jumped ship. If I treated him like I would a small boy, I had much more success than when I tried treating him like a man."

"How did he feel about it?" I asked.

"Honestly? I don't even think he noticed," she replied. "I believe I've earned the right to read that letter myself."

I got it out of my pocket, but before I handed it to her, I said,

"I already made a copy of it, so don't get any ideas." This was a lie, but I was hoping that she'd believe it and not try to destroy any evidence. "After you read it, I want it back. I'm showing the original to the police chief. He has a right to know what's going on, too."

"Okay, I can live with that. I just want to see exactly what it says."

I took the letter from its envelope and handed it to her. Jessie quickly scanned the brief note, and then her frown deepened as she read it again. "That skunk," she said as she stood there still holding the letter.

I took it back from her before she could damage it, since it was the only copy I had, and I quickly slid it safely back into its envelope. I really did need to make a copy of it for myself before I handed the original over to Kevin Hurley.

"He actually lied to me," Jessie said. "I never would have believed it if I hadn't seen that letter for myself."

"Are you really all that surprised?"

"I shouldn't be, I admit it," Jessie answered. After a few seconds, she shook her head and managed to laugh a little. "The guy played me like a pro, didn't he? If I could do it, I'd congratulate him right now for how slick he played it. I'm not easy to fool, but I'm not afraid to admit it; he got me good."

Before I could ask another question, her cell phone rang.

"Yes, sir," she said. "Yes, sir. Fine, sir. Right away, sir. Of course I'll hold, sir." Jessie put a hand over the phone to block it, and then said, "I'm sorry, but I've got a situation I have to deal with."

"Should I hang around until you're through with your call?" I asked.

She shook her head. "This is going to take at least an hour, but there's no need for you to stay. I don't know what else I can say. Benet played me, but I never found out about it until just now. What a guy, right?"

Instead of going back into Patrice's room, Jessie said into her telephone, "Hang on. The reception is lousy in here. I need to go outside to see if I can get a better signal."

She left me in the hallway, and I was dismissed from her mind as though I'd never been there.

I wasn't about to leave, though.

It was time I joined Maddy and Patrice.

I didn't even knock when I walked into the room. Maddy and Patrice were on the balcony, and as I stepped inside, Maddy stood. "Excuse me, but I need to go to the bathroom. I'll be right back." I wasn't sure if that were true, or if she wanted some time to snoop around.

I took the seat beside Patrice as she said, "I like your sister. She's got real spunk."

"So I've heard," I said. I reached over and picked up one of the two glasses on the table between the chairs and took a sip. Patrice might be drinking, but Maddy was having straight orange juice. Good for her.

Patrice, slurring her words a little, asked, "So, what rocks have you two ladies turned over today? Did you find any bugs scurrying out from under them looking for protection?"

"We haven't had time yet to do much rock turning lately," I said. "Pizza takes up most of our time."

Patrice picked up her drink and took a large swallow. I wasn't sure if it was my imagination or not, but she looked surprised as she took the drink. Had someone switched out her Mimosa with one that had more punch?

"Why don't I believe that?" she asked, her voice suddenly a little hoarse.

"Believe what you will," I said. "You must really trust Oliver."

"Why do you say that?" Patrice asked, shaking her head as she did so, as though she were trying to dislodge the cobwebs in her brain.

"Well, you sent him alone to collect your husband's things," I said.

"It was his idea, but I figured, why not? Oliver is many things, but a thief is not among them," Patrice answered. "Besides, in the end, what did Tony really have that was worth stealing?" Her gaze sharpened for a moment as she asked, "Why were you in my husband's room today, anyway?"

Oh no. It appeared that I'd said a little too much, and the chef's widow was not nearly as drunk as she first appeared to be.

Chapter 17

"We were making a delivery out that way, and we wanted to see if we could help make your life a little easier," I said as I stared out at the view, not risking making eye contact with Patrice.

I didn't know if she bought it or not, but I was saved when my sister finally came back out. "Eleanor, I hate to break this up, but we need to get back to the Slice. It's almost time to open again."

The hour we took every day was not enough to investigate, and I considered for a moment postponing our dinner service, but then I realized that our customers were counting on us, and I needed to be there for them.

"You're right, of course." I turned to Patrice. "Will you be okay until Jessie comes back?"

"You needn't worry about me. I don't need anyone to watch over me," she said defiantly.

"I didn't mean to imply that at all," I said. "I just know how it feels to be alone after something so tragic happens."

"Of course you do," Patrice said, her voice softer now. "I heard about your late husband, and I'm truly sorry."

I shrugged. "We do what we must to get by, don't we?"

Patrice was about to answer when Jessie opened the door and hurried into the suite. She looked honestly surprised to see that Maddy and I were there. "What are you two still doing here?

Don't you have pizzas to make?" At least she was off the phone, though probably for just a moment, judging by the way she was holding it.

"You asked us to stay, remember?" Maddy asked with a smile.

"I keep telling everyone that I don't need a keeper, but no one will believe me," Patrice said.

"Of course you don't," Jessie replied with some real sympathy in her voice. I had to guess that she really cared about Benet's widow from the way she spoke to her. "I just didn't want you to be alone. That's all."

"I'm fine with being by myself," Patrice insisted. "I've been alone before, and I will be again."

"Yes, of course, I know that," Jessie said.

Jessie escorted us to the door, and as we were leaving, she said, "I've just got a minute before the brass is calling back, but I'd like to ask you both for a favor."

"Name it," I said, curious about what Jessie was going to ask from us.

"Patrice is having a pretty rough time of it, no matter how lucid she might sound at times. We all need to have a heart and give her some understanding."

I nodded. "We get it, Jessie. We don't want to cause her any more grief than she's already dealing with."

"Thanks for understanding." She was about to add something else when her phone rang. "I'm sorry, I've got to take this."

She closed the door, and Maddy and I were once again standing in the hallway.

"Amazing," I said as we started downstairs. "I believe Jessie truly cares about Patrice."

"It's good someone's watching out for her," Maddy answered. As we approached my car, she said, "You know what? I'm glad you're driving. I'm not all that sure I could make it myself."

"I tasted your glass, you big fraud," I said with a smile. "That was clever of you to leave the alcohol out of your drink and just have straight orange juice."

"I don't know what you're talking about," Maddy said, clearly confused by my statement. "My drink had more champagne in it than juice."

"But the one I tasted was just OJ," I said.

"Then you must have grabbed the wrong one, because mine was absolutely spiked with liquor."

I thought about the way Patrice had acted earlier, and then asked my sister, "Why would Patrice want people to think that she was drunk when she was in fact, sober?"

Maddy shrugged. "Beats me."

"I have a thought," I said. "Maybe she wanted the people around her to take her for granted. If she appears to be a lush, folks might just start to drop their guard around her, thinking that she's a harmless drunk."

"So she might be doing some investigating into her late husband's murder on her own, is that what you're saying?" Maddy asked.

"It's possible," I admitted.

"But how likely is it?"

"I can't give you any odds," I said. "I just don't have enough information yet."

"She might be playing a pretty dangerous game. We need to keep an eye on her though, don't we?" Maddy asked.

"We do," I said.

"So, what should we do now?"

I didn't even have to think about my answer. "We go back to the Slice, try to sober you up, and get ready to work."

Josh was waiting for us up front when we got back to the pizzeria, even though he wasn't due to work until later that evening.

"Did I misread the schedule today, or did you?" I asked him as I took out my new key and unlocked the door.

"I know that I'm not supposed to come in for a few more hours, but we need to talk about something right now," he said firmly.

Maddy walked through the open door, and then said, "Why don't you two stay out here and chat? I'll go ahead and get things ready inside."

I remembered how tipsy she was, and started to worry about what might happen in my absence. "Don't go near the knives, and be careful turning the oven on."

"Got it," she said and gave me an okay sign.

"And drink a pot of hot coffee. We're opening in three minutes," I told her.

"That's plenty of time for me to get things right," she said.

As she disappeared unsteadily into the kitchen, I turned to my youngest employee. "What's going on, Josh?" A thought suddenly occurred to me. "You're quitting, aren't you?" I'd grown complacent with my little crew, but I always knew that it wouldn't last forever. The nature of my business meant that employees would come and go, but it was still tough to get used to seeing the good ones leave.

"No, why would you say that?" he asked. "You aren't getting tired of having me around, are you?"

"Of course not, but I know you're almost finished with high school, and you'll be going away before long."

He grinned at me, and I could see his father in him whenever he did it. "As a matter of fact, it's just the opposite."

"You're not thinking about dropping out when you're so close to graduating, are you? You can't do that, Josh."

"Tell me about it. My folks would kill me. They don't agree about much these days, but they both know they want me to go to school."

I was confused yet again. "So, tell me, how is that the opposite, then?"

He explained, "My folks want me to go to UNC–Asheville, but I want to stay closer to home. I figure if I go to the community college like Greg does, I can work more hours here. You're always saying how you need more help than you've got."

"Do you really think that Asheville is all that far away from us? It's not even an hour and a half from here, and I've heard great things about the school, and I love the town itself."

Josh frowned. "I'm not denying that it's all really cool, but why not wait a few years before I go? You'd think my mom would be happy that I wanted to stay, and that my dad would be pleased about the money I'm saving him, but neither one of them is crazy about the idea."

"And you're trying to convince me to talk to them?" I asked.

He grinned at me as he said, "Hey, I figure it might be worth a shot."

"That's where you're wrong. Josh, I'm just your boss, I'm not your parent. Work it out with them, and then come talk to me about what the three of you decide, but I can't afford to get in the middle of a domestic dispute."

Josh looked disappointed by my answer, as though he had been expecting me to say something else. "You're turning your back on me, too, Eleanor? I thought you'd be different."

I hugged him for a moment, and then said, "Don't get me wrong. If the three of you can work something out, I'd love to have you here as long as you'd like to work for me, but I'm not about to get into your family argument. I have enough trouble with your folks without butting in where I don't belong. Do you understand?"

"I guess so," Josh said.

"Now, I've got to open the Slice. Will I see you later?"

"Don't worry about me. I'll be here," he said, though he wasn't smiling as he said it.

I came back in and found Maddy in the kitchen downing a huge mug of coffee. "Where's Josh?" she asked. I wasn't sure if it was the caffeine or if the alcohol was just wearing off on its own, but she was already looking better than she had been when we'd left Patrice's room.

"He's gone," I said. "You are not going to believe the crazy thing that kid just asked me to do."

"I don't know; give me a clue."

As I unwrapped a few pizza dough balls from the fridge, I told her all about it, finishing up with, "Can you believe that he tried to drag me into that?"

"It's nuts, even for him," she agreed. "You know the Hurleys are going to put pressure on you to back them on this, don't you?"

"They can ask all they want to, but I'm telling them the same thing I told Josh. It's their family situation. I'm not in it now, and I don't plan to be. I'll tell you one thing, there's never a dull moment around here, is there?"

"That's one of the reasons I keep hanging around," Maddy replied.

We had a busy night, but I noticed that Maddy wasn't her usual chipper self. Whether it was from the mimosas she'd downed or something else entirely, I couldn't say. Added to that was Josh's sullen mood, and the pizza parlor had a grim feel to it all evening.

Greg came back around closing and said, "Can I take off early? It's like a morgue out there."

"There are no customers left?" I asked as I started cleaning up my work area.

"Oh yes, the diners are fine. I'm talking about my coworkers."

I nodded. "I guess they both have a lot on their minds."

"Well, I'll tell you this. They sucked the fun right out of this shift."

I glanced at the clock and saw that we had fifteen minutes until we were due to close. "Why don't you call it a night and slip out the back way?"

"You really wouldn't mind?" he asked.

"Are you kidding? I'd go with you, if I could," I replied with a grin.

"Why don't you? Maddy can come back here and finish your shift for you."

"I'm tempted, trust me, but I'd better not. It's too late for me, but you can still save yourself."

"I will," Greg said. He put his apron on its hook, and then let himself out the back door.

After I locked up behind him, Maddy came back. "Greg, table eight is . . ." Her words died off as she realized that I was alone.

"What happened to Greg?" Maddy asked.

"Isn't he out front with you?" I asked, trying to hide my grin.

"Eleanor, I may be getting older, but I've got quite a few years before my senility starts creeping in. I saw him come back here." She looked at the hooks with aprons and saw Greg's. Grabbing it, she waved it in the air. "See? I knew he was here. He left the back way, didn't he?"

"I let him go early," I admitted.

"It's not like him to skip out early on a shift," she answered.

I had two choices at that moment. I could ignore her statement, or I could tell her the truth. I opted for the truth. "He said it was like a morgue working with the two of you. What's going on, Maddy? Something's clearly troubling you tonight. Have you made up your mind about Bob's proposal yet?"

"No," she snapped.

"Hey, I'm sorry," I said, and turned back to my cleaning. "I shouldn't keep asking you."

Her expression softened instantly as she said, "No, I'm the one who's sorry. I shouldn't have lashed out at you, Eleanor. The problem is, Bob came by the Slice two hours ago."

"I didn't realize that. What did I make for him?" There were a great many folks who came in whose orders I knew by heart, so whenever I got a slip with their specialty on it, I knew they were dining with us.

Bob wasn't that predictable, though.

"You didn't."

"Do you mean that he didn't stay?" I asked, dropping my dishcloth for a moment.

"Not long enough to eat. He walked up to me, asked me if I'd made up my mind yet, and when I told him I hadn't, he walked right back out again. The thing is, when he got to the door, he turned back and looked at me as he said, 'I won't wait forever, Maddy.' Now what is that supposed to mean?"

"That he won't wait forever?" I asked.

"Seriously? You're trying to have a little fun with me right now?"

"I'm sorry," I said quickly. "You can't blame the man. He asked you a pretty important question. Why wouldn't he want the answer?"

"I'm not sure what to do," she said. "I keep going back and forth in my mind, but every time I do, I come up with a different answer."

"Do you love him?" I asked.

"It's more complicated than whether I love the man or not," Maddy replied.

"It wouldn't be for me," I said.

"So you're saying you think that I should turn him down?"

Was my little sister actually asking me for advice? I had a hard time believing that. "No, I never said anything of the sort. I'm just saying that by having trouble answering him, that's an answer itself, isn't it?"

"I think sometimes you forget that not everyone is as lucky as you were," Maddy said. "I'm not even sure I believe in true love anymore. As many times as I've been married, the decision gets tougher to make each time someone asks me."

"And yet they keep asking, don't they?" I said with a grin. "I'm still trying to figure out what makes you so irresistible to them all. It's a real gift."

"More times than not, it's a curse," she said. "Sure, I've said yes four times so far, but do you have any idea how many times I've said no? Trust me, accepting is much easier than declining."

"I wouldn't know. I've been asked only once, and I said yes before he could finish asking the question."

"Well, that's why I've been in a bit of a funk tonight. Josh is worried about his parents, but I hadn't realized we were both being so difficult to work with that Greg would feel compelled to sneak out the back."

"Cut Greg a little slack," I said, knowing my sister might just call him and ask him why he left. "We both need to remember that he doesn't have to work here; he's got plenty of money. But he still comes in every shift I schedule him for, and I for one am grateful for that."

"So am I," Maddy admitted. "He's a good guy to have around."

"Josh is, too," I said. "Though he's a little more high maintenance."

Maddy grinned at me, and it was good to see it. "Than who, an opera diva?"

"Hey, we're all different," I said. "It's not a problem covering out front for Greg until we close, is it?"

"No, we've got it," she said as she grabbed a toasted sub and went back out front. "It's all good."

And I knew that it would be, but I hoped their dispositions improved. The last thing I needed was losing customers because of my waitstaff.

* * *

The next morning, Maddy was at my house and ready to go ten minutes before she was due to arrive.

"You're early," I said as I glanced at the clock. "Did you call it an early night last night?"

She didn't look all that happy when she explained, "I didn't have much choice. Bob was waiting for me when I got home."

That could mean a number of things could have happened, not many of them good. "What happened?"

"He told me that until I could come up with an answer, he thinks the two of us should take a little break."

"I'm so sorry," I said as I handed Maddy a cup of coffee. "Are you okay?"

"He didn't break up with me, Eleanor. He just wants to give me a little time and space to think about his proposal."

I nodded, doing my best to understand and show my sister that I had her back. "So until then, you two aren't going out? How long do you think you have until he withdraws the offer altogether?"

Maddy didn't even have to pause. "I don't have to think, he told me himself. If I don't have an answer for him by the end of the week when he wants my reply, I'm telling him no. You're right. This decision just shouldn't be this hard."

Was she actually going to drag me into this after all? "Hang on a second, don't go by what I said. Everybody's different. If you need more time, take it."

"No, that's the only thing I've actually made my mind up about. Now, may we quit discussing this and get back to our crime busting?"

"I'm game if you are," I said.

"That's what I like to hear. What's the plan for this morning?"

I'd done nothing but think about what we should do next. "As uncomfortable as it's going to be, we need to talk to Cindy and Janet again."

Maddy didn't like hearing the news any more than I'd liked

sharing it. "What makes you think they're going to talk to us? We can't just bribe them with another pizza. We don't have any ready, and besides, it's going to take something more than that to get them to talk to us."

"I have a plan, don't worry," I said.

Maddy looked at me skeptically. "Care to share what that might be with me? I love hearing fantasies."

"Why don't you come along for the ride, and let me handle it? It might work better if you're not expecting it, either."

Maddy thought about that, and then said, "I think you're crazy, but when has that ever stopped me from tagging along in the past?"

"You drive," I said. "I need to fine-tune what I'm going to say."

"We could drive across the country and I wouldn't be able to come up with anything, so take your time."

By the time we got there, I was ready.

"It's not too late to change your mind," Maddy said as we parked in front of Janet's house.

"If I don't do this now, I'll probably chicken out." I completely meant what I was about to say. It was the only way it could work, and even if I didn't get anything else out of the coming conversation, it was still something I knew in my heart that I had to do. If I didn't at least try, I'd never be able to forgive myself.

"Okay, but remember, I'm right behind you," Maddy said.

"Thanks for your support," I said with a grin. "I appreciate that."

"Support nothing," Maddy answered. "I want to be out of the line of fire in case they start throwing things, so I figure the safest place I can be is right behind you."

That didn't make me feel any better as we walked up onto the porch together.

I took a deep breath, and then rang the doorbell.

Janet answered, and the look of sheer displeasure on her face was tough to miss. "What do you two want?"

I looked her straight in the eye, and then said, "Do you have it in your heart to forgive us for telling Chief Hurley about your connection to Benet?" I asked. "Maddy and I were trying to do the right thing, but we both realize now that we should have handled it differently. We wronged you by blindsiding you and Cindy like that, and we're here to make it right, no matter what it takes."

Maddy nodded as she said, "We're both truly sorry."

Janet looked hard at each of us in turn, and for a second I thought that door was going to slam in our face. It wouldn't be the first time it had ever happened, but I never liked it.

"I suppose it won't hurt to let you both come in," she said, stepping to one side to allow us passage.

"What are they doing here?" Cindy asked, clearly as unhappy with our presence as her mother had been.

Janet looked firmly at her daughter as she said, "Young lady, they came to apologize, and we're going to hear them out."

"They told Chief Hurley about my father," Cindy said, faltering as she spoke the last word. "That isn't anyone else's business but ours."

"If your father hadn't just been murdered, I would agree with you," I said. "Maddy and I were wrong not to warn you about what we were doing, but the decision itself was a sound one. Don't you want your dad's killer to be punished for what he did?"

"Of course I do," Cindy said angrily. "They didn't just kill him. They robbed me of any chance I ever had to get to know him."

"Then, in essence, we all agree," I said. "I just went about helping out in the wrong way. I asked your mother, and now I'll ask you. Can you find any way to forgive us? We would both hate to lose your friendship over this."

Asking someone for forgiveness is powerful. It's one thing to hold on to anger and let it grow from afar, but confronting some-one face-to-face is much harder to ignore. It didn't always work, but if you were sincere, it was always worth a try.

"I know you weren't purposefully trying to hurt us," Cindy conceded. "But it was tough hearing the questions Chief Hurley asked. He wanted alibis for both of us, and he wouldn't leave until he got them."

"Did you manage to convince him of your innocence?" I asked. I was dying to know what the mother and daughter had told him, but I couldn't ask flat out, at least not yet.

"I hope so," Janet said. "Cindy's right. It was uncomfortable, to say the least."

I was about to try to word a request for more information than that, something that wouldn't offend them since we were on pre-carious ground at the moment, but Maddy beat me to it.

"So, what exactly did you tell him?"

Cindy was clearly about to tell us when Janet put a hand on her daughter's arm, shutting her up before she could reply. "Ladies, I believe you've done what you set out to do," the mother said. "You've asked for our forgiveness, and we've granted it. Now if you'll excuse us, we have some things to see to."

"Thank you," I said, getting out of there as quickly as I could drag Maddy with me.

Once we were outside, Maddy protested, "She was about to tell us."

"Sis, there is no way that Janet was going to let Cindy say an-other word, and besides, my apology was sincere. If we have any hope of getting anything more out of either one of them, we're going to have to get them alone. They're too strong when they're together."

"Kind of like us, right?" Maddy asked.

"I'd say they're exactly like us," I admitted with a grin.

Chapter 18

"Do we have time to speak with Benet's posse?" Maddy asked as we drove away from the Rankin house.

I thought about all we had to do this morning before we opened, and then nodded. "If I speed the dough up, we should be fine. This is too important not to do right now while we still have the chance. Kevin Hurley told us he couldn't keep them from leaving for much longer, so we have to push them even harder than we have been."

"I'm not sure how we can do that and still stay on their good side," Maddy said. "We've been pressing them pretty hard already."

"We've run out of time to act delicately," I said. "I thought you'd be happy. You normally prefer the 'full speed ahead' method of investigation where we hammer everyone with accusations until someone breaks down and confesses."

Maddy grinned at me. "Don't get me wrong; you know I love a good manhunt as much as the next gal. I just want to be sure you're certain that we can burn some bridges in the process."

I thought about that, and then amended my earlier statement by saying, "Why don't we just try to scorch them at first, and save the burning only if we need it later."

"That sounds like a deal to me," Maddy said. "You know, if this wasn't about finding a murderer, it could be kind of fun."

It obviously matched my sister's definition of entertainment more than it did mine, but if it helped her to look at it that way, it was fine with me.

When we got to the hotel room, we found Oliver sitting alone, the door to the suite standing wide open. The poor man looked as though he'd just lost his last friend.

"What happened here?" I asked him as I walked into the room with Maddy on my heels.

"I lost everything," he said, tears tracking down his cheeks as he looked up at us.

"What do you mean?" I asked.

"They took my recipes back," he said, the words seeming to stick in his throat. "They were mine. I created them, but Jessie is exercising a clause in our agreement to release them in book form in Benet's name. I don't get a dime of royalties for them, and not a penny of the advance. I can't believe that fraud is going to keep cheating me long after he's dead."

"They paid for them in the first place, though, right?" I asked gently.

"I got fifty dollars a recipe," he said. "Using them, I could have started my own cooking empire. Now I've got nothing."

"You could always come up with more dishes," Maddy suggested. "You're brilliant at it."

"Nothing I could ever create would ever be as good as those were. I'm finished, and I know it. To think that I did all that work, and I still got cheated in the end. I just can't believe it."

"Believe what?" I asked. We needed to keep him talking. Maybe something would slip out. I hated taking advantage of Oliver when he was in such despair, but there was a window to get the truth, and I couldn't let emotion stand in my way.

"It doesn't matter if you know now or not, and I'm tired of keeping secrets. When Benet was murdered, I was in the back room of the bookstore with Cindy having a little fun, if you know what I mean. We had a connection from the moment our eyes met, but she didn't want any of you to know, so I pretended to be mean to her while you all were around. After you were gone was a different story altogether."

Was Cindy's mourning just a show? Could she really be that impulsive? Of course she could. She told us so herself. Like mother, like daughter.

"That was a little sudden, getting involved so quickly, wasn't it?" Maddy asked.

Oliver shrugged. "She's an impulsive woman, and I wasn't about to say no. And then she told me the truth about herself."

"What truth was that?" I asked.

"I know you already know, so there's no use pretending that you don't. When she told me that she was Benet's daughter an hour ago, I wanted to kill myself."

"What did you say?" I asked.

"I told her that there could never be anything more between us than the few times we shared together. She cried and tried to talk me out of leaving her, but every time I'd ever look at her again, I knew that I'd see that leering face of her father's instead of hers. There's just no way it would have worked."

"So, if we speak with Cindy, she'll confirm that you two were together even as her father was being murdered?" I asked.

"She might not want to admit it, but it's true. Go on, ask her."

"Can you prove any of this if she denies it?" Maddy asked.

Oliver nodded glumly. "She's got a strawberry birthmark on her left hip. Check that if you don't believe me."

It was too specific to be a lie, as far as I was concerned. Wow, the daughter was more like the mother than I'd ever imagined.

"Can't you see why everything has gone so wrong in my life? I lost my job, my recipes, and Cindy, all within a few days. I thought Benet was ruining my life while he was alive, but if I would have had any idea how much pain he could cause me when he was dead, I would have been his bodyguard instead of his ghost chef."

If what Oliver had just told us was true, he and Cindy both had an alibi for the time of the murder. "We'll check it out, but you should be in the clear if it's true," I said.

"I already told my story to the police chief, and he bought it, so why shouldn't you two? It happens to be the truth, but I don't care at this point whether you believe me or not. At this point, I've got nothing left to lose."

Maddy shook her head. "Quit feeling so sorry for yourself, Oliver. You've got it all exactly wrong."

"What do you mean?" He looked intrigued by her statement.

"Think about it," Maddy said. "One of the best times in my life was when I lost everything I held dear. Do you want to know why?"

"Because you're some kind of masochistic nut?" he asked, and it was all I could do not to laugh.

"No, because when you've hit rock bottom, there's nowhere to go but up, and the world is full of new possibilities."

"I'm having a tough time seeing it that way," Oliver admitted as his head dipped down again.

"Tell you what," Maddy said. "I'm willing to admit that you've earned a day of self-pity, but as soon as you're finished, start thinking about what you want to do next with your life."

"Can I have at least a week to feel sorry for myself?" Oliver asked with a slight grin.

"Twenty-four hours, and not another minute more," my sister answered with a smile of her own. "Do you happen to know where Jessie and Patrice are right now?"

"They're downstairs in the conference room. Since they promised the police they wouldn't leave town until tomorrow, they've convinced Benet's cookbook publisher to fly down here to meet with them. They'll be in meetings all day from what I heard, but by tomorrow, they'll be gone." Oliver stood, and brushed at the seat of his pants, as though ridding himself of dust. "I suppose that I will be, too."

"Where are you going to go from here?" Maddy asked.

"I don't know," Oliver said, and then began to smile with a full-blown grin. "You know what? You're right. That's kind of the beauty of it, isn't it?"

"Don't worry. I have a feeling that you're going to do just fine," Maddy said.

"Thanks."

After we were out of the room, I looked at my sister with a fresh perspective. "I never would have believed it if I hadn't heard it myself."

"What's that, their alibi? It's pretty strange, isn't it?"

"No, I'm sure Chief Hurley has confirmed that by now. I just never thought I'd hear Maddy Spencer giving a motivational speech to anyone."

She shook her head. "Don't expect to ever hear it again. The boy was in some serious trouble, and I thought I could help."

"I'm not complaining. I thought it was great. One thing, though. When did you lose everything you ever cared about?"

She bit her lip, and then admitted, "I might have embellished a little when I said that."

"You could have fooled me. You sounded as though you'd experienced it firsthand," I said, remembering how I'd felt when Joe had died.

"It was more like secondhand," she admitted. "I was using you as my example. I meant every word of it, Eleanor. The way you managed to keep going was truly inspiring, and I thought Oliver had a right to know that just because his dreams died didn't mean that he had to end with them."

I bit back the tears, but then I let them explode as I hugged Maddy. She calmed me, and after the brief flood abated, she asked, "You're not angry with me for doing that, are you?"

"I'm honored," I said. "Don't ever underestimate the role you played in it, though. If you hadn't come back to town when I needed you most, I wouldn't have made it, and that's a fact."

"You're stronger than you think," Maddy said.

"Maybe so, but I also know in my heart that I'm even stronger with you."

As we neared the hotel's conference room, Maddy asked, "Is there any reason to just wait around outside for them to take a break?"

"I don't think so," I said. I glanced at my watch and then added, "We probably just have to come back later. I'm not really sure how long we can wait."

"Pizza making sure gets in the way of our investigations sometimes, doesn't it?" Maddy asked with a smile.

"I can live with that," I said. "I only investigate these things because I have to. I make pizza because I love to. It's two completely different things."

"I'm glad you found your true calling," Maddy said as we headed out to her car. "I don't know if I'll ever find mine. Who knows? Maybe I'm destined to always be the bride, and never the bridesmaid." We got in and Maddy started to drive away.

"I'm not sure you got that exactly right," I said. "You've sacrificed a lot coming to work for me. I know your dreams have soared higher than being a server at a small-town pizzeria."

"Funny, I thought I was the assistant manager," she said with a slight frown.

I quickly amended my statement. "You are. But it's not quite up to your earlier aspirations; you've got to admit that."

"Dreams aren't all they're cut out to be," Maddy said. "At the moment, all I want is to be happy."

"Can anyone ask for anything more?" I asked.

"Oh, you can ask," she said with a wicked laugh. "But that doesn't mean you've got a prayer of getting it."

"Aren't you happy now?" I asked, concerned about my sister.

"I'm happy enough," she admitted.

"I've always wondered just how happy that might be," I said.

"Eleanor, sometimes it's greedy to want more, when you already have enough."

I wasn't exactly sure how to take that, but I never got a chance to spend any more time considering it as someone jumped out in front of Maddy's moving vehicle.

Maddy slammed on the brakes, and still narrowly missed knocking Janet Rankin to the ground.

"Are you insane?" Maddy screamed at her as she jumped out of her car.

"I thought you saw me flagging you down," Janet said, pale from the near hit.

"I did, but just barely," Maddy replied.

"Pull over to the side," I said to my sister. "We all need a second to catch our breath."

Maddy did as I asked, and in a minute, the three of us were sitting on a bench by the sidewalk.

"What were you thinking when you did that?" Maddy asked her, using a much calmer voice than she had before.

"I needed to speak with you both," Janet said. "I didn't know any other way to get your attention."

"What was so important that you'd risk your life for it?" I asked.

"It's nothing as dramatic as all of that. You're apologies meant a great deal to me earlier, and after thinking about it, I decided that I want to give you our alibis. You deserve at least that much."

"We've already got Cindy's," Maddy said, but before she could add anything more, I put a hand on her arm.

"But we'd appreciate it if you could tell us as well," I added.

Janet nodded. "I don't blame you for checking our stories. She was with Benet's assistant the entire time of the murder."

"And you believe them?"

Janet nodded. "My daughter is many things, but she's no liar."

Whether she was or not was beyond our scope of investigation at that moment. "That covers her, but where were you?"

Janet looked ashamed. "I told the police, so I'll tell you, but I'd appreciate if you don't tell Cindy."

It felt as though Maddy was about to agree, but I knew better than to make promises like that. "We won't say a word if we don't have to, but that's where it ends. I'm sorry if that's not good enough for you."

"It will have to do," Janet said. After a moment's pause, she said, "I was on the phone with Nathan Pane the entire time, and Chief Hurley has already checked my telephone records. There's no way I could have killed Tony, not without Nathan hearing every last bit of it."

"I thought Nathan was unreachable," I said, knowing that the town's millionaire recluse answered to no one but himself.

"For most folks he is, but I have an in with him."

I thought about my contact with Art Young, and the number and curious code he'd given me in case of an emergency. I couldn't imagine the circumstances that would force me to use it, but it was comforting nonetheless having him just a phone call away.

"What did you discuss?" I asked.

Janet couldn't even look at us as she spoke, instead staring down at the ground between her feet. "I was asking him for a loan to keep Cindy afloat. We were counting on the revenue from Tony's book signing to carry us six months, maybe even a year, but we lost every last bit of it when he was murdered."

"That had to have been hard to do," I said sympathetically. I'd never been forced to borrow money to keep the Slice open, but I knew that if I had to, I'd find a way to do it.

"Not as hard as it was asking Tony for the money first," Janet said.

"When did you do that?" I asked. "I didn't think you realized that you were in a jam financially until after he was murdered."

"We were operating too close to the edge as it was, and I wanted Cindy to enjoy her dream, and to have a little breathing space. After Tony stormed out of the Bookmark, but before he got to Paul's Pastries, I found him on the promenade shortcut and confronted him. When I told him he should do right by his daughter even before I knew that he wouldn't be able to host his demonstration, he laughed in my face. He said that I hadn't told him about her all those years ago, and then he said that he'd get to know her on his own terms, with no strings attached, and nothing expected from either one of them. Oh, Tony admitted that he might help her out financially someday, but not out of a sense of responsibility, and certainly not anytime soon. We had a fight, and he went into Paul's and continued having his little tantrum. I decided then and there that I needed another plan, and Nathan was the only person I knew with the means to loan us the money we needed."

"And did he?" I asked.

"It took some convincing, but he finally agreed. He's always had a soft spot for Cindy, and to my shame, I exploited it."

"Hey, there's no use beating yourself up about it. You did what you had to do," I said as I patted her leg.

"Well, that's it," Janet said as she stood. "I had to get that off my chest. I'm sorry about everything."

"We are, too," I said.

Janet walked away, and I could swear I saw a lighter movement in her steps. It was as though an actual burden had been lifted from her shoulders.

"Now who's the great inspiration?" Maddy asked with a slight smile.

"What can I say? It must run in the family."

As we got back into Maddy's car and headed to the Slice, I said, "That's three cell phone alibis we've come up with for five suspects."

"Most people live on their telephones," Maddy said. "It doesn't really surprise me all that much."

"I suppose not. Who do they all talk to?"

"Each other, I'm guessing. Think about it, though. Just about everyone you know works at the Slice."

"Not David," I answered.

"No, but he's tied up most days. You just don't have all that much time to chat, do you?"

"It works for me," I said. "It looks like we can strike another name from our list."

"It's finally getting to be manageable, isn't it?"

"Yes," I agreed. "We might have to close early tonight so we can see if we can stir the pot a little more with the ones we've got left, though."

"How are we going to do that? We have Patrice and Jessie left, and they're in meetings for the rest of the day."

"I don't know yet, but we'll figure something out."

I would have loved to know what Kevin Hurley had uncovered so far in the case. There had to be information he was privy to that we didn't know, but I couldn't just ask him directly. He'd tapped me for information once, but that didn't mean that I had the same privileges. I suspected that if I helped him enough, he'd throw a few tidbits my way, too, but if the two main suspects Maddy and I had in our sights had alibis they'd already told the police, no one had shared them with us.

Chapter 19

"Hey, Eleanor," Paul said as he poked his head through the kitchen door a little after one that afternoon. "I've got something for you."

"Any chance it's a cream-filled éclair?" I asked. Paul's pastries were addictive, and every time I saw him, it made me crave sweets.

"Sorry, I didn't bring any goodies with me this time. This is a letter that the mailman dropped off at my place by mistake. I think Bernie's starting to slip."

Bernie Hildebran had been our mail carrier since we'd opened the Slice, and he prided himself on his ability to sort and deliver our mail.

"Don't tell him that," I said as I wiped my hands on a towel and took the letter from him. "Oh, great. It's a bill."

"Sorry it wasn't better news, but I thought you might need to get it so you could pay it on time," Paul said. He took a deep breath, and then added, "I forgot just how good this place smells. How do you take working here all day and not weigh a thousand pounds?"

"I was just thinking the same thing about you," I said. "I'd be glad to make you something while you're here. Just say the word. Do you have ten minutes, or do you need to get back to the bakery?"

"You know what? I should stay open until three, but I'm thinking about closing early today. Have you lost much income since you started closing for an hour in the afternoons?"

"Not enough to matter," I said. "You're not getting burnt-out on running your shop, are you?"

Paul shrugged. "It's a long story. Why don't you make me a small cheese pizza and I'll tell you while we're waiting for it."

"I can do that," I said. As Paul grabbed a stool, I got the dough and made him a medium-size pizza instead. It was the least I could do after all the pastries he'd given me over the years.

As I worked the dough, I said, "Tell me about it."

"You know how much I love running the bakery," Paul said. "It's still my passion, and not practicing law when I passed the bar was the smartest thing I could have done for myself."

"There's a large 'but' hanging in the air, though, isn't there?"

He nodded. "I'm not denying that I've enjoyed being single, but I'm getting tired of being all alone. Do you know how hard it is to find someone to date, let alone to marry? I have to be in bed by seven-thirty or eight every night at the latest. It doesn't leave me a lot of options for a love life."

"Well, let's think about it. There have to be women around here who work on your schedule, too," I said as I added the sauce and cheese. "Nurses, factory workers, and late-night clerks might be a good place to start."

"If they're out there, I'm having a hard time finding them," he said, looking sadder than I'd seen him in a long time.

"What brought this on?" I asked as I slid his pizza onto the conveyor. "You didn't used to feel this way."

Paul looked around, and then said, "Don't tell anyone; I don't want anyone to make a fuss, but today is my thirtieth birthday."

Now I felt bad that I'd let one of my best friends' birthdays go by without celebrating it with him. "I'm so sorry. I didn't know. Happy birthday."

"Thanks, but that's just it," Paul said. "Nobody knew it was my birthday but my mom. It would be nice to have someone in my life to share the milestones with, you know?"

"Don't worry, Paul. You're a great guy and I'm positive that you'll find someone," I said.

"I used to think so, but lately I've been beginning to wonder."

"Tell you what," I said. "Let me ask around for you. I have friends all over three counties. There has to be a ton of women out there we can find for you."

Paul looked at me skeptically. "You're not going to put out an ad or anything, are you? My pride couldn't take that."

"No, I'll be discreet," I promised. "What do you say? Should I try my hand at a little matchmaking?"

"Well, I guess it's worth a shot," he said as he stretched his long legs. "I'm not doing so great on my own."

"May I tell Maddy?" I asked.

"I don't know about that," Paul said. "I don't want everyone in town to think that I'm desperate, even though I am. If she has to know, I guess that's okay, but don't say anything to Greg and Josh. They'd never let me live it down."

He was right on the money there. "Not a problem. They won't hear it from either one of us. The reason I want to bring Maddy in on this is because she works the front, so she knows who's out there better than I do." I reached over and patted his hand. "Don't worry. We'll find someone for you."

"I hope you're right," he said, "but you didn't have such an easy time finding David, did you?"

I laughed. "The funny thing was that he was there all along. It just took him leaving town for me to really notice him."

"Is that supposed to make me feel better?" Paul asked with a wry grin. He was a sweet and handsome man, and if he wanted someone in his life, he deserved the opportunity to find her.

"It should," I said as I pulled his pizza off the conveyor.

"Would you like to eat it back here with me, or should I set you up in the dining room?"

Paul frowned, and then asked, "Could you just put it in a box for me? I think I'll eat it outside in front of the pastry shop."

"You've got it," I said. Before I boxed it up, I dug into one of my drawers and picked out a candle stub. Sinking it into the pizza, I lit it and said, "Make a wish."

He grinned, did as I asked, and then said, "You know what? You're my kind of crazy, Eleanor."

"Right back at you," I said as I grabbed a soda for him, too.

"What do I owe you?"

"It's your birthday, Paul. It's on the house," I said with a smile.

"Does everyone get a free pie on their birthday?" he asked.

"No, just the folks I'm closest to," I said. "Don't spread it around, or everyone will want one."

He winked at me. "You got it. Thanks, Eleanor. I don't know how you did it, but you somehow managed to cheer me up."

"All part of the service we provide here at the Slice," I said.

Maddy came back a minute later to pick up a pair of toasted subs. "I'm not sure what you said to Paul, but he went in sad and came out happy. What exactly did the two of you do back here?"

I grinned. "I gave him his birthday present," I said.

"Is that what you kids are calling it these days?" my sister asked me with a grin.

"Keep it clean, Madeline," I said. "Paul can't meet any women with his odd work schedule, so he's asked us to see what we can do to help him find someone."

Maddy rubbed her hands together and smiled. "That's great. I just love matchmaking."

I remembered Paul's request, and added, "Don't tell the guys out front. Paul was embarrassed to even ask us for help, and he doesn't want anyone else to know what we're doing."

"You can trust me. I'll be the epitome of discretion," my sister said, her eyes sparkling.

"I mean it. This is important."

"I understand completely," Maddy said. "Now, who can we call?"

"I thought there might be someone at the hospital," I admitted. "Doctors and nurses tend to have crazy schedules too, don't they?"

"Leave it to me. I've already got a few candidates in mind," Maddy said. "But I need to think about it. This is going to be fun."

"Let's just hope Paul thinks so," I said.

After Maddy left to deliver the food, I took the envelope Paul had brought and put it back on my desk. Seeing it there reminded me of the mail Maddy had taken from Benet's hotel room. It had been an explosive letter, and I wanted to read it again. As I opened the envelope, something struck me. What if the seemingly random notes on the envelope itself held more information that the letter it contained? The notes were all in what I had to assume was Benet's handwriting, and it would make a doctor proud, it was so tough to read. In fact, it looked more like hieroglyphics at first glance than actual modern writing.

Some of the entries were mundane, a grocery list of things to buy, perhaps for one of his own recipes. There were also loads of random scribbles with various cooking- and baking-related items of all kinds, but as I studied the entries closer, I saw something that looked out of place. Instead of the common black pencil Benet had used to make the vast majority of his notes, there was one item printed in ink, and after looking at it closer, I saw that it wasn't in Benet's handwriting at all, but had been printed in block letters instead. It said:

Meet me alone at 2:30.

The most chilling part was scrawled just below that, though. With distinct trailing hooks on both *S*s, it said:

See you at the Slice.

So, that was how the killer had set Benet up for murder at my pizzeria. They hadn't just stumbled upon the chef there.

They'd set him up.

The only problem was, though, I didn't know who had written the note, and from the printing, there was no way to tell who had.

I glanced at the wall clock and saw that we were set to close for our one-hour break in forty-five minutes. I turned on the small combination copier/fax/printer in my office and made two copies of the outside of the envelope, blowing up and darkening the setting until the lure was easy to read.

I needed it to be legible, since it was going to be the bait Maddy I were going to use to catch a killer.

I left the copies on my desk and went out into the dining room. There was just one couple there finishing up their meal.

"What's up, Eleanor?" Maddy asked as I approached her.

"We're closing early," I said. "I'll tell you why in a minute." I walked over to the couple and smiled. "Folks, I'm afraid we have to close early today. Please accept today's meal as compliments of the Slice."

"We were going to order dessert, too," the woman said quickly.

"Gladys, you know full well that we're finished," the man replied. He stood, and the woman reluctantly followed.

"At least let me leave a tip," the man said graciously.

I didn't want to rob Maddy or Greg of their tip, so I nodded once. He dropped a few singles on the table, and they left, the woman still complaining about the man's behavior. I pitied him his situation, but what counted was that they were gone.

"Where's the fire?" Maddy asked as I locked the door.

"We have some errands to run," I said. I turned to Greg and asked, "Do you mind cleaning up and then locking the place after we're gone?"

He nodded, and then added, "I don't have a key, remember?"

"For goodness sakes, take mine," I said, chucking my whole key ring at him. "This is important, Greg. I wouldn't ask you to do it if it weren't."

"I know that," Greg said. "Go on. I've got it covered. Will you be back when it's time to open this afternoon?"

"I think so, but if we don't make it back in time, hang a sign on the front door saying that we're closed today, but we'll reopen tomorrow. Got it?"

"Got it," Greg said. "Unless you want me to come with you. I can be handy in a jam, you both know that."

"Don't worry," I said. "It's going to be fine." I put my apron in back, grabbed the copies to take with me, but left the original.

"Let's go," I said to my sister as I walked back out front. "We can take your car."

Maddy nodded, and I was amazed at how agreeable she was being.

It didn't last, though.

The second we were on the promenade and all alone, she stopped and asked, "What are you up to, Eleanor?"

"We're going to go find Benet's killer," I said.

"And how do you propose we do that?"

I handed her the copies, and after reading the note, Maddy asked, "Where did you find this?"

"It was on the envelope you took from Benet's hotel room. You're the one who found it."

She frowned as she studied it again. "I grabbed the letter, but we both know that I didn't see this."

"It was buried in the other writing," I said. "I'm willing to bet that either Patrice or Jessie wrote it."

"What makes you think it was either one of them?"

I shook my head. "It's the only thing that makes sense. If someone else did it, we don't even know about them. Kevin Hurley can track them down on his own, but I have a feeling in my gut that this is the crucial clue to what happened, and one of them is the real killer."

"So, we're just going to go confront them with this and see what they say?" Maddy asked.

"That's what I was thinking, unless you have a better idea."

She thought about it for a moment, and then said, "Not off the top of my head. Let's go."

As we hurried toward her car, I said, "You know we could just end up looking like a pair of fools."

To her credit, my sister smiled at me. "It won't be the first time, and I'm willing to bet that it won't be the last, either."

As we drove to the hotel, Maddy said, "Eleanor, I heartily approve of your plan, but I just want to throw this out there. Should we call Kevin Hurley and tell him what we suspect?"

"I don't think that's such a good idea," I said. "If we're wrong, I don't want Kevin witnessing it. Besides, it's broad daylight. What's going to happen to us in a hotel conference room surrounded by other people? This is the best place in the world to confront the women, if you ask me."

By the time we got to the hotel, my nerves were as tight as banjo strings. "How do you want to play this?" I asked Maddy. "Should we try to get them alone, or should we brace them together?"

"It really depends on how we find them," she said. "We should just play it by ear, in my opinion."

I couldn't find a reason to disagree with that. "Why not? It's worked for us okay up to now."

"Eleanor, in all fairness, we should remember that we only get one chance to be wrong here."

"I still say we take our chances," I said. "If we wait until they've both left town, we'll never get this opportunity again."

"If you say so," Maddy said as we got out of the car and started for the hotel's front door.

"You aren't getting cold feet, are you?" I asked.

"They're freezing, actually," she replied.

"Maddy, we can call this off, turn the envelope over to Kevin, and be done with it," I suggested. "It's not too late."

"Come on," she said. "I'm just a little jumpy right now."

"Don't worry," I answered. "I'll be right there beside you."

"Okay, let's do this," she answered.

"I thought you two were in meetings all day," I said as we barged into the conference room and found Jessie and Patrice alone. They were sitting at the table in front of piles of paper, and I noticed that Jessie's cell phone was in front of her.

"The publisher was called away for a teleconference," Jessie said as she stood. "They're having problems with one of their writers."

"I've heard they're all a little nuts," Maddy said, and then glanced at Patrice. "Though I'm sure your husband was the exception."

"He wasn't a writer, and he wasn't a chef," Patrice said as she stood as well. "But if we can get one more book out of him, I'll be happy."

"You don't seem as torn up as you once were," I said.

"What can I say? I've grown accustomed to the fact that my husband is gone. We had our differences, enough that I wanted to leave him a time or two along the way, but there was still some affection there between us."

Her story appeared to be changing yet again. Was she lying to spin what had really happened to soothe her own feelings, or was she trying to ease her conscience?

"What exactly are you two doing here?" Jessie asked. "I thought you had a pizzeria to run."

"We do, but this was more important. We found a clue," I said. "*The* clue, I suppose I should say."

Jessie shook her head. "Are you two still playing detective? Why don't you leave that to the police? They seem to know what they're doing."

It was time to spring the trap. "Look at this and see if you can say that it's just playing."

I handed them each a copy of what I'd found on the envelope, and tried to watch them both at the same time.

Jessie was the first to react. She threw the paper on the conference table and said, "So what? This could be easily be a setup."

"It could also just as easily have been how he was murdered," Patrice said. "You write notes in block letters just like this sometimes, don't you, Jessie?"

"I didn't do it until I saw your notes to Tony and decided that I liked the way the letters looked," she said. "He told me he just started it himself after you took it up to make things clear, and then he decided he liked it, too. That was clever of you, though, trying to shift the suspicion onto me."

"Why in the world would I do that?" Patrice asked.

"It's time to stop playing games, Patrice. You've been setting up diversions since you showed up here," Jessie said. "I bet you're even the one who started the trash-can fire near the bookshop."

"What are you talking about?" Patrice asked.

That was what I'd been hoping for. I said, "Jessie, I didn't think you arrived in town until you barged into the Bookmark. How could you know about a fire that happened before you were supposed to even be in Timber Ridge?"

"I must have heard about it from someone else," Jessie said. "After all, this isn't all that big a town, and when something out of the ordinary happens, it feels like that's all people want to talk about. Don't let her convince you that she's innocent."

"I am," Patrice demanded. "I'm no killer."

"So you'd like us all to believe," Jessie said. "You've been pretending to be drunk since Tony was killed, but I doubt you've taken more than a sip of alcohol the entire time you've been here. What's the matter, Patrice? Are you afraid you might let something slip if you take a drink? That sounds like a woman with a great deal to hide to me."

She took a step toward Patrice, and Maddy intervened while I reached for Jessie's cell phone, still on the table. She saw me after I moved toward it, and Maddy caught it, too. Bless her heart, my sister pretended to have a coughing fit, and one that was so violent that both women had no choice but to look at her. I took the opportunity to look at Jessie's phone. What a stroke of luck, it was just like mine.

I hit the section for call durations, and scanned quickly to the day of Benet's murder.

Jessie had indeed spoken to her bosses in New York, but she hadn't been on the phone for an hour. The duration was just three minutes, and in my mind, that left plenty of time to go to my restaurant, kill Benet, and then get back without being noticed. As I tried to slide it back where I'd found it so I could make an excuse to call Kevin Hurley, I glanced at the paper in front of her.

Every *S* had the same distinctive trailing hook I'd found on the note on the envelope.

And I knew at that moment who had killed Antonio Benet.

Chapter 20

Now was the right time to bring Kevin Hurley into our investigation. "Sorry we bothered you both," I said. "Maddy, we need to go. I was way off base on this one. Someone else must have killed Chef Benet."

My sister looked at me oddly. "What do you mean? Eleanor, you might not have realized it, but you were making real sense just then."

I tried to laugh it off. "That's my problem, isn't it? I have too much imagination for my own good." I glanced at my watch. "We need to get back to the Slice. I've got that sauce simmering on the stovetop, remember?"

It was the signal we'd created if one of us were ever in trouble, and Maddy picked right up on it. "You're right. We don't want to burn the place down. Sorry for the disturbance," Maddy said.

We were almost to the door when Jessie said, "Nice acting, but neither one of you are going to win any awards. Lock that door, then turn around and come back. We're not finished here just yet."

I glanced back and saw that Jessie was holding a gun on us.

I'd figured it out, but it was probably too late to do any of us any good.

After I locked the door, Maddy and I walked back to Jessie.

Patrice was in shock, just standing there with her mouth gaping open. "I don't understand what's happening right now."

"You never were the brightest star in the sky, were you?" Jessie asked.

"You killed Tony?" Patrice asked incredulously.

"Of course I did," she confessed. "He was going to ruin me, and if I couldn't make him stay, I was going to make sure that he was finished, once and for all."

"That still doesn't make any sense to me," I said. "You wrote the note for him to meet you on the envelope that held the letter saying that he wasn't even getting a new show."

Jessie looked really frustrated then. "I didn't read the letter," she snapped. "Tony told me what it said, and I believed him. What a liar he was. Oliver was right. The man couldn't do anything right."

If it had been a different situation, I would have loved the irony of the one thing that could save Benet's life being in the killer's hand before she committed the murder, but it was all just a little too sad for me. "You killed him for nothing, then."

Jessie shrugged. "Sure, in hindsight I wish I hadn't, but there was at least some satisfaction skewering him like that. You should have seen the expression on his pompous face when he realized that he was going to die."

"How could you?" Patrice asked, and I saw Maddy reach into her bag. I knew she kept an assortment of things in there that could be used as a weapon, but I hoped she was using her cell phone instead. Jessie was clearly deranged, and if Maddy attacked her, I was certain that some of us were going to get hurt.

"What I want to know is, why didn't you?" Jessie asked. "How could you live with him all of those years?"

"He had his good points," Patrice said.

"Name them on one finger."

Maddy glanced over at me, and I nodded. Whatever she was about to do, I had her back.

If she needed a diversion, she was going to get one.

"My heart," I said as I clutched my chest and collapsed. It should buy her the time she needed, if Jessie would only react to it.

It had an unexpected result, though. My sister dropped her purse, and then knelt down beside me. "Eleanor, are you okay?"

"I'm faking it," I whispered.

"Oh," was all that Maddy could manage before Jessie was looming over both of us.

"Nice job, Eleanor. You were pretty convincing, too, until your sister took the bait instead of me." As Jessie kicked Maddy's bag to one side, she added, "Now, both of you need to stand up. I've had just about enough foolishness from all of you."

What Jessie hadn't counted on was Patrice finally finding her will to move. While Jessie had been occupied with us, she made the mistake of taking her focus off Patrice, and from somewhere deep within her, the widow finally found the strength to act. Before any of us were aware of what she was doing, Patrice had a conference chair in her hands, and as she lifted it above her head to hit Jessie, the producer swung around to shoot her.

But then Maddy and I stepped up and took control of the situation.

Acting as one person, we both reached out for Jessie's legs and pulled her down to the floor toward us. The gun came clattering out of her hand, and Patrice stood over us with the chair, poised and ready to strike if Jessie tried anything at all.

Kevin Hurley got there thirty seconds after I called him, and as one of his officers led Jessie away, he said, "We were down to these two ourselves," he admitted.

"Why didn't you act on that?" Patrice asked. She was shaking now, as though the enormity of how close she'd come to dying was finally sinking in.

"You two weren't going anywhere," he said. "We were in the parking lot watching you so neither one of you could get away."

"All the while, she was in here ready to shoot all three of us," Patrice answered, her voice a ragged mess.

"It's okay," I said, doing my best to calm her nerves. "Jessie's under arrest, and we're all safe."

"I thought that heart attack was real," Patrice said.

"You're not the only one," Maddy added.

A paramedic came and looked hard at Patrice. "Are you all right?"

"Not really," she said. "I think I'm going to collapse at any moment."

"Let's see what we can do for you," he said as he led her out of the conference room.

Maddy, Kevin, and I were the only ones left.

My sister looked at me and said softly, "I can't believe I bought your act. I'm sorry I didn't do better."

"Hey, you did what you thought you had to do. You believed that I was really dying," I said. "I'm thinking that maybe I missed my calling. I might just have to join Timber Ridge's Theatre Troupe now."

"You'd be a natural," Maddy said. "I was impressed."

"What gave Jessie away?" Kevin asked.

I showed him the copies of the note, and then the paper in front of where Jessie had been sitting. "The *S*s matched on the rendezvous time on the envelope and her notes, and that's when I knew that I had her. She also made a mistake about commenting on something that happened before she claimed that she was ever in town, and I had to wonder if she weren't planning on killing him before he even showed up at the Bookmark. Something else must have happened, though, and she couldn't do it when she'd planned to kill him. I showed her the letter in the hallway upstairs, but I never let her hold the envelope. I'm just lucky she didn't kill me for it when she had the chance."

"Got it," Kevin said. "Officially, you both know that I have to scold you for the way you've been acting lately."

"And unofficially?" I asked with a grin.

"I'd pin medals on both of you if I could," he said. "You two need to come to my office later for some paperwork. I'm sorry, but you're going to be tied up for a while, so you won't be able to open the Slice this evening."

"That's fine with me," I said. "After all this excitement, it might be nice having a little quiet time to ourselves."

That wasn't going to happen, though, as the door to the conference room burst open, and both Bob and David came rushing in.

"Are you two okay?" David asked as he took me in his arms.

"You could have died," Bob added as he gave my sister the same treatment.

"We're fine," I said, though I honestly didn't mind the attention that much.

"You both take too many chances," Bob said.

Maddy pulled away, and then asked, "When we get married, you're not going to be one of those overprotective husbands, are you?"

Bob started to shake his head, and then he stopped and looked at her carefully. "What are you saying?"

"Having a gun pointed at you tends to clarify your thoughts," she said. "If the offer's still good, I'd be happy to marry you. Why not? You're probably the best I'm going to be able to do at this point."

Bob laughed so hard that I thought the walls were going to shake apart as he pulled out a beautiful engagement ring and slipped it onto her finger. "Life with you is going to be just one big adventure, isn't it?" he asked.

"Bob, you don't know the half of it," my sister said with that wicked grin of hers.

"We're both so happy for you," I said, but I doubted that either one of them even heard me. I took David's hand and said, "Let's give these two some privacy, shall we?"

"I can think of several ways we can accomplish that," he answered with a grin.

Once we were outside, David asked me, "Can you believe that?"

"You bet I can," I said. "That was the secret that I couldn't share with you."

"I understand," David said.

"You know, I had a feeling that Maddy wanted to say yes all along, but she couldn't come up with a good enough reason until we almost died a little bit ago."

"That would do it, wouldn't it? What flashed before your eyes when you thought you might die?"

I laughed at him, and then gave him a quick kiss. "I'm sorry, but I won't indulge your desire to be complimented," I said.

"Did I cross it at least once?" he asked, grinning broadly.

"You were there," I admitted, "but I'm not saying anything more."

I was about to kiss him again when Kevin Hurley approached us.

"Is something wrong?" I asked.

"You bet there is," he answered, clearly upset about something.

"What's changed since I saw you five minutes ago?"

"I just spoke to my son. What's this nonsense about him staying in town after he graduates and working for you? Did you put him up to it?"

I wanted to laugh out loud, but then I realized that it wasn't funny, at least not to Kevin. All I knew was that my life was back to the closest thing that could be called normal, and I was happier about it than I could express.

"Can we discuss this tomorrow?" I asked him. "Josh isn't doing anything for months, so we've got that long, right?"

"I suppose so," Kevin said, "But we are going to talk about it, make no mistake about it. What are you doing that's so important that we can't talk about it right now?"

"I'm taking my boyfriend out to dinner," I admitted.

As Chief Hurley left, I looked at David and added, "That is, I am if you're free."

He pretended to think about it, and then answered, "Well, this is kind of sudden, but I think I can squeeze you in. What are you going to do about the Slice?"

"We're closing, for one night only. After all, it's a special occasion. My sister doesn't get engaged every day."

"Well, no, not *every* day," David said with a grin.

"Tell her that joke," I said with a smile. "I'd love to be around when you do."

"No thanks, I don't have a death wish. Seriously, I'd be glad to take you wherever you'd like to go. Bob and Maddy can come, too, if you'd like."

"Thanks for the offer, but I have a feeling they're going to be doing a little celebrating of their own."

As David drove me home so I could change, I realized that Maddy hadn't been the only one having an epiphany during the confrontation with Jessie Taylor. While I wasn't anywhere near ready to consider getting married again, I was thankful that I had someone in my life I could share it with. I hoped we could find the same thing for Paul, but in the meantime, I was going to do my best to enjoy what I had.

And I knew in my heart that my late husband, Joe, would have heartily approved.

DESSERT PIZZA #1

We like dessert pizzas when we really want to indulge, so I've come up with a couple of recipes to make any pizza meal end with a sweet treat. These are a lot less involved than most of my recipes, but that doesn't mean they aren't delicious. I've included a few variations as well, in case you're feeling adventurous. Try your own combinations, and enjoy!

Ingredients
1½ tubes sugar cookie dough (16.5 ounces each, about 24 ounces total; I like Pillsbury)
10-ounce jar strawberry spreadable fruit or preserves
½ cup strawberries, cut horizontally into rounds
6-ounce package chocolate chips, semi-sweet
6-ounce package white chocolate chips

Directions
Cut the cookie dough into rounds approximately ¼-inch thick. Arrange them in a circle approximately 13 inches wide on a piece of parchment or wax paper and work the dough together until you have one solid cookie. Wet your fingers from time to time, as it really makes the job go smoother. Place another piece of parchment or wax paper on top and roll out the dough until the base is smoothed. Transfer the round to a 13½-inch pizza pan, adjusting as necessary. Crimp the edges of the dough to make a ridge all the way around, and bake in a 350-degree oven for 40 to 60 minutes, until the cookie crust is golden brown. While the cookie is cooling, melt the semi-sweet chocolate chips in a double broiler or a microwave, mixing and working slowly on low power so the chocolate doesn't seize. Repeat for the white chocolate chips, and set aside. Coat the top of the cookie crust with the spreadable fruit, or preserves if you'd like a more delicate flavor. On top of that, place the cut strawberries around the pizza, treating them

as though they were pepperonis on a regular pizza. Then take the dark chocolate and drizzle it across the top in a crisscross pattern using a spoon. Finish by doing the same with the white chocolate, and serve.

Serves 6–8

DESSERT PIZZA #2

Sometimes a bite of a treat is enough to satisfy, so we like to make these when we don't have a lot of time. Try them with your own toppings. They are delicious.

Ingredients

16-ounce (24 count) Pillsbury Ready to Bake! Sugar Cookies packet
½ cup Nutella
½ cup Marshmallow Fluff
1 cup cream cheese (reduced fat is fine)
6 ounces chocolate chips, semi-sweet
6 ounces white chocolate chips

Directions

Bake the cookies as directed, 350 degrees for 8 to 10 minutes, until golden brown. Immediately indent the center of each cookie with a quarter cup measuring cup bottom to create a rim around the outside of each cookie. While they are cooling, mix together in one bowl ½ cup cream cheese and ½ cup Marshmallow Fluff, until smooth. In another small bowl, mix together ½ cup cream cheese and ½ cup Nutella, again until combined. Melt the semi-sweet chocolate chips in a double broiler or a microwave, mixing and working slowly on low power so the chocolate doesn't seize. Repeat for the white chocolate chips, and set aside.

Top half of the cookies with the cream cheese–Fluff mixture and the other half with the cream cheese–Nutella mixture. Drizzle semi-sweet chocolate on the Fluff-covered cookies and white chocolate on the Nutella ones.

Add sprinkles if desired, but the plain white-on-chocolate and chocolate-on-white looks really elegant all by itself.

Makes 24 cookie dessert pizzas